ROOM39 AND THE
LISBON
CONNECTION

ROOM39 AND THE LISBON CONNECTION

A Novel

ANTHONY WELLS

To order additional copies of this book, contact:
Xlibris
844-714-8691
www.Xlibris.com
Orders@Xlibris.com
829560

DEDICATION

This novel is dedicated to the memory of Vice
Admiral John Godfrey, CB, Royal Navy,
Director of Naval Intelligence in the British Admiralty 1939–1942,
the very first M,
and
his personal executive assistant, Commander Ian
Fleming, Royal Naval Volunteer Reserve,
and
the author's mentor, Sir Harry Hinsley, Bletchley Park Code
Breaker and Master of St. John's College, Cambridge.

CONTENTS

LIST OF PHOTOGRAPHS

PREFACE

THIS IS A novel that brings together the career of Ian Fleming in British Naval Intelligence during World War II and how his activities in Portugal, and Lisbon in particular, not only shaped his future James Bond novel plots, but developed in detail the character of James Bond himself. The story unfolds from the famous Room 39 in the British Admiralty and introduces a key character who was Fleming's boss and became the role model for M in the Bond novels, Vice Admiral John Godfrey, CB, Director of Naval Intelligence, in the critical years 1939–1942. However, this novel is more than this. It takes the reader into the center of one of Winston's Churchill's greatest strategic concerns until the Nazi era began to implode after D-Day and the Soviet success at the Battle of Stalingrad. This is neutral Portugal, led by the dictator Dr. Antonio De Oliveira Salazar, who, by sheer necessity of survival, played the Allied cause off against the Nazis until he realized that Hitler was doomed. Portugal was at a critical strategic crossroads, straddling the approaches to and from the Mediterranean, the US, and the Eastern Atlantic, South America, and Cape route from the Far East. If Portugal was invaded like France in 1940, then the threat to the Allied cause would be intense, with key ports like Lisbon and Oporto potential bases for Kriegsmarine submarines and German naval and air forces—a strategic nightmare. Shortly after France was overrun, Lisbon became the center of intrigue and espionage, with the German Abwehr and Gestapo playing hard against British Naval Intelligence, the British Secret Intelligence Service (SIS) or MI6, the UK Special Operations Executive (SOE), and the British Ministry of Economic Warfare (MEW). Into this unique and hugely challenging world steps, Lieutenant Commander Ian Fleming, Royal Naval Volunteer Reserve, is a debonair, multilingual, very astute, and extraordinarily resourceful instrument of pursuing the goals of British intelligence. This is both

Fleming's story and also how the broader detailed aspects of the intense drama of wartime Lisbon played out and the impact on the course of World War II. It is no exaggeration to state that Lisbon in World War II was the ultimate center of the spying business ever. This novel will capture the imagination of every generation, young and old, because it is a timeless story of courage, determination, amazing inventiveness, and leadership in the face of formidable foes. This novel will make a very good movie because unlike the Bond movies, the characters, settings, and events portrayed in this novel bring to life the essence of what became an extraordinary genre.

The chronology is as follows. The novel begins in Room 39 in the British Admiralty in June 1940, a month of crisis for Winston Churchill and Britain, making a solitary stand against the Nazi onslaught. On June 4, the Battle of Dunkirk is over with the greatest ever military evacuation from a beachhead, and the Battle of France ends on June 25, 1940, with the capitulation of French forces and the occupation by the German Army, the Gestapo, and the other odious instruments of Nazi power, the SS and the Abwehr, of France. Portugal and Lisbon now have become huge strategic concerns for Churchill and British intelligence. Will Portugal be invaded too, and will this open up a whole new set of vulnerabilities as the Battle of Britain ensues followed by the Luftwaffe's bombing onslaught on RAF airfields, London, and key industrial and military and naval centers? The story concludes in the period between the end of 1942 and June 1943, following first the successful second battle of El Alamein on November 11, 1942, the Operation Torch landings on November 8, 1942, by British and American forces in Tunisia and Morocco that concluded with the highly successful North Africa campaign on May 13, 1943, and with all German forces driven completely from North Africa by June 1943, with 250,000 Germans prisoners following the surrender on May 13, 1943. In parallel to the British-American victory in North Africa the Battle of Stalingrad that began on July 17, 1942, ends in February 1943 with a colossal defeat of the Wehrmacht on the eastern front. The novel concludes at this point because Portugal is now secure from Nazi invasion and British intelligence will continue undermining all

Abwehr and Gestapo operations in Lisbon until the war's end. Mid-1943 saw the pressure come off regarding Lisbon because the great strategic concern dissipated as the Allies prepared for Overlord in June 1944. The epilogue comprises a description of the large treasure trove of gold that Salazar accumulated from Nazi purchases of wolfram and other war materials from Portugal, as well as the biographies of the main characters.

INTRODUCTION

OUR STORY BEGINS in June 1940, in the Admiralty in London. It is another month of crisis for Winston Churchill, his Cabinet, and the British people, making a solitary stand against the Nazi onslaught. On June 4, 1940, the Battle of Dunkirk is over with the greatest ever military evacuation from a beachhead in history. The British Army is saved to fight another day. On June 25, 1940, the Battle of France ends with the capitulation of French forces. France is occupied by the German Army and Air Force; and in addition the other odious instruments of Nazi power, the Gestapo, the SS, the SD, and the Abwehr begin their insidious infiltration of French society at every level. France is now under siege from not just an occupying German Army but the whole apparatus of Nazi surveillance, counter intelligence, and corruption, dominating the daily lives of both those who have capitulated and those who will fight to the end. German infiltration will create a divided French citizenship of collaborators and those who will continue the fight with the support of British intelligence and its newly formed Special Operations Executive, the SOE. The Battle of Britain is raging over the towns and countryside of southern England, and soon the German Luftwaffe will begin its Blitzkrieg campaign of bombing British cities, airfields, and military installations. The British people are under siege, alone, with no allies as yet; and the Royal Navy is fighting desperately to keep the sea lines of communication open so that Britain can continue to feed itself, import critical oil and other vital war materials, and challenge the German U-boat threat. Hitler is amassing a large force across the English Channel in northern France, and his generals and Luftwaffe chiefs are planning an invasion of Britain. In addition to these dire challenges, Churchill and his political-military leadership now face another daunting threat with the occupation by the German Navy and Air Force of key Bay of Biscay ports that now permit the Nazis quick access to the Atlantic, a massive strategic shift and advantage for Hitler's Kriegsmarine and particularly its U-boat force led by Admiral Karl Donitz, who will eventually succeed Grand Admiral Erich Raeder as head of the German Navy in 1943. Churchill now fears that the Germans can potentially either invade or seek the total submission of both Spain and Portugal to the Nazi will, with the fearsome concern that the Mediterranean and the whole western European seaboard comes under Nazi control from Spanish and Portuguese naval and air bases. Churchill and his key intelligence staff now have to plan against the possibility that two dictators, General Francisco Franco in Spain and Antonio De Oliveira Salazar in Portugal, will fall under Nazi control with dire strategic consequences for Britain. This is the story of how British intelligence, and one key component of it, contributed to keeping Portugal free from total Nazi domination.

CHAPTER 1

Room 39, the British Admiralty

WHITEHALL IN LONDON in peacetime is a busy street, with black cabs swinging their way between Trafalgar Square at one end and Parliament Square at the other. Off to the right at the Nelson column end, heading toward Parliament and Big Ben, is an impressive building with many radio antennas sprouting from its rooftops. Today, June 26, 1940, the peacetime ambience of one of Britain's best known thoroughfares, competing perhaps with the Mall, Oxford Street, Regent Street, Bond Street, Piccadilly, and the like, is broken by a sense of foreboding. As dawn approaches, black-out curtains are pulled back and air-raid wardens head for breakfast after a night of patrolling central London in the event of an air raid by Adolf Hitler's Luftwaffe. The sun is barely up and breaking through a dull overcast as the postsummer-solstice warm air wafts down Britain's center of government. There are multiple uniformed persons scuttling in both directions, some coming off watch in the Admiralty and others preparing for a long day, not at any kind of office, but the heart and soul of the British Navy, fighting to keep the sea lanes open and prevent an invasion the like of which this country has not witnessed since the formidable Bonaparte harbored such a false ambition. The column behind those entering through the gates of the Admiralty, identity cards checked by armed sailors and Royal Marines, is testament to success and failure, the glorious defeat of the combined French and Spanish fleets by Vice Admiral Horatio Nelson, a man that, with just one eye and most of one arm missing, led his fleet to victory, losing his own life at the height of the battle. Today, on what will become a warm and balmy English summer's day, the odds are stacked against this island people, and those now entering through the ports of the Admiralty have not just a great tradition to uphold, but to find new, ingenious, and effective ways to stop an enemy encamped across the English Channel in northern France.

"What's the latest from Coastal Command about the sighting of the U-boat transiting through the Greenland-Iceland gap?" asks the duty operations officer overseeing the North Atlantic plot. A young female officer from the Women's Royal Naval Service, WREN for short, barely out of training, responds instantly to the commander's request, "It's still on the surface, sir. We've got an intercept from four and half hours ago. It's heading southwest and looks like it's heading to join with two other U-boats out of the bay. At the moment, sir, we're not sure whether they're from the first and ninth out of Brest, the second and tenth out of Lorient, or the seventh and sixth out of St. Nazaire, and it's also possible they could be from the third at La Rochelle. We've overnight been talking with our source about who left when and where and their likely estimated RV point." She takes a deep breath and looks the intense commander straight between his steely eyes. "I wish we had a more precise fix, sir, on the others, but we're hoping to get something soon." Before the commander can ask further questions, Captain William Stephens comes through the security door behind where the WREN officer and her team of WREN plotters and typists are busily manning the north Atlantic plot, showing who and what was where and when, both friendly and German. Everyone stands at attention. The deputy director of British Naval Intelligence has entered the most important intelligence plot in the United Kingdom, Room 39.

"Stand easy, everyone. I know it's been a long night." He looks at his watch. "At the change of the watch, I want to talk to both watches, so you'll all be having breakfast a little later today, but it's important, very important. But before I get into what's on, let me hear the latest about the U-boat positions and what Coastal and Western Approaches are doing. By the way, everyone, we're thinking about moving Western Approaches from Plymouth to Liverpool. The Director and First Sea Lord now think with Gerry just across the Channel, it's too vulnerable to have Western Approaches Command stuck there like a lame duck ready to be bombed by Hermann Goring's Luftwaffe. Moving to Liverpool, at least farther away for his Dorniers and Junkers and the like, to transit through our fighter defenses." Stephens takes a breath, and he glances at the third officer WREN, who instantly responds. She instinctively knows it is her turn to let the captain know the latest. With meticulous skill and clarity, the twenty-four-year-old young woman gives him a precise account of what is where and, most of all, likely intentions. "Sir, it's pretty clear that they're planning on rendezvousing with the units out of the Bay of Biscay. We should have more pretty soon once they start transmitting again. It's a question of time. We've estimated their speed of advance, and the OR people are doing some calculations for us."

"Good work, ladies. Excellent. What's Patrick Blackett and his boys got to say for themselves? They've been pretty well on the ball so far. His fellows Zuckerman and Waddington are two very smart men?" He pauses.

"Well, sir, Mr. Blackett was in with us earlier. He was here to just after midnight. He's gone home to get some sleep and do some more calculations, and said he'd be back as soon as he was finished. We've got some pretty good estimates. Here are the coordinates on the plot."

Stephens stretches across the plot.

The WREN plotters working the miniature submarines stand aside and then indicate what the small flag indicated.

"You'll see the estimated RV point, sir. It's there. Here's the coordinates. We've already flashed to Western Approaches and Coastal at 0320 this morning."

"Good, very good," says Stephens.

He stands back, folds his arms, and looks again at his watch. As he turns to the duty officer, the security door opens and the guard lets through Patrick Maynard Blackett.

"Good morning, Captain, I think I may have some answers. The other chaps and I have got what we think are some pretty reliable numbers."

"Please give me some good news, Patrick, we're due in with the Director at 1100 this morning, and we've got a pressing new problem on top of this current operation that the PM himself is concerned about. So what have we got?"

Blackett goes over to the plot and lays several sheets of paper on the plotting table and, in a very gentlemanly manner, asks one of the WREN plotters to stand by to lay her plotting tools on the table.

"Look," he says, "we've calculated their likely positions using our best knowledge of the ocean current and wind speed and direction, and also working on the assumption that they will transit at night on the surface on their diesels, they'll need to recharge their batteries, and by the way, we've used the best intelligence we've got on their recharging cycles, assuming that they're proceeding at best speed on the surface. Based on all that we know about Donitz's wolf pack tactics, we calculate that they'll spread themselves across this arc here."

He turns to the young WREN and says, "My dear, please use these coordinates to plot all three boats' position—here's the data." She meticulously does this, with her second officer WREN unobtrusively looking on, but not wishing to disturb her as she figures out Blackett's various latitudes and longitudes.

"Perfect," says Blackett. "Now let me show you where that nasty chap is that sneaked through the Iceland-UK gap. He's likely to be here, with all of their positions, by the way, are at 0800, 1200, 1600, and 2000 today, GMT. We projected out so you can decide what course of action you may want to take William." Blackett was senior enough in his civilian capacity that all but the Director himself were addressed on a first-name basis. It was in his nature to be personable. Stephenson, however, given Blackett's both status and position as the preeminent operations research genius of his generation, always showed marked respect, and Blackett was always "sir."

As the WREN finishes her plotting, the deputy director says to his duty team, and with Blackett all ears, "You'd all better use to one thing. Donitz has us by the tail right now. He's got Brest, Lorient, St. Nazaire, and La Rochelle in his grasp. The game's changed. Transit times, air support from the Luftwaffe, while we are running ragged trying to keep the Atlantic convoys alive and well."

"Thank you, sir, for this invaluable lot of calculations," he says, turning to Blackett. "This kind of information shifts the initiative back to us. We're all grateful to you, sir, and by the way, many of you may not know that before he became a fellow at King's College, Cambridge, and all the great things he's achieved at the Cavendish Laboratory, our chief technical advisor started life at Osborne and then Dartmouth when it opened. So Professor Blackett was a naval officer first and then a distinguished physicist. Sir, we are lucky to have you. You know as much about life at sea as any of us. So please, all of you, do give Professor Blackett your maximum support."

Blackett is a kindly man, and he retorts in a low-key and friendly way, "William, thank you, but it's all of you in this room and the others off duty who will help win this war. We've got a lot of very brave people out there right now facing the odds against the Nazis, but your brains here, in Room 39, can change the whole war, believe you me."

Stephenson then proceeds to give the duty watch a short lecture on the planned convoy cycle and why the one that has left the East Coast of the United States with critical war materials is in danger from the German U-boat wolf pack heading into the transit zone.

Stephenson can be abrasive at times and certainly does not mince his words when wits needs to be sharpened or he thinks someone is slacking, but he is, underneath it all, a kindly and considerate man; and he knows from decades of leading sailors and junior officers that stricture has to be balanced by humanity and occasionally spiced with a little humor.

"Well, sir, you are welcome to stay. I'm just about to brief the outgoing and incoming watches on the key meeting that Admiral Godfrey has called for 1100 this morning. I hope that you can stay for that, unless you've got other pressing Whitehall business.

"The word came down to me about the PM's meeting tomorrow, and I'm sure Admiral Godfrey will want a gathering of the minds. I've got one or two things to do before 1100, but let me listen in now and I'll be back for the admiral's meeting."

Just as Stephens is about to expound, the security door opens and the guard lets in a man carrying a heavily locked security pouch and escorted by two armed petty officers.

The regular visitor, a Royal Air Force wing commander Frederick Winterbotham, a courier from Bletchley Park, announces in a calm and collected way, "We'll need to have all noncleared people for the material to depart, please," at which point the duty staff slowly departs, leaving all but Stephens, Blackett, and the duty commander.

Stephens turns to the duty commander and orders in a low-key voice, "Go have the PA round up Ewen, Patrick, and Frederick at the double, please. Tell him to pass on that it's most urgent. I need them here now."

"Yes, sir," is the instant response.

"Oh, if Commander Winn and Commander Hall are in the building, I think they may be with the admiral, have him let them know that I would like them to come to Room 39 as soon as possible. By the way, let Lieutenant Commander Kemp know too. He's working a special DF task for me right now, but if he's available, I'd like him here too."

"Aye, aye, sir," comes the instant response.

"Let's have a coffee while we wait for the others," Stephens suggests to Patrick Blackett.

He then turns to Winterbotham and orders him in a low-key voice, "Fred, if you can open up the pouch, please, I'll sign for it, and then it will be time for you to head north."

Winterbotham is a courier, but he clearly does not have access to whatever is in the pouch. He distributes, but is unknowledgeable of the content, just where it originated. He hands two copies of the receipt document to Stephens, who duly signs, and has the duty commander countersign, and then hands one copy to the duty commander for safe keeping and one for Winterbotham to return to Bletchley Park. Winterbotham gathers up his pouch, bids all good day with the parting comment, "I should be back later today, sir, with more material that's being worked on."

"Sounds good, Fred. Safe journey. Thank you." The deputy director gives Winterbotham a smile and a hand shake. Winterbotham departs, joining his escort outside the security door.

While having their coffee, Stephens and Blackett discuss the situation after the fall of France. The wing commander had unlocked the security device on the pouch, and the duty commander retrieves a large manila envelope that is encrusted with red sealing wax, and says in bold letters "DNI EYES ONLY." He opens the outer envelop and then examines the inner envelop, marked "Top Secret ULTRA." He opens this and lays the material on the plotting table. He begins to examine the content, reading intently the critical product from Hut 4 at Bletchley Park, otherwise known as GC&CS, or the Government Code and Cypher School. The latter is a misnomer for the highly secretive code-breaking facility house in a nineteenth-century country house and several huts near Milton Keyes in Buckinghamshire. On top of the material is a typed cover letter signed by Alan Turing, Gordon Welchman, Hugh Alexander, Stuart Milner-Barry, and Harry Hinsley, and stating that they are in concurrence with the findings. There is a supplementary note, marked again "Top Secret ULTRA," detailing the plans to build an automatic machine that they describe as a "Programmable Digital Electronic Computer." This is underlined in red. The name that is given to this highly secure program is Colossus.

Within about ten minutes, the security door to Room 39 and the treasures of the Operational Intelligence Centre, or OIC as it was better known, are open to several key people—Ewen Montagu; Lieutenant Commander Patrick Beesley, Royal Naval Volunteer Reserve; Frederick Wells, an Oxford don now in Naval Intelligence for the duration of the war; Commander Roger Winn, Royal Navy; Commander Richard Hall, Royal Navy; and Lieutenant Commander Peter Kemp, Royal Navy. These are the backbone of the director of Naval Intelligence's key staff. They had been handpicked by the DNI.

"I think that we've got everyone," announces Stephens.

The door opens, and enters the DNI's personal assistant, a stock broker in peacetime and especially recruited by Vice Admiral Godfrey himself after a long and serious search, ending in a lengthy one-on-one interview over a lengthy lunch in a nearby private club. The man is young, fit looking, dapper almost to the point of being suave, and sharply dressed in the uniform of a lieutenant commander, Royal Naval Volunteer Reserve.

"Come on in, Fleming, thanks for herding the team."

"Yes, sir," says Fleming, and he joins the group around the plotting table.

"All right, what's the latest, let's have it," says Stephens.

The duty commander, having studied the material, lays out the very latest intercepts of German communications, not just the U-boat dispositions and intentions, which he describes later, but what the German high command plans are after the fall of France and, in particular, Raeder's and Donitz's plans to bring Britain to its knees by total unrestricted U-boat warfare. He reads out the translations from Bletchley, emphasizing what the Abwehr's (German Intelligence) plans are not for just subjugating French citizens to their will, but also plans for coercing both Spanish and Portuguese citizens and bringing as many new agents into the Abwehr's orbit as possible so that the Kriegsmarine can add Lisbon, Oporto, Cadiz, Palma, and Valencia into the German Navy's sphere of influence. There is mention of Bilbao being a key port in the north if the British Navy can be stretched to the point of breaking.

He then turns to the latest U-boat transmissions and the situation in the northeast Atlantic. He has already adjusted the German U-boat positions on the plotting table. He then provides intercepts of communications between Donitz and Raeder, and between Raeder and Hitler and his staff in Berlin, and in particular transmissions to and from Adolf Heusinger and Franz Halder. Hitler's personal assistant, Albert Borman, sends Hitler's personal comments to Donitz, with a commendation. One critical intercept from the head of the Abwehr, Admiral Canaris, directly to Hitler, with a copy to Heinrich Himmler, makes clear his intention to widen his espionage net across France and the Iberian peninsular. Canaris mentions Lisbon in particular, and its key value as a port facing the eastern Atlantic and a source of wolfram.

The deputy DNI thanks him for his analysis and then turns to Blackett and with a smile says, "Sir, you hit the mark. Your projected positions match what Bletchley have intercepted. This is very important if they cease to transmit or they switch from Enigma."

"Thank you, William, we do our best, and based on all the data we can amass."

"Send flash messages, Commander, to both Western Approaches and Coastal Command, with the usual caveats. No sources, nothing. Dress it up—oh, and call them in advance. If the AOC and the CINC need to chat with me, let their chiefs of staffs know I'm here and can discuss on the secure link. We need to engage and destroy those U-boats before they get near to attacking that convoy."

He grabs his coffee and takes a breath.

"Gentlemen, the DNI wants us in his office at 1100. It's a dress rehearsal for his meeting tomorrow at 0700 with the prime minister, the war cabinet, and chiefs of staff. I'm told that 5 and 6 will be there with Admiral Godfrey. I'm not sure whether I'm invited or not. Only Enigma cleared will be allowed at the meeting. What I want to do between now and 1030 is to prepare the DNI's talking points for the PM. Ian, I want you to coordinate, please. I want to focus our attention on one key topic—Portugal, and the likely consequences of either a Nazi occupation or major infiltration, and then for us to provide the DNI with draft counteraction plans. The PM's going to want answers, solutions, not problems. Remember Winston's turn of phrase that I like so much: 'A pessimist sees the difficulty in every opportunity, an optimist sees the opportunity in every difficulty,' so let's be creative and put your fine minds to work, between now and 0930. We'll then have a brainstorming session, and, Ian, you'll be responsible for coordinating the paperwork with the cleared first officer WRENS. Any questions, gentlemen?"

"Yes, sir," Fleming retorts.

"Roger, you're the chairman of this meeting," Captain Stephens says, turning to Commander Roger Winn. "I'm going to meet with the DNI. I'll be back promptly at 0930. Go to it, gentlemen."

"Yes, sir," they all universally retort.

Captain Stephens leaves Room 39.

Roger Winn leads an intense discussion, with the whole team contributing, listing the likely issues and problems, and then the possible solutions, with Ian Fleming scribbling rapidly on his notepad.

An hour later, they have a plan.

Winn says, "Time for a coffee break while our WREN writer types up Ian's notes, and I want Ian to have time to edit and make sure we're all ready to brief the DD."

Fleming works assiduously to collate and edit the point paper for the deputy director. As editor, he uses his privileged position to add his own nuances and some additional ideas. His literary skills shine through in this paper, with added vitality to an important step in the process that will end with a briefing to Prime Minister Churchill early the next day.

Captain Stephens returns to Room 39 and calls his assembled team to order.

"Well, gentlemen, let's hear what you've come up with. We're running against the clock. Admiral Godfrey wants us to meet promptly at 1100. He's leaving at noon for Bletchley, and he wants to ensure that his briefing to the prime minister and the war cabinet is in fine shape because he won't be back in London until late tonight and will head straight to the Cabinet War Room first thing in the morning. Over to you, Roger."

Commander Winn expounds. After a series of exchanges and iterations, the finalization of the draft briefing for the DNI is agreed by consensus, with Captain Stephens adding some final touches. The DDNI instructs Winn to have it typed in its final format, and he orders the key people to assemble in the director's office, Room 38, promptly at 1100.

The director of Naval Intelligence, always known as the DNI, is Vice Admiral John Godfrey, handpicked for the job by the First Sea Lord Admiral Sir Dudley Pound with Winston Churchill's concurrence. His personal assistant, Lieutenant Commander Ian Fleming, has delivered the draft briefing and is completing a short prebrief with the admiral when the admiral's secretary announces that Captain Stephens and the staff are ready to meet.

"Come on in, gentleman. Make yourselves comfortable. Fleming's given me the gist of what you've all come up with. It looks good. Because of time, I want Captain Stephens to go over the highlights and for you all to chip in when William's finished. Ian, you take notes, and we'll get this in final shape on the drive out to Bletchley. When we return later this evening, William, I'll need you to be here in case something new has come in the meanwhile that I'll need to know about. I'm meeting the First Sea Lord for after-dinner drinks in his apartment at 2100, so he's totally knowledgeable of what I'm going to say to the prime minister and war cabinet at 0700 tomorrow."

The group spreads themselves around Room 38.

Captain Stephens begins. He's precise, concise, and after a brief introductory statement of the current situation, launches into a point by point proposal for addressing the dramatically changed situation on the Iberian peninsular. He concludes. Admiral Godfrey asks for additional comments. There are none. The staff has already done their work, and their boss has now said it all.

Godfrey leans back in his chair, looks at the gathering, and says, "Good work, gentlemen. The key is going to be coordination and cooperation with 6, SOE, Double Cross, and Bletchley. We're going to have a very special role. I'm not sure that SOE is ready yet. They're a fledgling outfit. We're going to have to come up with alternatives. The PM's going to want an action plan. Let me think about this between here and Bletchley and back, and William and I will discuss before I see Admiral Pound tonight."

Everyone silently breathes a sigh of relief, including the deputy. The DNI is pleased.

"Go to it, gentlemen. I'll make sure that you're all kept informed of the outcomes from tomorrow's meeting. Thank you."

They all leave.

"William, I'll have Ian call you as soon as I'm back in the building."

"Yes, sir, good luck at Bletchley. We just plotted their latest gold dust. All good stuff."

"Good to hear, I'll tell Denniston," comments the DNI.

The admiral and Ian Fleming depart the Admiralty main entrance and climb into a staff car and head to Bletchley Park. En route will be laid plans that no one could have envisaged except the bright, charismatic RNVR lieutenant commander sitting with Admiral Godfrey, pen and writing pad in hand. As the miles tick by to Bletchley Park, John Godfrey muses to himself what a wise choice he made in selecting Ian Fleming as his personal assistant.

CHAPTER 2

Bletchley Park and Hut 4

GODFREY ALWAYS INSISTED that he be driven in an unmarked car with no three-star insignia plate or flag on the bonnet. He and Fleming are in plain clothes as their driver weaves his way northward from London in lunchtime traffic. The driver, specially vetted, is a trained Royal Marine Commando, and he has a loaded pistol on the front passenger seat.

"Tell me, Roger, have we missed anything for tomorrow's briefing?"

Fleming pauses, wishing to be diplomatic and not imply that he is going above and beyond what Stephens and the NID team has devised.

Godfrey surmises wisely, "Ian, we're alone. If I'm going to get value out of recruiting you, I want total candor from you at all times. Give it to me straight. Let me be the judge of what you say and contribute. I hired you for your brains and ingenuity, not to be a yes-man. Do you understand that, Ian?"

Fleming pauses and says with a slight smile and a twinkle in his eyes, "Sir, I very much appreciate the confidence you've shown in me. I promise to always, without fail, give you my very best, totally unvarnished opinion. If I turn out to be totally wrong from time to time, please don't hold it against me."

"Good, very good, that's the whole point. We've an understanding, Ian. Now, let's get down to brass tacks, are we missing anything? The PM is incredible astute. He's a fighter. He wants action, not words."

Fleming takes a deep breath.

"Well, sir, what we didn't include and what I would recommend we do is form a special operations group, not a big outfit at first, but made up of seasoned and very experienced commissioned, noncommissioned, and relevant civilians like I was a year or so ago who have special skills.

Quite a few will also have fluent language skills like I have—French, German, Russian—and now we are going to need fluent Spanish and Portuguese speakers."

"Go on, Ian, I'm all ears."

"They're trained beyond where SOE is right now in its organization, barely off the ground, and full of people from the good old boy network. We want fighters, but also smart, tough, intelligent, and ingenious men with skill sets that SOE just don't have."

"And how does all this fit in with the Iberian situation?"

"With Menzies' people that we can trust, we insert these people into Lisbon, Oporto, and other key locations, have them stash away the necessary weaponry and explosives, recce the environment and fade into the background so that Salazar's thugs and the Abwehr don't even know they exist. They need to ferret out locals whom we can trust beyond a shadow of a doubt, and pay them well, better than the Germans. None of the usual spy craft that 6 peddles. A lot of those people are going to be spotted very soon, given all the incestuous things going on between us and the Germans chasing shadows in Lisbon."

"So what do you want to do, what do I recommend?"

"Authority to proceed and special funds for a highly classified outfit, with well-defined mission objectives that I have in mind, and by the time we leave Bletchley, if I can have an hour or so in an office with a typewriter, I'll have for you, sir, to review on the way back to London."

"How many bodies, Ian?"

"No more than a hundred, perhaps a hundred and twenty, each specially selected and all as fit as a fiddle, no slackers, no one who won't be prepared to give his very utmost, kill, but not be killed."

"Ian, I'm glad I found you. Never ever hesitate to tell me what's exactly on your mind, even if it contradicts what I might say from time to time. None of us are infallible. Even Winston's crazy Plan Catherine had to be shot down. First Sea Lord took the flak, but he was right, Winston was terribly wrong."

"Well, a couple more things."

"Go ahead."

"Lieutenant Commander Denning, Ned, he's been away for the past few days liaising with Western Approaches and planning the new operational relationships after they move to Liverpool from Plymouth. He's as smart as a whip. Yes, he was a paymaster early on, doesn't have that seamanship pedigree that you have for example, sir, but he's extraordinarily bright and innovative."

"Go on, Ian. What's the plan for Ned Denning?"

"The OIC that we have is Ned's baby. He's read the old reports and knows what we did twenty odd years ago when Blinker Hall was in your job. He wants to go several steps further. He wants to turn the OIC into the hub, the place where we coordinate all our key ops, where the rubber meets the road, where just us NID—with no SIS, SOE, and certainly no 5 Wallas anywhere in sight—run a separate, highly secure show. Own code words, own specially selected and trained people, and perhaps only C himself in on most of our stuff."

"Ian, I'm warming to this. Keep going."

"Ned and Commander Denniston's people are joined at the hip. The navy's running Bletchley. We can exploit all the Ultra material with 6's inputs, plus our own special ops group, plus other additions, like what Donald McLachlan brings to the party."

"He's a good man, I agree, what special job or jobs do you have in mind for McLachlan?"

"Propaganda, psychological warfare, and deception. We need to exploit the weaknesses in the Nazi mindset, the very nature of their odious empire. Donald sees inherent weaknesses, flaws that can be exploited, playing their own propaganda back to them in clever, unfathomable ways to the Nazis' key weakness, their own ideology."

The DNI is about to say something but senses that Fleming has not finished.

"He's convinced that we can play games with Donitz and his staff, deceive them, make them drink their own bathwater, and choke on it without ever knowing who poisoned the well."

The DNI smiles to himself, enjoying every word from Fleming.

"Concur, again, Ian. I'm going to have you read into something we won't talk about now. You'll be making a visit shortly. I'll set it up. What you and McLachlan are cooking up here falls nicely in place with one of our other silver bullets."

As the DNI's car stops at the security checkpoint, he turns to Fleming and makes one short comment.

"Ian, make it so."

"Yes, sir."

"You have my full support and authority. Don't take no for an answer. Tell them you speak for me and ultimately the PM. Remind them that 'action this day' doesn't mean next week or the week after, but now. Any nonsense, come straight to me."

Fleming beams. "Yes, sir."

"I'll keep Captain Stephens in the picture, no one else for the time being. I'll have the treasury people work out the funding through the secret vote."

As Godfrey's driver opens the car door, a stiff-looking commander in full uniform steps forward from the steps of the Bletchley Park entrance and salutes the admiral, which Godfrey returns.

"Welcome back to Bletchley, sir."

"Thank you, Alastair, we've got a busy afternoon ahead of us, the PM's briefing is at 07 double O tomorrow. I want the latest, please."

As they walk into the entrance, Godfrey pauses, looks Denniston in the eye, and says in a direct tone, "What you've got here, right now, is the best thing we have in our locker. We're on the defensive on all sides, except here, in this building and in these precious huts. Before we get down to it, I need a cup of tea."

"Yes, sir, all ready in my office."

As they wound their way to Denniston's office, Godfrey makes two somewhat personal remarks.

"I've always wondered why you're called Alastair when your name is Alexander."

"Family quirk, sir. I think a father-mother naming issue. I've lived with the change."

Godfrey notices Denniston visibly wince.

"Are you all right, Alastair?" he says in a kindly tone, with a worrisome look.

"You noticed, sir, I've got a bladder stone that every so often decides to irritate. I'm waiting to get it fixed."

"Don't leave it too long, we don't want you becoming a casualty. Get it seen to, please, you're too valuable."

Godfrey settles in one of two comfortable chairs in Denniston's spacious office overlooking the Bletchley lawn and gardens.

He has visited before but never noticed on one of the shelves a photo of Denniston in field hockey rig and underneath what looks like a medal.

"Didn't know you were a hockey man, Alastair," Godfrey questions, sipping his tea and eating a biscuit.

"Yes, that was taken in 1908, summer Olympics, managed to win a medal with the team."

"Very good, quite an achievement, I knew you were in Bonn and Paris for your studies when you were a young man, but didn't know about you wielding the hockey stick."

No sooner had the DNI finished his quips about Denniston's hockey skills than the door opens and Commander Denniston's secretary announces that the briefing team was here.

Denniston summons them in. Godfrey finishes his tea and stands to greet five of Bletchley's finest—John Tiltman, Dilwyn "Dilly" Knox, Josh Cooper, Oliver Strachey, and a fifth who is a little late by seconds, Nigel de Grey.

"Good to see you, gentlemen. You have my undivided attention for the next two hours. Ian, find a quiet room and go work on what we discussed. I'll fill you in on our meeting here on the way back. Make sure you have it typed up, easy to read, and so on."

"Yes, sir," quips Fleming, glancing at Denniston. He bids the others goodbye and departs with Denniston's secretary to find a private room.

They then first get into the detail of one of two pressing issues that Godfrey's wants resolving.

"It's critical that I know where Donitz is going, not just with his operational plans, but equally important with his building plans, how many U-boats on the building ways, where, when, the production rate, likely types, and all that you've managed to glean about capabilities. The reasons are clear. How many U-boats Hitler can put to sea in the next year, into 1942 and beyond, will determine not only our operational priorities but whether we'll be able to counter the numbers game."

Godfrey pauses and pours himself another cup of tea.

"Then there's the prime minister's current question of the day."

They all look intensely at Godfrey from their different angles.

"The Iberian peninsular. What will Hitler do now he's taken France? How will he deal with Franco and Salazar? Will he simply keep moving west and invade, or will he rely on coercing Salazar while it seems he still has Franco in his pocket. What can you reliably tell me, gentlemen? This is top priority. In a few days, it may be something else. Tomorrow the PM wants answers from me and SIS."

Dilly Knox, a brilliant veteran cryptanalyst steps forward and hands Godfrey a briefing paper covered in bright red code words, TOP SECRET UMBRA. He says that he and Nigel de Grey will address both questions. The other three present will field questions as people who have worked both issues over the preceding days and nights.

Godfrey sits back in his chair and makes one simple statement.

"Gentlemen, please proceed. Much depends on the next couple of hours and your conclusions and recommendations."

Denniston draws down the blackout blinds, while Josh Cooper and John Tiltman set up the magic lantern projector, and Oliver Strachey sets up two easels with various maps and drawings overlaying the maps.

While this is going on and Godfrey is enjoying his tea, Denniston's secure phone rings.

"Denniston." He pauses, listens, and says, "All right, I'll be over."

He turns to the DNI and says in a low-key voice, "Sir, if you'll excuse me please, Hut 4's just come up with some new data. It's important, they need me over there. You're in very good hands here, sir. I'll be back as soon as possible."

"Go to it, Alastair. Fill me in when you return."

Yes, sir."

Dilly Knox begins a lengthy detailed exposition of Donitz's building plans.

Commander Denniston strides across Bletchley's parkland and enters Hut 4 via a secure double door with a sentry outside who checks his ID, though he's the director.

Inside he's facing something more than just a group of hard-working, dedicated cryptanalysts.

Inside Hut 4, a small group is crouched together looking at what seems like endless reams of paper on top of a plotting table with a series of maps on top of each other. Around the room are heavy-duty secure filing cabinets, desks with individual chairs, no personal effects or decoration, but lots of photos pinned to a series of blackboards, with one large board full of chalk scribblings. The windows are blanked out. The overhead fans are running slowly so the myriad pieces of paper do not get airborne.

"Good afternoon, Commander," says Alan Turing. "I came over about an hour ago to deliver to the team the latest intercepts and translations. They've been working on them, and it's important you know the latest, given the DNI's meeting with the war cabinet tomorrow."

"How recent is it?"

"Right up-to-date. We translated it immediately. The ladies did a superb job. Picked up on all the nuances, the lot."

Denniston look at the other familiar faces, all animated as if they had just received a huge surprise birthday present.

"Tell me, I can't wait."

"My team did the decryption, I'll let Gordon and the rest of the team explain what this all means. They're the analysts. Gordon, why don't you start?"

Gordon Welchman is one of five others in the room—Alan Turing, Stuart Milner Barry, Hugh Alexander, and Harry Hinsley.

"I'll let the others add their comments, Commander, but let me get the ball rolling. We've got the latest Abwehr thinking and policy after the fall of France. This has come straight from Canaris himself, his chief of staff and operations people, a series of signals that went to key centers in Paris and, most important, given the war cabinet's concerns, to both the Abwehr heads in Madrid and Lisbon. Canaris has advised Hitler that the Abwehr can control both Franco and Salazar in Germany's interests, while undermining the British in both countries."

Welchman pauses. "Stuart, why don't you explain our interpretation of the war materials and economic aspects."

"Well," says Stuart, "Canaris is telling Hitler that through Abwehr controls the flow of iron ore and wolfram will go totally uninterrupted while they will guarantee any or minimal supply to the British. The Führer's being advised in strong terms that Franco and Salazar will toe the Nazi line." He then adds a most important rider: the undermining of British vital supplies passing through neutral Spanish and Portuguese ports to Britain. "Stuart and Hugh, why don't you explain the other key aspects that you worked on."

Stuart Milner Barry looks at Hugh Alexander and retorts, "Well, more good news. Canaris wants authority to run the show in both countries, a big development given Heinrich Himmler's almost pathological desire to have control above and beyond the Abwehr by using the Gestapo and the SS. He's advising Hitler that the network he has in place will be multiplied, he doesn't go into numbers, just hyperbole, and that shortly he will have control of all intelligence and operations in both countries."

"Furthermore," adds Hugh Alexander, "he's claiming to know where all the weaknesses are in the British presence in both Madrid and Portugal, implying the Abwehr knows whose who on the British side."

Denniston frowns, holds his chin with his left hand, and slowly massages his lower jaw, clearly in thought.

"So there's a power play in Berlin. Are you sure Canaris is convincing Hitler? We've seen how that evil toad Himmler operates. Who's Hitler really listening to?"

"The after actions tell us that, Commander," Welchman immediately quips. "The messages that went out after the Abwehr's signals clearly came under Hitler's personal command. Let me explain. Hitler trusts his ambassador in Lisbon, Hoyningen-Huene, as does Hitler's foreign minister lackey, the evil Ulrich Friedrich Wilhelm Joachim von Ribbentrop, whose signals to and from Lisbon we've intercepted. Von Ribbentrop has bought into Canaris plan, and Hitler likes it because

Admiral Raeder and his henchman Admiral Carl Donitz are convinced that they can manipulate both Spain and Portugal in their favor with Canaris's clandestine operations against Britain."

"Over to Harry on this," says Welchman. "He's handles all those aspects."

"Remember one critical factor, Commander, and as a naval person, you will appreciate this." Harry Hinsley pauses, with Denniston listening with bated breath. "Canaris, Raeder, and Donitz are part of a well-established and powerful old boys club called the Kriegsmarine." Denniston is all ears. "None of them like Himmler and the other die hard Nazis, just as many of the German general staff detest the Nazi upstarts who have Hitler's ear, but in this case, Himmler seems so far to be the loser."

"And the impact for us?" questions Denniston.

"It means that we'll have firsthand knowledge of what the Abwehr are up to—who, where, what, and when."

"Great work, gentlemen. Any other key aspects?"

Hinsley says directly, "Oh yes."

Denniston turns to Hinsley, all ears.

"We're beginning to see how Donitz will use the new bases on the French Bay of Biscay Coast, none of it good news, but so far, we see zero intent or any kind of plans to recommend moving into neutral Spain and Portugal. Furthermore, Commander, I think the submarine group has come up with one critical factor that should be brought to the attention of the war cabinet."

"Go on, Harry, with the DNI over in my office, tell me some good news, I hope."

"Well, the submarine build rate is not going well for Donitz. He started the war, thank goodness, with fewer submarines that the Kriegsmarine needed to seriously not only challenge the Royal Navy but also bring British merchant shipping to its knees. The submarine supremo is not getting the resources he'd like to build his force up quickly enough to sink more merchantmen and Royal Navy surface ships. The traffic between Donitz and Berlin is not indicating a big win for him—more submarines, yes, but nothing like the numbers that he both wants and needs to come out on top. It's all there. Hitler has other plans for his military that will take up resources, that seems to be the issue."

Denniston pauses, frowns, stands tall, stretches, and says, "What's your best assessment, or educated guess, gentlemen?"

Hinsley looks at Gordon Welchman.

"Very premature, but we've all put on our thinking caps, and we're in agreement."

"Well?" says Denniston.

The Hut 4 group pauses.

There is silence.

"The Soviet Union, Stalin, the Communists," said Welchman, "it's in everything that Hitler and his Nazi creed have espoused. The evil Slavs to the east, the antithesis of German culture, all the bogus Aryan nonsense, and the like. We think that he's planning on doing what Bonaparte failed to do. He's saving all his resources for invading the Soviet Union. It's part of his inbred pathological culture, however strategically irrational. It could be our savior."

There is a huge pause in Hut 4.

"By God!" Denniston exclaims. "This is dynamite. Do you have the synopsis for me? The DNI will want to study and take with him back to London."

"All typed up, classifications in order, ready to go, sir," says Alan Turing, the mastermind who had delivered the raw goods to Hut 4.

"I need to run," says Denniston.

"One thing before you go, Commander," remarks Turing.

"Go ahead," says Denniston.

"We urgently need more resources if we're to keep up the current level of effort, and as the workload increases, as it undoubtedly will, we are urgently going to need more staff, professionals, and support staff, plus more technical capabilities that I'm working on with my people."

Denniston is curt. "Out of the question. We're all under pressure. You all have to make do with what you've got. Remember what the prime minister said to the House of Commons. He meant it. Blood, toil, tears, and sweat. No more of it, gentlemen," at which point, he replaces his navy cap and departs.

The team are aghast.

"Well, we asked for it, and we got it," says Turing. "What do we do next? We cannot go on with the limited resources we have. We're overloaded. We'll break."

Hinsley comments, "What's our next move then?"

"Nil desperandum," says Turing, and he turns and picks up the secure line and dials a Bletchley secure extension.

"Turing here, Commander Travis, it's most urgent. Would you come over to Hut 4, please, when convenient?"

The voice on the end of the line can be heard by the others, saying, "I'll be right over. Give me ten minutes. I have one call to make to London."

"He's our man," says Turing. "He understands the situation we're all in. He's not a Denniston. He's with us, but he'll have to be careful, very careful."

Ten minutes later, Commander Edward Travis, Royal Navy, is striding across the Bletchley pathways to Hut 4, resolute as always, a distinguished veteran of the code-breaking community.

The next thirty minutes after Commander Edward Travis's arrival will save Britain in ways that no one, not even those in Hut 4, could possibly envisage, let alone surmise.

CHAPTER 3

Godfrey and Fleming to London While Denniston and Menzies Talk

ADMIRAL GODFREY THANKS Commander Denniston for a hugely beneficial visit. They shake hands just after five thirty, on what was now a sunny afternoon outside Bletchley's main entrance.

"Give my thanks again to your team, Alastair. They're the best. I hope that I gave them the encouragement and support that they need, every day, indeed every hour."

"I will indeed, sir, thank you," snapped Denniston.

Denniston saluted smartly as the Royal Marines driver closed the doors of the staff car. Godfrey wound down the window and, in a cheerful, friendly, yet direct tone said, "Alastair, do take care of yourself, we can't afford to have you going down at this crucial time. Do get that stone fixed." Godfrey paused for just a second or two. "That's an order, go see the doctor tomorrow."

Denniston made eye contact with the DNI. "Aye, aye, sir, will do."

The security guards come to attention and salute as Godfrey's car departs Bletchley and heads back to the Admiralty.

"Ian, I've got gold dust in the pouch. These people are not just remarkable, seriously capable people. They're a national asset, a treasure. I want Denniston to understand that they need every support that can be mustered. Best comes from Captain Stephens to follow through, you understand."

"I do indeed, sir," Fleming retorts, pausing before considering what he is about to say next, not wishing in his mind to undermine Denniston, before saying, "After I finished the briefing for you, I went over to Hut 4 because I'd heard from the director's secretary before she started to type my paper that Commander Travis had been requested over at Hut 4. Thinking this was a good opportunity to catch up with all those players, I went over."

"And," says Godfrey, "what was going on besides all the good things that came back to me late in the afternoon?"

"Resources, extra people, equipment, sir, that's what I heard. Commander Travis is on top of it. It was all good. The deputy left shortly after I arrived. It was if they didn't want me to be in on all that was transpiring."

"Interesting," says Godfrey.

"They all shut up like clams as soon as Commander Travis said he would have...whatever...in hand, and I took the hint and got on with hearing the very latest, what's at your feet, in the pouch, sir."

"OK, Ian, let's talk more about your special ops group. I'll read your paper in a moment, between now and the Admiralty, but give me the gist, in a nutshell. I've got a lot to read and mull over before I meet First Sea Lord."

"Riley, sir, Quintin Riley, he's my man that I recommend heads-up what I'd like to call Number 30 Assault Group, innocuous in some ways, but emphasizes the key mission. I know Lieutenant Commander Riley well—first class, made for training and leading a clandestine undercover group that can deal with the Portuguese problem, and many more like it."

"Good, go on."

"The other key section leaders that I'm contemplating include a naval intelligence specialist, Patrick Dalzel-Job, who's as tough as nails and knows how the Nazis operate."

"I saw his file when I became DNI. Good man, I agree, but I've never met him."

"The other initial leader is Charles Wheeler, he's a broadcaster, a journalist, in Civvy Street, and you may have read his stuff. Fit as a fiddle and knows the Germans and how we can foil them."

"Interesting," says Godfrey, "I think C may want to recruit him. Get him on board soonest. I don't want him stolen by Menzies if you need him that much."

"I do, sir, he's top-notch."

Godfrey says that he'll address the funding issues after the war cabinet meeting.

"You're going to need a special facility, hidden in the country, no one to know what's going on. The less people who know, Ian, the better. And for now, no communications with either SOE or C's people. Understand."

"Yes, sir, got it."

Fleming sensed that his boss now wants time to read and think. He adds gingerly, "I've got a list of others that I'll send to you, I know you want to read, but one of the more interesting people I want onboard is a gent called Johnny Ramensky, who—and don't be alarmed, I know all about this character—he's a professional safe blower and can get into anything and everything without leaving a trace. He's been a bad boy, career criminal you may say, but he's the best. I know him, need him, as both a trainer and as a field operative."

"Ian, I know you are acquainted with a lot of different people, from the top to the bottom, but I didn't realize you included jail birds in your long list of social acquaintances," John Godfrey says, beaming.

"Well, sir, I won't be taking him to my club, but I'll be glad to have him break into Abwehr, SS, and Gestapo safe houses and leave without a trace."

"Ian, go for it, now it's time for me to read. Stand by to take notes when needed."

The DNI's car sped south toward the capital, and Fleming took out his pencil and pad, at the ready to scribble indecipherable notes that only he could understand and which would be committed to the burn bag once used back in Room 39.

Back at Bletchley, Denniston is aching all over. His back is in spasm. He takes three aspirin tablets with a large glass of water, thirsty after a busy afternoon with the DNI. The bladder stone is kicking in and his kindly secretary asks if there is anything she could do.

"I'll be fine, thank you though, you're very kind, let me get through the 1800 call, and I'll take a nap before the evening reports from the huts at 2000." He walks around his office, stretching his arms overhead, and then leans back on his haunches to alleviate the pain from the bladder stone.

"Are we all set up for the secure call? I hope we can get a clear line?"

"Yes, Commander, we're all ready at this end. The specialists are prepared in the communications center, they told me a few minutes ago they did a test call. Just the usual cleared people for the call to your person, sir. The encryption is working."

"Thank you, Mildred. Good work. I've got a few minutes to stretch a little more and hope this bloody pain goes away."

His secretary sighs, concerned that her boss is in pain.

At 1800 precisely, the classified switchboard operator calls Denniston's secure red phone.

"Your call is connected, sir, the other party is on the line, ready to go."

Denniston says in a demonstrative fashion, "Denniston here, do you copy?"

"Loud and clear, Alistair, C here."

On the other end of the line, the director of the British Secret Intelligence Service, or SIS, Stewart Menzies, has a series of critical questions before the 0700 prime ministerial meeting in the morning. Menzies is not known by his first and last name. He was simply C. His identity is highly classified, together with his location in London. He reports to the British foreign secretary and, through him, directly to the prime minister. Winston Churchill takes a direct and daily active interest in C's product, together with that of Bletchley Park and Godfrey's NID. C is derived from the first incumbent of the SIS, sometimes referred to only in cleared official circles as MI6, Commander Mansfield Cumming, who always signs his personal documents not with his name but C. The tradition lived on, and does today. When Captain Sir Mansfield George Smith-Cumming, KCMG, CB, died in June 1923, aged sixty-four, he left a fine legacy that Denniston's fellow telephone partner has to maintain.

"Stewart, we've had a hectic day here. Admiral Godfrey left about half an hour ago and he's scheduled to meet with the First Sea Lord this evening before tomorrow's meeting. He's fully up to speed. My people are preparing a pouch for you as I speak, and I should sign off on this in the next thirty minutes of so. It will have the latest."

"Good, very good," says C, "but I've got some key things that I need to go over, stuff that we're working on here. Are you ready?"

"Go ahead."

"First, are you going to be able to reliably intercept the Abwehr and the Sicherheitsdienst communications in Portugal now that the Nazis have overrun France? The PM's going to ask first off what's next, is Hitler going to move further west?"

Menzies is referring to the security service of the Reichsfuhrer-SS, the intelligence agency of the German Nazi Party, or SD, formed in 1931 as the most sinister of Hitler's agencies, together with the Gestapo, formed in 1933. The SD leader, Reinhard Heydrich, reports directly to the sinister Heinrich Himmler, who also controls the SS, the Schutzstaffel, a major paramilitary organization, together with the Gestapo, the Geheime Staatspolizei, the Secret Police. Heydrich headed the Gestapo too, reporting to Himmler.

"They're our best source, we believe here, but we could be wrong. We're basing this on what I think are reliable assessments of the culture and daily practices that seem to be the hallmark of who Hitler trusts, and doesn't by the way, and how key decisions are flowing from Berlin to his key people in Lisbon. This raises one other question, are you still able to track Hitler's movements and communications when he's either at the Berghof or the Wolfsschanze?"

Menzies is referring to Hitler's home near Berchtesgaden in the Obersalzburg and his headquarters in East Prussia, where he spends much of his time.

"All this is critical because we think Hitler's not consulting his generals and admirals as much as the usual Nazi Party hacks that have been around since the beginning. The one exception is Wilhelm Canaris, the Abwehr head, and he still seems to have the daily ear of Hitler in spite of Himmler's clear jealousy. If all this is correct, we think here at 6 that we can best understand their next moves more by tracking the Nazi hard-liners and Hitler's darlings than concentrating on his general staff in Berlin and the field commanders."

"You have it correct," Denniston adds. "Von Brauchitsch and Halder seem to have little or no influence compared with the Nazi personal elite and political sycophants who have been with Hitler since the early days. The OKH"—he's referring to the Oberkommando des Herres, the high command of the German Army under the high command of all the German Armed Forces, the OKW, the Oberkommando der Wehrmacht—"have little or no influence but, and this is a big but, he clearly trusts and relies on Canaris."

"Well, Alastair, this is where we are going tomorrow, placing a lot of reliance on the toadies, not the senior uniformed leadership. Your material and some gems we have point in this direction. Question is, how will this emerge as policy? What will be in effect, the party line, the Nazi line, not that of the Wehrmacht leadership?"

"Every Hut here is seeing the same trend. Hitler's heavy reliance on his party followers, who he's been with forever, and who, most of all, he trusts. The Wehrmacht will execute, no doubt at all, but they may not be in on these crucial initial strategic decisions."

"We're in total agreement."

"Can I answer your other detailed questions Stewart, I've got several reports coming in from the key Huts, and we need to get these off to you, DNI, and the foreign secretary as soon as possible."

"Absolutely, let me give you several more detailed operational and communications questions my staff have for you, all related to exactly what we just discussed.

"Go ahead.

Over the next forty minutes or so, C and Denniston discuss these points. Denniston is able to answer all C's questions to his entire satisfaction.

About seven o'clock Denniston's secretary knocks gently and enters, indicating that the night pouch is ready.

"C, if we're finished, I have to break off and go over the latest material in the pouch for you and the others"

"Go ahead, Alastair, we're nicely finished, been a very good conversation. I'll see you in the morning in the Cabinet Office. Have a good night. Many thanks."

"You're most welcome. Goodnight, Stewart."

Wing Commander Winterbotham enters Denniston's office with the latest assessments and key translations from the encryptions. Commander Travis enters a few minutes later as Denniston is examining the material.

"What are your thoughts, Edward, is it all good to go? I'm both tired and in pain and want to rest before the night's work gets underway. If you say yes, let's get Fred on the road to London. People are waiting."

"It's all good, ready to go."

Commander Travis has done a most thorough review.

"Thank you. Off you go, Fred, parcel this all up, and get on the road."

Mildred knocks, pokes her head round the door, and announces, "The car's ready, sir."

"Thank you, Mildred."

After Winterbotham leaves, Edward Travis and Denniston exchange a few words about the night's work and who is on watch in the various Huts. Travis bids Denniston goodbye and says he would see him later this evening.

The ever watchful Mildred comes in, bearing what she calls "a nice hot cup of tea for you, sir, it'll help that back of yours."

"You're most kind, Mildred, thank you, the good old British remedy for every ache and pain, a good cup of tea."

Mildred closes Denniston's door. He downs his tea, put his feet up, and dozes off.

ANTHONY WELLS

CHAPTER 4

Churchill's War Cabinet Meeting

B Y 0730, THE various military staffs has delivered the current military situation, navy, then the army, followed by the air force. Churchill likes short, sharp, and incisive briefings, not long, protracted diatribes. They are each allowed ten minutes. It is all informational, current situations at sea, on the ground, and in the air. The respective navy captain, army colonel, and air force group captain salutes and departs. No highly classified intelligence is involved. Plain facts about who is what, where, and why, and their current operational objectives and where the various German threats are both located and their likely intentions and actions over the next two to three days. Churchill works at night. He is already up to speed by the time the war cabinet assembled just before 0700. As he marches in; they all stand, and he gives them his familiar greeting and invites them to sit and say without further adieu, already knowing the agenda, "Let the battle commence, gentlemen. The navy's on first, as usual," he quips. "Let's hear the latest."

The room is full of Britain's leadership that heads the sharp end of the stick, those who are leading and managing the war, not the economy or military production or any of the other peacetime affairs of state. These are Churchill's political-military-intelligence brains trust. Churchill knows that the quality and capacity of the people in this room will decide the fate of the empire. After his late-night bath in his tight space in the underground war room, he had enjoyed a cigar and whiskey and then proceeded to look at all the latest intelligence and other state papers. He had spent three hours digesting and thinking about the content before falling asleep. He knew what he now wanted to know.

Sitting closest, first on his right, is his foreign secretary, Lord Halifax, Churchill's bête noire, who will be posted off to Washington as British ambassador on December 22, 1940, paving the way for the man who sits on his, Halifax's, right, to succeed him, Churchill's favorite and right-hand man, Anthony Eden, the secretary of state for war. On the prime minster's left is Clement Atlee, the Lord Privy Seal, nominally the leader of the opposition but, in the new cabinet arrangement, the deputy prime minister of a shared government, a coalition. Churchill has wisely brought in those from the Labor Party whom he knows would add value to his cabinet. He has been magnanimous, and his willingness to share responsibility between Conservative and Labor Members of Parliament is working. Halifax is the odd ball, a leftover from the Chamberlain days and mindset. Churchill already knows where Halifax is headed, out of sight if not out of mind in Britain's most important embassy, the United States. The military leadership are in fine fettle, having a combined chiefs of staff meeting over dinner the previous night, ending with drinks. The chief of the imperial general staff, Field Marshall Sir John Dill, soon to be replaced by Field Marshall Sir Alan Brooke, sits next to Atlee, with the First Sea Lord, Admiral Sir Dudley Pound, on his left, followed to the left by the chief of the Air Staff, Air Chief Marshall Sir Charles Portal, with the chief of combined operations, Admiral Sir Roger Keyes, on his left. The key civilian staff sit at the end, to Churchill's right, the chief scientific advisor, Sir Frederick Lindeman, Alexander Cadogan, the permanent undersecretary at the Foreign Office, the secretary to the war cabinet, Edward Bridges, with two highly trusted personal aides to Churchill, John "Jock" Colville, his assistant secretary, and his military aide, Royal Navy Commander Charles "Tommy" Thompson. Across from Churchill sits the three people that the prime minister most wants to hear from and what he regards as the crux of the meeting. In the middle is C, Stewart Menzies, the head of the British Secret Intelligence Service; Vice Admiral John Godfrey, Director of Naval Intelligence, on his right; and on Menzies' left sits no other than Commander Alastair Denniston, Director of Bletchley Park. Conspicuous by their absence are the representatives of army and air intelligence. Churchill has made it clear that he could read their reports and briefings in his bunker under Whitehall. If he has questions, he would send for them. What he wants to hear would become very apparent.

He has insisted, against the advice of the cabinet secretary, not to invite the heads of either the fledgling and emerging Special Operations Executive and the Ministry of Economic Warfare. He tells Bridges that their time would come, once roles and missions for them became clear. Churchill is adamant; they are not fully organized and needs time to get underway. That is that; Bridges always bows to Churchill's wishes, as indeed he should.

After his May 13, 1940, opening speech in the House of Commons, when he had offered the British people nothing but "Blood, toil, tears, and sweat," he had formulated his own strategic thinking routine. It was this. Hear the current operational situation, then hear the current intelligence briefings, and then, with these two key elements in mind, formulate key strategic and detailed planning and execution with the combined chiefs of staff and the civilian political-military leadership.

Top of his priority list at now 0730 on a June summer's day is Hitler's next moves, after the subjugation of France, while never leaving his eye off Britain's lifeline, the sea, and vital protection of seaborne trade. He knows from World War I, a close run thing he used to say, paraphrasing the Duke of Wellington at the battle of Waterloo, simply because Britain as a maritime nation depended on imported goods, and particularly oil. Nazi submarines could cripple Britain, bring it to its knees, in which case the situation in France would become moot. Britain is incapable of changing the strategic position on mainland Europe, but on the sea, absolutely yes. Churchill is perceptive enough to realize the connection between his naval strategy and the emerging new situation, not just in France, but more important, what might next happen regarding the Iberian peninsular.

"Gentlemen, what's done is done in France. The Nazis are in control. I want to hear from Admiral Pound, C, and Bletchley what the impact is on our maritime lifeline with the Nazis in control of those key Bay of Biscay ports and Hitler's submarine force, plus what will he do next regarding Franco and Salazar. Will he move on Spain and Portugal next? What do we know now, today, not yesterday or last week, but right now? If Hitler takes over Spain and Portugal the odds become sadly seriously worse, with the Med and the eastern Atlantic exposed more than they are now with U-boats shortly running out of French ports."

Churchill pauses. "Please smoke, gentlemen," he says as he lights a cigar.

"Admiral Pound, how do you want to proceed?"

"Prime Minister, I'm going to hand over the answers to these urgent and pressing questions that you have to Vice Admiral Godfrey, C, and Bletchley Park, Commander Denniston. Over the past several days, we've been working in unison, weaving together our various sources and methods into what we believe is a very reliable picture. With your permission, sir, I'll invite Vice Admiral John Godfrey to open our briefing to you."

"Good, John, always good to hear from my DNI. Splendid."

Admiral Godfrey begins to stand, but the prime minister puts his hand up. "John, stay seated, everyone can see you, and hopefully hear you. Go ahead."

"Thank you, Prime Minister."

The DNI gives an erudite and perceptive picture of where collective intelligence indicates with a high level of confidence that the German U-boat force will be disposed, providing numbers and capabilities, and most of all, providing DNI's and Bletchley's current use of Enigma and its Ultra data to both anticipate and warn of the disposition of Donitz's U-boats. Churchill interrupted with questions about which ports on the Bay of Biscay and what the numbers difference was compared with when they were running from the north German bases, a much longer and dangerous transit. Godfrey spells out the detail. Then he says he has a little sunshine in among the gloom after the fall of France. He explains the likely German submarine build rate, providing numbers, where they will be built, and classes. He looks Churchill dead in the eyes. "Sir, Hitler is not thinking as a maritime strategist, and we know this, for sure. If we can keep hammering at his U-boats, we think that his build rate will not eventually be sufficient to beat our growing antisubmarine capabilities. He's thinking like a Nazi propagandist, which he is, not a naval strategist. The team here are in total agreement based on the most sensitive Enigma and C's data."

Godfrey pauses as Churchill smokes, and he can see Churchill's mind working, anticipating his next questions.

"This Nazi mindset, I've always thought, underwrote what Hitler will do, step by step, what do you three think?"

Godfrey turns to Denniston.

"Sir, the report that we sent over last night shows a clear trend about who's clearly calling the shots in Berlin, and at his other retreats. It's not the military leadership. Let me provide the detail."

Churchill raises his cigar. "Not necessary Commander, I read all of your material. Excellent assessment and the material—simply superb. God forbid if we lose Ultra data."

Everyone focuses on Churchill.

"What these three have will determine the outcome of the war."

Everyone then focuses on C, Denniston, and Godfrey.

"You're into Hitler's mind and all those other odious sycophants that fawn at his evil court. This is good. Now tell me straight—I've read all the intercepts, each and every one, and your conclusions, and I agree with these—what is his next move with Franco and Salazar? I read all the Canaris material, Abwehr, the SS, SD, and those evil thugs in the Gestapo. Now tell me about your recommendations."

The three looks at each other, with C having said little so far.

The DNI takes the lead.

"Sir, this is what the intelligence shows, and out of this comes, we assess, the following actions. First, we are confident that Hitler will invade neither Spain nor Portugal. That's the good news. The bad news is that we know, almost one hundred percent sure, no shadow of a doubt, that he has given specific directions, originating mainly from Canaris, the head of the Abwehr, to undermine and obliterate British interests in Portugal in particular, with two objectives of continuing the supply of vital wolfram and iron ore from Portugal to Germany in neutral ships not subject to our blockade, while totally undermining British trade interest with these two neutral countries and using their clandestine network to gain intelligence particularly regarding British shipping in the North and South Atlantic and in the Mediterranean. They are going to flood Lisbon in particularly with agents from all the Nazi agencies and aim to keep both Franco and Salazar under Nazi subjugation without risking invading two dictatorships, one of which is a fascist pro-Nazi state, namely Spain."

Godfrey takes a sip of water, at which point Churchill turns to C and asks, "And how are we placed Stuart in Madrid and Lisbon?"

"Poorly, sir, we had all our key assets in northern Europe rather than the Iberian peninsular. We're going to have to build up quickly. We will, rest assure, Prime Minister."

"Well, gentlemen, you've got your hands full. What else?"

Godfrey continues, "We're laying plans, sir, as we speak here. I should have some highly classified plans for the secret vote within the next few days. We will action these soonest after your review and approval."

"Good, very good, John, and you too, Commander, and C, of course.

Churchill then summarizes the findings, recommendations, and not just his thoughts, but Action This Day go-to-it directives.

"Gentlemen, I have great confidence in all that I've heard. Let's remember one key thing. Portugal is our oldest ally. Franco, no, he's a Nazi look-a-like, another Hitler dressed up as the savior of Spain. Salazar is definitely not in the same mould. He's living on the edge, politically and internally keeping his people both fed and watered and under his knuckle, but—and this is why—what these gentleman and their people provide is so critical, we know he's playing one off against the other, the British versus Hitler's worst organizations, and they're not the German Army or Navy. So, Admiral Godfrey, let's have your plans soonest, and, C, we'll chat after the meeting please."

"Gentlemen, we'll break for thirty minutes. Go have coffee. I want to discuss things with C. When we return I, want to hear from the combined chiefs about our immediate and short-term military plans and needs. Thank you, and I'll look forward to seeing the DNI shortly."

Churchill stands, cigar in hand. They all stand, and Churchill indicates to C that they will meet in the prime minister's private office adjacent to the war cabinet briefing room. The cabinet secretary asks if he is needed, and both Colville and Thompson stand by to see if the prime minister needs them. He indicates to all three that he wants to be alone with Menzies.

CHAPTER 5

Churchill and C Behind Closed Doors

THE DOOR IS closed behind the prime minister and C. Churchill invites Menzies to take a seat and says, "Stuart, would you like a cigar or maybe coffee."

"I would love a cup of coffee. It's been a busy twenty-four hours, but no cigar, sir, thank you though." Churchill presses his buzzer, and coffee is on its way.

While they wait to have Menzies caffeinated, Churchill goes over to the window and looks out, holding his cigar. He turns and looks C in the face.

"You inherited a great tradition, and I'm very pleased—no proud's the word—of what you've accomplished. I remember Commander Cumming well, the very first C, a fine naval officer, and he and I used to converse a lot. I loved being First Lord"—Churchill is referring to his time as First Lord of the Admiralty—"and I was so very pleased when Neville"—he is referring now to his predecessor as prime minister, Neville Chamberlain—"invited me back as First Lord. Best job of all, but now, you and I have the greatest jobs and tasks of all."

"Indeed, sir," said Menzies. "We have fine people working for us, and most of all we've started with some aces in our hands."

"That's just want I want us to discuss, Stewart, to make sure there are no jokers in our pack, in amongst the winning cards."

"Yeah, verily to that, sir."

There is a knock at the door, and the steward delivers Menzies coffee, with some traditional English biscuits, politely asking C, "Is there anything else that I can get for you, sir?"

"No, thank you, this is just perfect."

The door closes quietly.

Churchill sits in an armchair close to Menzies.

In a low tone, almost as if he didn't wish to be heard, he says, "Warlock, are you absolutely sure her material is as good as it is?" Churchill says "her" empathically, not "his."

"Sir, I can give a one hundred percent guarantee, it's gold."

"How do we know?" Churchill quickly interrupts. "I'm all ears, Stuart."

Menzies is a veteran SIS director. He comes from a wealthy family, educated at Eton, joined the Guards, and fought with great distinction in the World War, receiving the Distinguished Service Order from King George V. After being injured, he transferred to Field Marshal Douglas Haig's intelligence staff. At the end of the war, he joined SIS, or MI6 as it is better known. He kept his army rank and was prompted in due course to major general, succeeding Admiral Sinclair, who was C, his boss, in 1939. He is greatly trusted by Churchill, and at this moment in time, his long-time relationship is on the line.

"Sir, we have several confirmations, from separate sources, none of which are connected. Plus her information correlates in both time and content with Enigma data, incontrovertible, Prime Minister."

"But is it possible, Stewart, and I know you've seen it all, that the Germans have a massive deception operation against us?"

"Impossible, for these reasons."

Churchill takes a puff of his cigar in anticipation.

"We've known her for years, run one counterintelligence operation after another on her, and all she's been associated with ever since she and her husband were in Berlin together. They hate the Nazis, just as much as you and I. We've been into their innermost personal lives for years. She knows how to play the male penchant for attractive women."

Churchill exhales. "Keep going, Stuart, what about Enigma?"

"That's where we know that her information is gold."

"Go on."

"It all cross checks from several hugely classified sources that Bletchley has decoded. On top of that, we have regular contacts with her in Switzerland. We pay her typically in Bern, other places. We run counterintelligence against both her and the Germans in Switzerland. There is virtually zero Abwehr and certainly no SD, SS, or Gestapo presence in Switzerland. Money issues with the gnomes are all handled through our number one source. That source confirms everything, plus Enigma. The latest reports yesterday and in the night tell us one thing: Theodor is good, very good."

"Ah, Theodor, I would love to meet him," Churchill interjected. "My kind of traitor if ever there was one. A good human being, hates Hitler."

"Exactly."

"I'm much happier now, Stewart."

"I should have mentioned that the other key source, in Zurich, handles Warlock's comings and goings. We've looked at every angle, been totally counter intuitive, making sure not just that there may be deception, but analyzed and frankly paralyzed every possible loop hole."

Churchill then gives Menzies the nearest he would come to a direct order.

"C," he begins in a very formal tone, "I want you to ensure that within the next few days, you begin planning to outwit the Nazi menace in Spain, and most of all, Portugal. Franco is a fallen angel, has been forever, nasty man, dictator, no better than his friends in Berlin, but Salazar, he's different. You need to ensure that I want him scrupulously watched so we know his every move, and be ready, Stuart, heed my words, to do the worst we can in the event that he becomes a turncoat and ends the longest alliance in British history."

Menzies is awestruck at Churchill's resilience and presence of mind.

"Sir, you have my absolute assurance that no stone will be left unturned. I fully understand your order."

"SOE and the economic warfare people are good and will get better, but right now they're barely off the ground. They have to grow, and quickly, but it's no good you and I, and DNI, kidding ourselves they are in any way ready to set Europe alight, as I have so directed. It will take time. Meanwhile, we must use all the experienced and valuable resources that we have."

Churchill smiles. "You and your people are doing a good job, Stewart. I know that. Never fear. Now to another key aspect I want you to pursue, and it's related to what I just said. I'm not telling you your business, but I've been around as long as you, and I am, frankly, a self-confessed navy man. You cannot be First Lord of the Admiralty twice without developing loyalties, plus the fact I firmly believe that the navy is, and always has been, our main hope."

Churchill gets up and goes over to the cabinet, pours himself a whiskey, offers one to C, who declines, and sits down again, with his glass in hand.

He turns and raises his glass to his right eye level. "Stewart, you need to get close to NID and Godfrey's people, work together, you don't have to give away your nuggets, he knows that, and he's got his silver bullets too, but work together, that's what I want, and why?"

Menzies stares at his prime minister, hanging on every word.

"Because, Stewart, believe you me, this country right now, and for the foreseeable future, depends on the navy first and foremost to keep us fed and watered and to prevent invasion, then NID, SIS, and Bletchley. These four, they, you, will save this country over the next year or two."

Menzies stands up, as if his military background automatically demands that he stand to attention and salute. He stands still and upright in front of Churchill.

"Sir, you have my solemn word, I will immediately start work integrating between SIS and the others. I will be in touch with Godfrey and Denniston as soon as I'm back in the office. I'll make it happen."

"Stewart, if you need something, funds, authority to act quickly, just call Jock or Tommy, don't bother with the cabinet staff and Halifax. Come straight to me through one of them, whoever's available first. Understand?"

"Yes, Prime Minister."

"Thank you, Stewart. The future's in the balance.

Churchill offers his hand.

Menzies shakes the prime minister's hand and turns to depart.

"Now to deal with the chiefs of staff, Stewart, I hope they've worked up plans that are indeed workable, and by the way, I will ensure that their staff keep you fully in the loop. Godfrey's has Pound to keep him informed, I'll make sure that you have full and constant liaison."

"Thank you, sir."

Menzies closes the door behind him; Churchill sits back in his armchair, takes a swig of whiskey, yawns, and takes a short nap before he faces the chiefs of staff.

He has had about ten minutes of snooze time when Tommy Thompson knocks on the door, enters, and says quietly, "Sir, Anthony wants to discuss several things before the meeting."

He is referring to Anthony Eden, the minister of war.

"Very well, give me five minutes. I need to visit the heads as my navy friends say. I much prefer heads to privy!"

"I couldn't agree more, sir," the former navy man quipped.

Churchill's day is well underway, and in just two short hours, he has set various key actions in motion.

CHAPTER 6

Room 39, Godfrey Sets the Wheels in Motion

A S THE NIGHT watch comes off duty in the Operational Intelligence Center and breathes the fresh air of Whitehall and Trafalgar Square, the morning watch and the nonwatch keepers are settling in to the day's tasks. The night's developments have been passed on and assimilated, with more material arriving by courier from Bletchley, together with urgent signal traffic from Headquarters Western Approaches and Coastal Command.

Admiral Godfrey is finishing his second cup of morning coffee when his assistant, Lieutenant Commander Fleming, knocks on his door and enters with the latest reports and a synopsis from the outgoing watch.

"Thank you, Ian. While I'm studying all this, I want you to gather the key staff together for a 0900 meeting in Room 39. Let Captain Stephens know first. He's over with Stuart Menzies' people at the moment, and he called to let me know he's on his way back. He should be here any minute."

"Yes, sir."

"Ian, I've some positive thoughts about how we convert your ideas into action. The prime minster has given us strict directives, and C and I are the key action officers. What we've discussed fits well with the way ahead. So stand by to brief the team on your ideas. I know I've your paper, but at this stage, we need to keep things very well hidden and classified. Minimum paper trail. Got it?"

Yes, sir, I'm glad my thoughts are timely. If we move quickly, we can get ahead of the Abwehr before their counterintelligence machine clicks into gear, and Lisbon is flooded with Canaris's and Himmler's stooges."

"You've got it, Ian. Stewart Menzies and I are one of the same mind. We'll need to be extremely cautious and keep closely held. Let me read all this and make some calls, so go ahead and get things set up for 0900."

"Yes, sir."

Godfrey muses to himself what a good decision he's made selecting Fleming from what had been a short list of people recommended from a wide variety of sources. The city people had come up with a winner. As he finishes his coffee the secure line buzzes, he picks up the receiver to hear the commander in chief, Western Approaches, on the other end. As Godfrey listens intently to Admiral Martin Dunbar-Nasmith, he quickly reads through the reports that Fleming had left with him. They both check each other's data, with Godfrey looking at the latest signal intercept data of German submarine movements in the Atlantic. Dunbar-Nasmith lets Godfrey know that he is speaking not from his personal office, but in Western Approaches' newly established operations room in Derby House in Liverpool. He has, listening in on the line with him, his staff officer convoys and the duty officer. OIC in Room 39 has done a good job during the night of keeping Derby House well informed. Godfrey listens as Dunbar-Nasmith describes the moves he is putting in place to forestall the latest convoy from the United States being attacked.

Godfrey than makes a telling point, after the three men in Liverpool had spoken.

"Martin, one key point from my end. We just cannot afford in any way to tip off the Germans that we're reading their signals. Disastrous if this happens. The PM will have our guts for garters." He pauses while Admiral Dunbar-Nasmith says dryly, "I hear you, John, couldn't agree more."

"So do have your people in the know be extremely cautious in all your signal traffic. We just cannot afford for them to think we're acting after we've learned something that we're not supposed to know."

"Trust me, we'll be hugely discreet. Very bland movement instructions, etc."

"Good, thank you," the DNI quips.

After some further operational points and pleasantries, the two Admirals bids "Out here."

Godfrey returns to prepare for his 0900 meeting, scoops up all the necessary papers, and heads to Room 39.

Stephens has returned from his meeting with SIS and has his key staff assembled, waiting for the DNI's arrival.

Godfrey bids them all good morning and does not take his usual seat but stands facing his people.

"Why I want you all here at a time when I know you're already overloaded is this. The prime minister has given us and SIS a clear directive. We've got to counter the Nazis in Spain and Portugal, with total emphasis up front on Portugal. The reasons are clear to you all. If Salazar breaks with our historic alliance and uses his neutral position to either align directly with Hitler or show total support for the Nazis versus us, we're in deep trouble. The Atlantic not only becomes more vulnerable but the Mediterranean and shipping from South America and coming around the Cape and West Africa become more threatened. The Abwehr are already there in a modest way, and we know that is going to intensify, plus the other usual suspects will up their game too, the SS and the Gestapo, but it's the Abwehr that we have to worry about, the real intelligence people, not Hitler's private sleuths and hitmen run by Himmler. They're bad, really bad, but it's the Abwehr we have to not just watch and know their every move, we have to be ready to take them on if it looks like one of two worst contingencies." Godfrey pauses and takes a sip of water.

"The Nazis invade, unlikely from what we can see at present, or they go the most likely course, which is to undermine Britain in every way possible inside Portugal. That's where we come in, with C and his people. Any questions so far?"

No one responds.

"All right. What do we do? The PM's made it clear. One word: cooperate. With whom? Simple, SIS and SOE, in a coordinated way, not tripping over each other and certainly not trying to be top dog in a kennel full of pure breds. We have lots of advantages because of the clear crucial naval aspects. No need to explain those. You've all got what those are. The question is, what, how, and when?"

Godfrey pauses and turns to Fleming.

"I've asked my assistant to put a draft together, which he's done. It's good, it meets my instructions from above, and I'll have this circulated after our meeting for comments and inputs. Captain Stephens, if you'll coordinate, please. Now to my key message for our meeting now, beyond the Portuguese requirements. Security. We have several golden eggs. We're protecting the golden geese that lay them. Whatever you all do, in the spirit of cooperation with C's people and the emerging SOE people, do not, in any shape or form, give any of these aspects away. Please never forget this. That's an order."

Godfrey takes a pause to see if there is a reaction. None, except for total nodding of heads in agreement.

"SOE is a fledgling. It will grow and no doubt will have success in due course, but right now, they're simply not ready and equipped to do what I want us to achieve, with C and his people. Bletchley, as always, will be totally crucial, especially the intercepts of Abwehr plans and movements, who's going to be doing what and to whom. The Ministry of Economic Warfare, gentlemen, is, in my opinion, a different kettle of fish. Some very bright and very knowledgeable people, just like our civilians here in Room 39, similar backgrounds to quite a few of you. They've got very good data on Portuguese war products and movements, all extremely valuable to our new mission. I want us to work closely with MEW. They know exactly where Salazar produces his wolfram and iron ore, how it's distributed and the like. We need to know all that, including of course shipping details, and overland routes for products moving east through Spain and France to Germany. The Germans we know are using flags of convenience plus neutral shipping, including obviously Franco and Salazar run ships. They need vital war materials from Portugal. We have to stop this, keep Salazar soft towards Britain, undermine the German presence in Portugal, and, most of all, have plans and materials in place in the worst case situation, Hitler decides to either occupy Portugal directly or turn it into a puppet state that both loses its neutral position, whereby we're thrown out as PNG in a Nazi controlled state."

The room is silent. Captain Stephens breaks the silence.

"Sir, are we getting into the clandestine business, above and beyond where we are today, the traditional NID agent links, and so on?"

"William, you have it. Yes is the answer."

There are smiles all round. Fleming beams.

"Everyone in this room has more than enough on their plate already. William and I are working hard to get more staff, but meanwhile, I need a lead person for these new tasks. I'm putting Lieutenant Commander Fleming, my assistant, as the lead coordinator. I want you all to contribute to his planning. I've tasked him to have a plan no later than two days from now. All of you, please contribute. His existing blueprint looks good, but we all know there's no pride of authorship. Please give it your best, gentlemen. The prime minister is looking to us with C to make all this happen. Any questions?"

There are a series of questions about process and security and time lines. Commander Roger Winn asks one pertinent question.

"Sir, resources? Where will we operate from? We don't have either the space or the people here in Room 39."

"Spot on, Roger. I'm requesting secret vote funds for another Bletchley-like facility, plus all the people that Ian has detailed in his paper. I'm advised by Tommy Thompson that the PM will give us whatever we want, and the key is sooner, not later."

"Sounds good, sir," replies Commander Winn.

"If they're no more questions, we'll adjourn. Ian will be available shortly to work with you all. Study his paper first. If you prefer group discussions, that's fine, whatever works best. William and Ian, let's go to my office and get this all underway. The clocks running. The prime minister wants answers."

In Godfrey's office Stephens and Fleming settle down, coffee in hand.

The DNI then sits back, looks at Fleming and gives him a series of orders.

"Ian, you're to visit both SOE and MEW soonest, make arrangements after this meeting. Get your recruit list through personnel and start the security process, background checks etc. I take it you've talked to some of your people, and they're actually available or can make themselves available in a timely manner?"

Fleming nods an affirmative.

"Now to two very sensitive aspects, with which William is familiar. I'm arranging for you to visit a facility where you'll meet a man called John Masterman, an Oxford don before the war. You're going to be read into some things that you don't know about, just a few of us here in NID. Next, C has agreed that you're to be read into one of his most sensitive and highly prized sources, and all that goes with it, which includes others I cannot discuss here. You're one of the very few. The prime minister will be apoplectic if anything goes wrong with the management of these vital sources. I've made the arrangements. My secretary has all the details in a classified envelop. She's waiting to give it to you when you leave. Any questions, Ian?"

Fleming is a little overwhelmed, somewhat unusual for the confident and self-assured wealthy stock broker, whose pedigree has enabled him to live in prewar Europe and master three foreign languages. He would now have to add Portuguese to his repertoire.

"William, if you would stay please. I've a call I want you to be in on. Ian, go to it. Let's move quickly and silently. On our side only, the First Sea Lord and the First Lord will be in the know."

"Yes, sir," retorts Fleming, who stands up and departs briskly.

Godfrey looks at Stephens.

"OK, William, time for us to talk with C. Stewart's expecting my call about now."

The DNI buzzes his secretary to call C on his secure line.

"Good morning, Stewart. Hope all is well with you. We've set the wheels in motion here, and I want to bring you up to speed on what NID's planning."

Menzies is clearly pleased to hear Godfrey's positive tone, mindful of Churchill's private conversation, and verbally applauds.

"That's good, John, carry on, please."

"First, I want to let you know that we've a very capable man here on the NID staff, my personal assistant, a city man, old Etonian, speaks three key languages fluently, and is as sharp as a razor. I personally recruited him from a group of very worthy people. He understands the German mindset and has the Nazis well-taped."

C interrupts, "Does he know Europe well? Can he mix with the worst of the Nazis like the best of us?"

"Oh yes, indeed. He's lived in Switzerland and Austria for a long period, in and out of Germany all the time, and knows the culture, who's who, and what's what in the hierarchy. Frankly, he's better placed than most of my people, and by the way, that includes me. While I was doing my thing in the thirties, working my way up the naval ladder, he was busily figuring out, on the ground, the Nazi mindset."

"John, relieve me of the suspense!" Menzies exclaims.

"Who's this person that's your right-hand man, besides my good friend, William Stephens, of course?"

"Name's Fleming, Ian Fleming."

"I'll check him out if you don't mind."

"Please, Stewart, no. We don't want security busy bodies, least of all 5 asking questions in light of what I'm about to say. Plus the fact he's been vetted thoroughly by our own naval security. We know more about Fleming than he knows about himself. Totally reliable and highly secure. His penchant for the ladies is well under control. He knows how to play that game with the fair sex to our advantage."

"So what do you have in store for Mr. Ian Fleming?"

"He's currently Lieutenant Commander Ian Fleming, RNVR, in for the duration, hostilities only, not a career navy man. But he's good, in fact he's the best."

Godfrey pauses, takes a breath, glances at Captain Stephens, and continues. "He's going to run a brand-new one-hundred-plus outfit, under cover, totally clandestine, under my direct control, and totally with your full knowledge. We're recruiting already. Separate from the plans SOE have afoot, which is largely going to be working with the French, Dutch, and Belgian underground. You and I know that there are risks, people who are doubles, people who will crack if the Gestapo get their hands on them, and people who will be in it for what they can get. I'm not suggesting that the majority of the small number of Resistance people that we've set up before the collapse of France are risks, but nothing's perfect, Stewart, we both know that. Fleming's people will be totally separate, no connection whatsoever with SOE and their planned modus operandi."

"So what missions, at least initially?"

"Portugal, as Winston directed."

"OK, go on."

"Once they're fully trained, we'll insert small teams, maybe no more than three, possibly four, where certain skills are needed. They'll infiltrate, work the key areas, Lisbon, Oporto, and the supply centers and routes for the key resources Hitler needs, wolfram, iron ore, and so on. But most of all, they'll prepare for the worst and be ready to execute at a moment's notice."

"Go on, John, this sounds all good, exactly what the PM wants now."

"Yes, indeed. They'll need all the intelligence that you and Bletchley can provide, but only a tiny few will be in the know. None will know the whole picture, with the exception of Fleming himself. The foot soldiers that will work with some of Fleming's finest don't need to know what he'll know."

"Agreed, but if you plan on inserting Fleming, that's a risk. We don't want him stripped and tortured in some Gestapo cell by Himmler's gorillas, pumped with drugs, and electrodes, telling them in a delirious stupor all that you and I know."

"Stewart. I'll only send him into Portugal if absolutely needed. The good news, it's not an occupied country, it's officially neutral, our oldest ally, and we'll have plenty of top cover, rest assured. But that's all down the road. It will be his trained people who will go in, get set up, store all the explosives, communications, and weapons that may be needed of the worst happens. Meanwhile the linguists amongst them who know Portugal well, have lived there, and have good, reliable contacts, will have business top cover, all reliable, like a lot of your people in Germany before the war,"

"Sounds good. Go on."

"The ports are critical. The Abwehr and Himmler's lackeys are going to be working to both undermine British shipping activities while working their intelligence routines, particularly ours, and friendly ships that are en route from Portugal to Britain. We know that they'll play games. We have to counter, undermine, but all covert. No obvious signs of NID meddling with Salazar's people, otherwise he'll both be angry and also possibly likely to turn to his friends in Berlin, whose gold he needs to prop up his economy."

"Good, John, very good, I'm impressed. What can I do while you all set this in motion?"

"If you agree, Stewart, I'd like Fleming to visit you, and for you to brief him on three things. First, where you are on the ground today in Portugal, so he doesn't tread on British toes in due course. Second, please brief him into Warlock and Theodor. Third, give him an introduction to Masterman and his operation and set up for him to visit Masterman's place."

"Are you one hundred percent sure that Fleming really needs to know?" stresses C.

"Yes, Stewart. He, indeed we, need to know every move in advance of the Abwehr, the SS, SD, and the Gestapo. The enemy in Portugal is not the Wehrmacht, or Donitz's U-boats, it's Himmler's people, and of course the Abwehr. If we cannot trust opening up these sources to Fleming, we're in trouble. You and I might be gone tomorrow, Stewart, killed in an air raid or moved on or retired. Who knows? We have to ensure continuity of operations and build a small elite group that's both fully trusted and in the know. Admiral Pound will agree with this and your boss too."

"My boss hopefully will be out of my hair soon. Anthony's the man. Winston cannot wait to see Halifax on his way to Washington and Eden in the Foreign Office, where he truly belongs."

"You'll be a much happier man, Stewart."

"What's this that William mentioned about Roosevelt?"

"Glad that you asked. While the US Congress sits on the fence, the PM and Roosevelt have secretly agreed that we'll deal with the

Nazi menace in Portugal, with the US lying low, but—and this is an important but—the US through their Office of Naval Intelligence will continue to provide intelligence. ONI is their one star. That's it. There is no SIS, no C, no covert operations running in Madrid, but their ONI is good, very good. It's a navy-to-navy thing. We're working with their people in Washington and Hawaii on a daily basis. Relations are good. Denniston and his people at Bletchley are all in the picture. Commander Edward Travis is our lead US coordinator, very good man."

"No more fighting over who has what, the old numbers game, John?" says C wryly.

"We're all on the same page. Roosevelt's a navy man, like Winston. He knows what's what when it comes down to saving the day. Plus the fact ONI has some good data, very good data."

"John, agree, totally agree. Send Fleming over soonest. Have your secretary set it up with mine. I'll await his visit, with interest. I should have known about him and recruited him." He pauses. "Joking, John, my predecessor missed some other great people too. You have many of them, plus Denniston's people out at Bletchley."

"They're all part of the same team. Thank you, Stewart. I'll be back in touch. Keep pressing," ends the DNI.

"Bye, John."

The secure line goes dead.

The DNI has accomplished all that he wants with the director of the Secret Intelligence Service.

He takes a deep breath, turns to Captain Stephens, and says, "William, bull's-eye, please tell Fleming what he now needs to do and tell him to make it so, soonest, please."

Yes, sir," says Stephens and, smiling, leaves Godfrey's office with a clear lift in his gait, as if he'd just won first prize in a draw.

CHAPTER 7

Berlin
Canaris's and Himmler's
Staff Meet

BERLIN'S FAMILIAR LANDMARKS were filled with an assortment of uniformed Nazi personnel of all ages and ranks, from the lowest recruit in their late teens, to aging black and brown shirted fifty-year-olds, bedecked with various insignia reflecting the Nazi culture. It is a warm morning in the heart of the Third Reich, and the Führer himself is in residence, gloating over victories in northern Europe and being fawned upon by his innermost servile and obsequious party supporters. As he drives in his large Mercedes through the Brandenburg Gate heading to the Reich Chancellery on the Wilhelmstrasse, he is puffed up with elation at his conquest of France and the rest of northern Europe. He does not trust his military leaders in the way that he relies upon the party faithful, those that has been with him since the beginning, the dark days of servility during the Weimar Republic, and then the supreme victory in 1933. The old guard Prussian military elite might be professionally the best, but they are not inwardly subservient to the little upstart from Austria, Schicklgruber by name, and physically no true Aryan, born in the Austrian village of Braunau Am Inn in 1889. The cultural, social, and historic disparities does not warm either Hitler or his generals to one another. The navy men are different in many regards, and Hitler has gravitated to the head of the submarine service, Karl Donitz, and to a lesser extent his boss, the head of the German Navy, the Kriegsmarine, Admiral Erich Raeder. Hitler's trust in navy leaders is reflected in his choice for the head of the Abwehr,

Admiral Wilhelm Franz Canaris. The German military intelligence service has been headed since 1935 by Canaris at the personal behest of Adolph Hitler himself.

Born in January 1887, in Aplerbeck in Westphalia, to a wealthy family, and joining the Imperial Navy in 1905 at the age of eighteen, Canaris has a distinguished navy career. Without Hitler's inner personal staff, or the Nazi Party's elite, ascertaining that his loyalty is in question at the time of the Munich Agreement, Canaris is now in one of the most powerful and significant positions in Nazi Germany.

Canaris, like the army leadership, had to weave his way around the Nazi Party established security and quasimilitary organizations, the SS, the SD, and the Gestapo. Canaris's rival in the intelligence domain is Heinrich Himmler, the Reichsfuhrer of the Schutzstaffel, better known as the SS. He is a key Nazi Party member and will, in due course, become the main architect of the Holocaust. On this day though, he has other things to consider, specifically instructed by Hitler to meet with Canaris and develop plans not just for the post conquest of France and northern Europe, but operations in and associated with neutral Spain and Portugal, and their two dictators, Franco and Salazar.

Himmler sees Canaris as his rival for Hitler's attention in all things related to intelligence and what he sees as the associated domains of secret police activities, counterintelligence, and the use of force to subjugate any opposition to the Führer's wishes and orders. A navy admiral is not what Himmler wants as the key leader of German intelligence. However, he has to be subservient. Hitler admires Canaris and has elevated him personally. Himmler has to admit to himself and his inner circle that he has been defeated for the Abwehr leadership. He would bide his time.

The contrast with Vice Admiral John Godfrey in London could not have been starker. Canaris is in the midst of a totalitarian regime, with fixed, almost messianic ambitions derived from an ideology that is not reflected in the history and the traditions of the post 1870 Germany of Bismarck and the victors of the Franco-Prussian War. The cultural and professional divide between the educated and rational elite of Canaris's

Abwehr on one hand and the fixed, unwavering, and at times irrational elements of the Nazi creed is huge.

Canaris and his key staff are in session at the Sicherheitsdienst (SD) main headquarters, together with key representatives from the SS and the Gestapo. The agenda has come down from the Führer. Canaris has been briefed personally by Hitler ahead of this meeting. He knows the objectives. He knows what must be achieved, all in keeping with Hitler's thinking and that of his inner circle, irrespective of other inputs from the Wehrmacht (the German Armed Forces).

Himmler is late to arrive. His aide has called to announce that he is awaiting a meeting with Hitler and for the meeting to proceed without him. One of his faithful, the lead in the counterintelligence section of the SD will represent, and the message for Canaris is that his representative present will speak for him. Canaris proceeds and, without recognizing the SD person, turns to the SS Gruppenfuhrer and indicates that after his Abwehr Kapitan zur See has laid out the Abwehr's plans for Portugal he will take comments from the Gruppenfuhrer as representative of the SA, SS, and Gestapo combined. Canaris continues after this brief statement with a commanding policy position.

"The Führer has directed me to lead and coordinate how we will proceed with Salazar's Portugal, a key country with important raw materials vital for our war machine. Without a regular flow of wolfram and iron ore from Portugal, the Reich will have serious difficulties in producing critical weapons. We must ensure that Portugal remains loyal to Germany while undermining and destroying all influence of Portugal's oldest ally, the British. Churchill needs goods coming in by sea from Lisbon primarily and, to a lesser extent Porto, though the British weakness for their precious port drink will be their undoing if we play our cards correctly." Canaris is interrupted by laughter, and one of the Gestapo representatives comments, "And, sir, we will ensure that they choke on it."

"Yes, indeed, Mein Herr. My staff will distribute to the SS, SD, and Gestapo staff members present the plan of attack that the Führer has approved. I will spend a few minutes outlining the strategy."

There is discernible shuffling within the ranks of the non-Abwehr officers present.

This will be Abwehr run, directed, and controlled.

"One question, before you begin, sir," proffers a Gestapo colonel equivalent, a particularly young and clearly ambitious Standartenfuhrer.

"Who will run counterintelligence? Who will ensure, sir, that all our people in the Abwehr are playing on the right side, all of the time? Will the fox be guarding the chicken coup?" he asks in a singularly direct and aggressive tone.

"Colonel, the Abwehr, as you know, has a separate and highly experienced counterintelligence arm, totally separate from the operational side, including all our covert and clandestine operations. We will be taking care not just of the Abwehr but also"—Canaris pauses for effect, looking the Gestapo colonel dead in the eye—"the SS, the SD, and indeed the Gestapo."

So do we have a role?" quips the colonel in a less than respectful voice.

"Certainly, the Abwehr plan clearly specifies where the SS, the SD, and the Gestapo will play roles. We will, in effect, draw you all in as the situation demands and as our operations develop on the ground."

Canaris pauses, draws a deep breath, considering his next statement to a less than friendly audience.

"My senior analyst that heads my team responsible for collating our sources about the British will now give you all a short and concise picture of the latest intelligence that we have on the British situation."

A youthful Abwehr major explains with considerable enthusiasm the output from the latest coded radio messages coming from agents located in and around London. He describes a dispirited nation, and Churchill facing opposition to continuing the fight, with a group of members of the Conservative Party wanting to sue for peace and negotiate with the Führer. He says Churchill's position is precarious. He turns to intelligence from Portugal. He describes how the as yet few Abwehr agents in Portugal are exploiting British and other nonaligned merchant ship crews to find out British convoy movements. He says indiscreet talk by sailors from British merchant ships and flags of convenience heading to British ports that are docking in Lisbon is yielding valuable intelligence that the Abwehr is passing on to the navy and the Luftwaffe. He then turns to a senior Abwehr officer, indicating that his briefing is over.

Canaris's chief of staff pulls down a map of Portugal.

Canaris points to Lisbon.

"This is where most of the action will be, Lisbon, the capital and primary port. Most of the trade is through Lisbon. This is why the navy elements within the Abwehr will play several roles, and in particular undermining the British and their Portuguese friends, and at the same time gaining vital intelligence on British ship movements carrying vital supplies to what is now a beleaguered Britain." Canaris hands a pointer to his two-star chief of operations, a Konteradmiral. He invites him to show the audience the geographic and political implications of Lisbon's role in the future to help cripple the British, and particularly the British merchant marine and the Royal Navy, the Konigliche Marine, Canaris emphasizes with a lilt in his voice.

The Konteradmiral plays to the gallery of non-Abwehr staff present. He lays out in considerable detail the significant number of additional Abwehr agents who will be inserted into Lisbon and other key locations in the very near future to augment current numbers. He describes their missions. Most of all, he stresses the need for security and separate, discreet communications, off line from the German embassy and coming via secure encrypted links to Abwehr headquarters in Berlin. In anticipation of the usual Gestapo and SS questions about counterintelligence, he lays out who will know what, do what, report to whom, with each Abwehr officer, and the agents that they will run, kept to very small operational numbers, the least the better, he stresses. "Am Wenigsten desto besser," he says and repeats it. "If compromised, our plans ensure that each officer and his agents will only know their small part. It is the big picture that we, here in Berlin, will control, the one that the Führer likes and has approved."

The SS and Gestapo officers visibly wince.

"So was ist unsere Rolle?" remarks one senior Gestapo officer tersely.

"Your role," says the admiral boldly, "is to stand by to stand by."

There is quiet in the room.

"When the Abwehr needs your special skills, and these are considerable," he says with a tactful and deferential voice. Canaris quietly smiles to himself at his chief of staff's comment. "We expect to bring you all in once the Abwehr has consolidated its position on the ground, and we find that your special skill sets are required."

"Wann wird das sein?" questions a SS Gruppenfuhrer.

"When we are ready," the admiral says assertively.

There is tension in the room.

An SS colonel looks at Canaris, and without the respect that a colonel should show a four-star admiral and head of the Abwehr, sounds off in a high-pitched voice, "Schutzstaffel Head Heinrich Himmler will be watching very carefully the Abwehr's performance in Portugal. He expects nothing but one hundred percent of effort and total annihilation of British intelligence operations in Lisbon in particular. I am advised, too, Admiral, that the Gestapo under Herr Heinrich Mueller reporting through Herr Reinhard Heydrich directly to the Führer will be watching too Abwehr counterintelligence operations to ensure that there are no weaknesses as you press ahead in Lisbon." This is a disrespectful statement that no Wehrmacht officer should say to a four-star member of any of the German military services under direct Wehrmacht leadership. It is not just disrespect, but a blatant challenge by one part of Hitler's inner nonmilitary staff to a very senior member of the old guard German military elite.

Canaris and his chief of staff are quietly seething, yet without showing any sign of annoyance or indeed the aggravation that is warranted.

Canaris states in a cool, calm, and totally controlled voice, "The Führer has given me these orders directly and personally. He has, by the way, in addition to all that you have heard in this meeting, instructed me to visit Franco in Madrid and Salazar in Lisbon as soon as possible. I will be ensuring their continuing loyalty to the Third Reich."

Canaris inwardly thinks to himself, *And funding them accordingly, with the Reich's gold.*

Canaris turns to his chief of staff and asks if he has anything to add.

No, sir," retorts the chief of staff.

At this point, Canaris stands and says that unless there are further questions, the meeting is adjourned. His final comment is strident.

"Gentlemen, you will be privileged to read the plan for Lisbon. It is crucial that this is not shared beyond all of you in this room. The detail of our clandestine and covert operational plans are not included, for obvious reasons. You all have the objectives, the main aspects with which you need to be familiar." Canaris pauses. "This is all you need to know."

He scans the group, smiles, and says, "Heil Hitler."

They all responded in unison, "Heil Hitler."

Canaris and his chief of staff departs for Abwehr headquarters.

The two admirals sits back in the staff car, look at each other, with Canaris's chief of staff wishing to break the ice.

"Sir, you were incredible. You kept your cool in there. I would have found it very difficult not to give that SS colonel both barrels."

"Never fear, Jurgen, we haven't heard the last of this. Himmler will be watching our every move. I want to talk to the key staff. Set up a meeting please. We need to be very wary of what Himmler and his people are up to, as much as we are the British. By the way, I want you to do something very special for me and just share this only with Gunter."

"Whatever you say, sir."

"Make sure that none of our people who are really in the know about our plans for dealing with Salazar's and Franco's people are working both sides, ours and Himmler's. I don't want any Himmler spies inside our own camp. Understand?"

"I do indeed, sir. I have just the right person to handle checking who of our people might meet with any of the SD, the SS, or the Gestapo, or call them."

"What about private calls from their homes?"

"We have that in hand too, sir. All private calls by our people are routed through our own special communications group. I'll ensure that the head of special communications knows of your wishes."

"Perfect, absolutely perfect," says Canaris in a soft voice.

As their car reaches Abwehr headquarters, Canaris shows a slight chink in an otherwise full mental armor.

"My biggest concern is not the enemy, it's the people within, those who are rendering very bad advice to the Führer. I just hope, indeed pray, that he will not pursue what I think could become our undoing."

"Sir, what is that?"

"I can't say, much too sensitive. We'll have to watch how things unfold. Meanwhile, watch Himmler and his people, like there's no tomorrow."

"Yes, sir. Count it as done."

Canaris heads to his office, knowing that ahead lay a very rocky road with Himmler and all whom he controlled.

ANTHONY WELLS

CHAPTER 8

Fleming Meets Kim Philby

THE DNI INSTRUCTS Fleming to get close to SIS and specifically connect with the MI6 lead person in London for the Iberian peninsular, the man who is overseeing covert operations in both Spain and Portugal. Godfrey has agreed with C that there should be no crossing of wires, no confusion over who was doing what and how. As his new head of a special operations group, the DNI wants to keep whatever Fleming created organizationally completely separate from C's agents and the MI6 people running them on the ground in Lisbon and elsewhere. The DNI has a natural and singularly intuitive sense of good security. He knows one key aspect. In every large barrel of apples, there is always at least one that's either rotten or going that way. As much as Godfrey trusts C implicitly, he knows very little about his people, those who manages agents overseas and back at MI6 headquarters collate reports and send on to the key end users in the Foreign Office, the Admiralty, the War Office, the Air Staff, and the Joint Intelligence Committee in the Cabinet Office. As a navy man, he always wants to know everything he could about his crew. When it comes to C's people, he has no such knowledge. His message to Fleming, as he set out from the Admiralty to visit with C's lead person for Spain and Portugal, is simple. Do not tell them anything about our plans. Only C knows, and I, John Godfrey, will keep him in the picture as things move down the pike. Fleming is, therefore, under no illusions as his black cab weaves its way through the London traffic to an innocuous looking building on the south bank of the Thames, near to Waterloo railway station. As he tips the driver, Fleming recalls the DNI's final words, ringing in his ears, "Ian, don't tell them a thing. Understand!" Fleming had responded with the traditional, "Aye, aye, sir. I have your message, loud and clear."

Godfrey even suggested a little deception, "There's no harm, Ian, in sowing a few dead seeds either. They'll come to nothing, but they won't know that."

Fleming is surprised at the minimal security, two uniformed security guards just inside the entrance, and a gentleman in a smart black suit, white pressed shirt, and black tie sitting in a glass-protected booth, reception by another name, a super porter who is the very first person one meets when entering the hallowed turf of MI6.

"Good morning, sir, who may I ask have you come to visit?" the graying man in his late fifties greets Fleming with a pleasant smile and cheerful demeanor.

"I've an appointment with Mr. Kim Philby," replies Fleming. "He's expecting me about now. I'm a few minutes adrift," responds Fleming, using a nautical metaphor.

"I'll just buzz him, sir. You're on the visitor list. He'll be down shortly. If you'll kindly take a seat."

The porter never once asks for Fleming's name or to see any form of identification. He is clearly expected.

"Thank you."

Within less than a few minutes, Mr. Kim Philby descends the stairs adjacent to the reception booth.

Fleming stands, and they both greet each other, never having met before.

"Welcome, Commander Fleming. Let's go to my office. Just a couple of floors up. Like some coffee?"

"Sounds like a plan."

As they enter the secure area where Philby, and whoever else does their work, Fleming notices several things. There are no security guards in place, either the usual government uniformed security staff or plain-clothes staff. But there are cipher locks on the doors, and these are all open as they go through an open area with several secretaries working away, pass half a dozen offices, some with closed doors, and then reach what looks like an inner sanctum, where Philby is clearly located. Within it there are several people, about four men and three women, working at a large table, all examining a map, with papers strewn over the table in a haphazard fashion.

"I've a visitor from the Admiralty. I'm going to be busy for the next hour and then I have a lunch engagement. I'll be back in the office about two o'clock." Fleming notices that Philby does not use military time, and his secretary, who is sitting at a separate desk outside his office, is a frail-looking, almost wizen older lady whom Philby addressees as if she was his chamber maid.

"Marjory, keep all calls on hold, and no visitors. Understand?"

"Yes, sir," replies the frightened little Marjory.

"Very well, come on in, Commander. Would you like coffee?"

"That would be nice please, black, no milk and no sugar, thank you."

"Marjory, do your thing," Philby brusquely says to his secretary. Not one "please or thank you," Fleming notices.

They both sit. Although there are several chairs in Philby's office, he sits in his chair behind his desk, a large oak table littered with papers that Fleming can see clearly the security markings. Some say clearly, Top Secret. He has clearly felt not obliged to secure them while he had descended to meet Fleming.

"Let's get down to business. I gather you're going to be involved in Portugal and that Nazi rat hole, Lisbon, and C's instructed me to brief you on our operations."

"I think that's the idea," replies Fleming in a low voice, almost nonchalantly.

"If you'd like to tell me what you're up to that might be helpful," Philby states in a fairly direct manner. "Give me some context."

"We're just looking at where we are, nothing specific in mind, trying to get our arms around the waterfront side of things," Fleming replies disarmingly.

He than makes his position clear, without any ambiguity. "I heard you mention to your staff that you have an upcoming appointment after our meeting. Maybe we should cut to the chase? The DNI was told by C that you would bring me up to speed on 6's current operations in

Portugal, where we are on the ground, and what NID can, or maybe cannot expect from the Iberian section, your section."

"Well, here goes, Commander. By the way, the front office sent down a short bio on you. You've been around, I see. Spent a lot of time in Europe, in and out of the Third Reich before Doomsday, got educated there, or maybe it was Austria, speak several languages fluently, and know the city like the back of your hand, eh?"

Fleming pauses, and without being either immodest or adding to Philby's description, simply says, "And you, how did you end up here?"

Philby is taken aback. He pauses, gathers himself in his chair, and without looking Fleming directly in the eye, says, "I was a Cambridge man, Trinity College to be precise."

"Oh, I guess we all have our problems in life," quips Fleming mischievously, smiling as if to disarm Philby and make him realize his comment is a joke and to be taken as such.

But Philby is not amused. He continues, "One of my Cambridge friends, Guy Burgess, brought me in after the fall of France. We were all part of the good old boy network from our Cambridge days, good thing, people who know each other, from the right schools, right breeding, and all that."

"Really," replies Fleming, noting that Philby is becoming passively aggressive in a somewhat strange but nonetheless alarming way. Fleming is then a little provocative.

"I gather that some very smart chaps from Cambridge are doing great things elsewhere, that none of us know about, and quite a few of them started life as working class lads who happen to be a lot brighter than me with my Eton education and you, at where, I think it was Westminster?"

"How do you know that?" retorts Philby in a startled manner.

"Like you, I was shown a little crib sheet back in the Admiralty, you're an interesting fellow, Kim, born in India, Punjab I recall, lots of journalist experience around Europe. I see you're out of here and on the way to SOE, that new place out at Brickendonbury manor, in Hertfordshire, I believe."

"Not quite, old man. I'm head here of what we call a subsection of Section 5, running our people in Madrid, Lisbon, Gibraltar, and Tangier. I help train SOE recruits out at the manor, when time permits. I'm not moving any time soon unless you know something I don't."

"Very good, you've moved up quickly since you weren't one of the Sinclair golden boys in the 1930s."

"No, you're right, too busy traveling and writing for the lead dailies. Made some serious money too."

"Do you know a Cambridge chap that I ran into, name's Hinsley, if I remember correctly."

"No, but I've heard of him, much younger than my Cambridge group, very bright, first and all that, at King's, I think?"

"Maybe, I was told St. John's, one of those less privileged scholarship boys from the Midlands who will help us win the war."

Philby then totally dissembled, recognizing a different mindset to his.

"The working class will one day run things, Fleming, mark my word."

"Well, we'll see. This is a war where every class has to pull their weight and make contributions." He pauses. "And sacrifices." He quickly gets off this subject and notes, "You're in a hurry. Tell me about Lisbon and what I can learn."

"OK, let me see. My Section 5 subsection is about one thing only in Lisbon, basically Portugal since it all happens in Lisbon. It's all about offensive counterintelligence, watching Abwehr agents who are clearly detailed to watch our naval base at Gibraltar, and upset the apple cart for us in Lisbon. They're monitoring all our supply ships coming and going in the Mediterranean. I've got some very good people running Spanish and Gibraltarian agents for us, and by the way, we try to recruit German merchant sailors or non German nationals who are working on a whole variety of flag of convenience vessels plying the Mediterranean, some of which come through the Suez Canal from the Red Sea and beyond."

Fleming notices Philby is becoming slightly irritated and is looking at his watch, an expensive-looking Swiss make.

"Let me show you my organization chart, my Subsection. You can't have a copy of this, but I'll explain who's who and who does what and what we have achieved to date."

Over the next ten minutes, Philby elucidates, clearly not wanting questions.

Fleming is singularly unimpressed. He's secretly thinking that he's glad he doesn't have to work for a man who is a clear and unadulterated control freak.

After what is in effect a diatribe, a quasi-lecture, Philby asks directly, "Now tell me about your plans. What are the heirs and successors to Blinker Hall got up their sleeves, what you see yourselves doing in Lisbon?" he asks with a slight smirk.

"Do nothing. We have nothing in the works. Too busy chasing U-boats. DNI wanted me to see if you had anything that might help us keep tabs on Donitz's U-boats and what might happen if Hitler decides to add Spain and Portugal to his conquests,"

"We can't help you there. That's all navy stuff."

Stuff in this context is not a word Fleming would have chosen for what the Royal Navy is doing round the clock to keep Britain fed.

Philby is glancing at his watch for about the fourth time during their meeting.

"Time for me to depart. You have to go. Let me walk you out of your own building. Maybe we can share a cab?"

"No, that's not necessary, but thank you," Philby comments in an insincere way that Fleming could not help but notice.

On the curbside, Fleming lets Philby take the first cab that arrives to their beckoning. He tries to listen to what he asks the driver. He thinks he heard, "Bond Street," but no address. While waiting for his cab, he reflects that the only secret place on Bond and Oxford Street is the secret communications center under Selfridges store, unless of course, he muses, he's off to some MI6 safe house or maybe a visit to their, MI6's bête noire, MI5, the domestic counterintelligence organization that vetted Fleming together with the Royal Navy's special security group.

"The Admiralty, please."

"Yes, sir, traffic's not bad for a change," the cab driver states in a cheerful tone.

Fleming sits back and reflects. There is something about Philby that he simply did not like. Arrogance, overconfidence, a certain smugness that although Fleming came from a well-to-do and wealthy family, he simply found bordering on distasteful. Most of all, Philby's Subsection is, no question, underachieving in Lisbon, at least based on what he'd revealed, unless of course there is more that he simply did not wish to share. Fleming is not impressed.

What Fleming notes on his pad for when he would, in due course, give his director a report, is the paucity of any really thorough British counterintelligence in Lisbon, who is watching the watchers? Who is checking on Philby's so-called recruits? Philby seems to be Spanish and Gibraltar centric. Most of all, there are zero plans equivalent to what the DNI and he has in mind. At one level, Fleming is secretly glad. "We can run our own covert undercover show, no MI6 busy-bodies getting in the way. It'll be us versus the Abweht and whoever else Himmler throws into the mix." These inner thoughts silently give Fleming a sense of great satisfaction.

As Fleming's cab draws up outside the Admiralty building, Kim Philby alights from his cab outside Bond Street underground station on Oxford Street.

Philby crosses Oxford Street, umbrella in hand, knowing that the BBC weather report that morning indicates showers. He slows his pace, glancing in several shop windows, looking at reflections, as if he is running a countersurveillance operation. Indeed, he is.

He enters the large and busy Selfridges store on Oxford Street. He makes a cursory walk through Selfridge's store, looking askance all the time, stopping occasionally to look at gift items in the ladies' cosmetic section and glancing over his shoulder as he moves on. He increases his gait and leaves Selfridges by the rear doors, and then crosses the road into a pub opposite, where he leaves through the rear, and then doubles back toward the Marble Arch area at a brisk pace, umbrella in hand being used like a drill sergeant's baton. He almost marches toward the Edgware Road, just north of Marble Arch. He enters a café and heads to the very rear and sits down at a table for two, with only a handful of shop assistants and clerical workers at lunch. Philby becomes nervous because he notices as he entered the front door that the American reporter, Edward R. Murrow, is sitting in a window seat to the left in the front main area, clearly interviewing someone. The great American reporter, a tried-and-true Anglophile, who has seen the British enduring hardships and sacrifices unknown to his American readership and listeners to his popular broadcasts, is busily writing on a pad. Later this day, he will address the American people from London with his signature opening, "This is London, and this is Edward R. Murrow." As Philby enters, Murrow is totally engrossed in interviewing the head of London's air-raid warning organization. He is busily asking about the use of the London underground network as makeshift air-raid shelters for London's beleaguered citizens. He does not notice Philby come in and does not look up. Edward R, Murrow will notice neither Philby nor the person he meets eventually depart. The quintessential reporter is doing what he does best, gathering the facts from real Londoners under siege from the German Luftwaffe. He will never know who just entered and the purpose of his rendezvous.

Philby orders coffee and a sandwich. After about ten minutes, a heavy-set man comes in, about five feet nine, clearly overweight, and in his fifties. Without any comment from Philby he sits down at Philby's table.

He speaks reasonable English with a strong accent. The latter is clearly East European. To the listener casually hearing him, maybe Russian? They speak in inaudible low tones, muffled as if deliberately not wishing anyone who enters the back room of this coffee shop to overhear their conversation.

Who is Philby's guest? Is he an MI6 agent reporting in to the head of Subsection 5? He's clearly not Spanish or Portuguese. Is Philby receiving information?

The answer becomes unequivocally clear. Philby passes under the table an envelope.

The man says, in muffled, inaudible tones what a recorder if such a device had surreptitiously been implanted close at hand, would clearly pick up as instructions, for the "Next tasking, Comrade Philby."

This man is Philby's Soviet KGB handler. Philby, the privileged epitome of his class, he who exploits the inner sanctum of those who believe that all Cambridge men of a certain breeding must be fine people, "Hail, Fellow, well met," and all that, is about to pass on his country's secrets. What Philby has handed him under the tablecloth in a buff envelop betrays all MI6's secrets to which Philby is privileged. They then have an inconsequential conversation, at a higher decibel age about the effects of the bombing, the weather, and other trivia. The man from Moscow tells Philby the time and place for their next meeting, in three weeks' time. The man finishes his coffee and hands under the table a small envelop to Philby. He gets up, smiles at Philby, looks over his shoulder, and leaves, not noticing for one moment that to his right on departure is America's finest reporter, engrossed, committed, passionately loyal to the British, and in his own unique way, a true hero.

When Philby departs ten minutes later, Ed Murrow is still busily chatting with his interviewee.

Philby takes a completely alternative and circuitous route back to his office. In the first of two black cabs that he takes, he decides, somewhat nervously, to open the envelope that his handler had given to him.

He checks that the driver is fully occupied in navigating his way to his first stop on Piccadilly. He looks behind, out of the rear window. He opens the envelope.

Philby discreetly and, without the driver noticing, places in his coat pocket one thousand pounds, tightly bound. He leaves the envelope on the floor of the cab as he alights. At first he follows a similar routine to his outbound route. Eventuality he quickly, as if impetuously, hails a second cab and gives Waterloo station as his destination. As his ride begins, he sits back with a sense of smug satisfaction, smirking to himself and thinking about how this large amount of money will fund his expensive habits and tastes. Philby is the quintessential ideologue, and one with a taste for the good things of this life, far from the madding crowd, and the poverty of the Soviet masses. Philby has never known what it is like to be poor, just a theoretical sense of how the proletariat will one day overwhelm capitalism. Meanwhile, he will live off and enjoy the fruits of the Soviet KGB.

Fleming is back in the Admiralty, sitting in his office adjacent to the admiral's. He is writing a brief report on his meeting with Philby. It is direct, nonjudgmental, and does not reflect his personal observations of the head of Subsection 5 of the British Secret Intelligence Service. Inwardly, Fleming reflects that it is most important that people such as Philby are not in the Bletchley loop, unaware thank goodness, he surmises, of the nuggets coming from the brightest minds that Britain produces. His report is a summation of MI6's clear lack of extensive coverage in Portugal, and Lisbon specifically. He stresses the weaknesses. There are no strengths to commend. His conclusion is simple and clear cut. The NID needs to move ahead quickly with their covert plans. Moreover, the prime minister wants it so. Churchill gets what he wants. Fleming decides that he will deliver and, in doing so, will have to weave a web around C's Section 5 scant and none-too-effective agents on the ground in Lisbon. Fleming has a clear idea of how he will achieve this, and to the entire satisfaction of the man he respects most in his life, Vice Admiral John Godfrey, the DNI.

CHAPTER 9

Fleming Meets Masterman: Synergism on Steroids

THE FOLLOWING DAY, Godfrey listens carefully to Fleming's account of his meeting with the MI6 Iberia section head. He weighs every word and makes notes. The DNI then makes a series of definitive statements, after which Fleming is both impressed and, at a personal level, delighted with what he hears.

Godfrey clearly wants to change the subject. Fleming backs off and listens.

"We're moving ahead quickly with our own plans. We don't need the likes of Philby messing with our operations planned for Portugal. I'll deal with C. He and I have an understanding."

Godfrey takes a breath and looks at Fleming with one of those authoritative looks that means only one thing, "Pay attention, I'm about to give you your marching orders."

"You're all set for your meeting with John Masterman this afternoon. You'll need to get on the road soon, but before you go, I want to give you a heads-up on what this is all about, though I'll leave it to him, naturally, to brief you into his program. It's all good stuff, it's the best, and Masterman is the ideal person to lead this operation."

"I don't think I've ever heard of him, let alone what he might be doing."

"That's all right. Most people haven't, and that's good too. What to expect? Well, let me see, he's about forty-nine, if my memory serves me correctly. Bit like you, but older, insofar as he spent time, in addition to Oxford, Worcester I think, Worcester College, getting better educated and teaching in Germany. University of Freiburg, I think."

"Freiburg im Breisgau," interrupts Fleming, "beautiful city, in southwest Germany, in the Black Forest, very cultured and a great university."

"Yes, indeed," proclaims the DNI, seemingly not too interested in the merits of Freiburg University.

"What I really like about John is that before he went up to Oxford, read modern history, he was a true-blue navy man. Started life at Osborne and moved to Dartmouth when it opened. Interesting thing is that after Oxford, he got a job lecturing at Freiburg, and in 1914 when the war started, he was interred by the Germans, place called Ruhleben Internment Camp, for the duration of the war, would you believe."

"For the whole war?" queries Fleming.

"Yes, four years in some awful internment camp, bit like being captured on day one of the war and being a POW for the duration."

"Poor devil," comments Fleming sympathetically.

"Well, being John Masterman, he made the most of it. Perfect German, understands the Hun mindset, and talks and acts like the best of them, German that is, when required of course."

"Even so, hats off for sticking it for four years."

"He made up for it. He's a seriously accomplished sportsman. I'm surprised you haven't heard of him, though I guess you were off gallivanting around Europe while he was playing cricket and tennis with great success."

"Impressive," comments Fleming.

"Indeed, he did a tour of Canada with MCC, and on top of that, he played at Wimbledon, I think he did them all—singles, doubles, mixed doubles, the lot. Quite the star."

"Looking forward to meeting him."

"Yes, you're going to like him. I'll tell you just one thing before you head out. He heads what we call the Twenty Committee, it's nominally an MI5 outfit, but it's got a life of its own. You'll understand once you meet the intrepid John Masterman. He's cunningly called his operation very appropriately, enough said."

"Well, sir, I can't wait."

"You'll meet his key right-hand man, very good chap, army, Lieutenant Colonel Robertson. Top-notch fellow. Masterman thinks the world of him. Be on your way. Let me know how you get on in the morning."

"Yes, sir." And Godfrey leaves the DNI's office.

Before he departs on his visit to the English countryside that Godfrey has arranged, he gives a short synopsis to Captain Stephens of his meeting with their boss.

"The admiral's clearly not enraptured by Mr. Kim Philby and his Iberia Section. It wasn't because I gave Philby and his people in Portugal low marks or muddied the waters of cooperation between us and 6. Though I must admit, sir, I did give Philby and what I observed over there low marks."

"So what's the boss's position, Ian?"

"Simple, sir, we go it alone, while working closely with the MEW people and, of course, always with Bletchley. The director's not ruling out 6. He and C clearly have some understandings to which I'm not privy, so there could be another agenda."

"Very likely, very likely indeed, Ian," Captain Stephens observes, as if he's both agreeing while indicating that he knows something that confirms this.

"Enjoy your visit to the Twenty people. You'll be amazed. Masterman is something different. Puts Philby and his people in the shade."

Fleming climbs into the unmarked navy staff car.

The Royal Marines driver, in plains clothes, stops twice toward the end of the journey while navigating narrow country roads and asks directions to the country house where his occupant, Fleming, is headed. Fortunately, he has allowed time for discourse with two locals—one an elderly gentleman pushing an aged Raleigh bicycle that has seen better days, and the other a charming lady in what turns out to be the local village, who did not have the brogue of the cyclist and was more intelligible. She sets him straight, literally and metaphorically, as she gives the polite marine and his passenger, in addition to precise directions, an earful about how her "dear friends the Davenports" has to leave their mansion for their summer home in Cornwall as the government has, at virtually no notice, requisitioned the house for the duration.

"I so miss our teas, and those wonderful cocktails, to die for!" she exclaims, at which point Fleming could not resist from the backseat, "Ah, a lady after my own heart. I'm totally sympathetic. A fine martini at the end of a long day, unbeatable. Are you a G and T lady or perhaps like me, a Martini aficionado?"

"Oh, a dry martini, the only way, the finest cure for all our problems, my dear!"

"How do you take yours, may I ask?"

"There is only one way, young man," she replied with a smile. Bear in mind that this attractive aging lady is well into her sixties. "Shaken, of course, never stirred, never."

She then said, in impeccable English, "I'm your match, a Martini aficionada," emphasizing the *a* with great clarity.

"A great pleasure, ma'am, a great pleasure. Thank you for your help, we'd never have found the manor without your impeccable guidance. If I have the good fortune to meet you again, please allow me to treat you to your favorite martini."

She beams.

"I would love that. Our local barman knows exactly what I like. The Red Lion, just down there on the left. Goodbye, 'til we meet again."

Fleming is charm personified.

The driver smiles and cannot resist an immediate off-the-cuff comment.

"Sir, if you don't mind me saying, we simple marines have a saying for it."

"Go ahead, please tell me what the *it* is between us."

"Well, sir, with chat like that, you could charm the knickers off a nun!"

"Thank you," Fleming says in a cordial way, appreciating the moment and the basic, if somewhat sordid, nature of the young marine's observation.

"Being nice never hurt anyone. Remember that when you're next chatting up the ladies in Pompey or Guz."

Fleming is referring to the Navy's and Royal Marines' colloquial names for Portsmouth and Plymouth, respectfully.

"Yes, sir, you bet."

At which point the driver stops in front of two civilian guards at the gate in front of a long driveway that led a good half mile to the front entrance of the manor house.

After the customary identity checks and the more senior of the two checking a sheet on a board in his hand, they bid them to proceed.

On alighting from the car, Fleming notices the tight security, with an inner perimeter area that's clearly been secured with high barbed wire fencing and dog patrols walking the fence lines. He observes multiple antennas on the top of the main part of the building, and over to the left in an adjacent field, he can see what looks like a recently erected set of high antennas. At the base is a purpose built radio shack large enough by Fleming's estimation to house about ten or more people.

"Good afternoon, Commander Fleming. The director's expecting you. My name's Claire. I'm his personal assistant. Please come with me. Would you like some tea while you await the director? He's on the telephone right now."

"Thank you kindly, Claire, but first I would like to pay my respects to the heads."

"Follow me. Over to the left, down the passage way, on the right. I'll wait for you here."

Fleming returns, and they proceed along two winding corridors, pass what in peacetime is clearly a large lounge, and then a superb dining area, now totally full of men and women in plain clothes busily working from government-issue desks, with typewriters hammering away and batches of telephones being worked by the staff. There appears to be two, maybe three, supervisors moving between the different groups. The dining room group, the second group that he observes, seems to be more professional both by their dress and the fact that they appear to enjoy better everything—smarter desks, chairs, and armchairs in which to relax. Three secretaries appear to support this group. He can overhear German being spoken between two of the lead people.

They reach a large oak door to what must be the smoking room for the now dispossessed family, the place where the gentlemen convene after dinner, without the ladies, for smoking, after-dinner drinks, and private men's talk.

They enter. It's an impressive room, with a lovely view over the rear garden lawns that lead down to a large lake with swans and a deck.

Fleming's host says a final, "Goodbye, Minister," puts the phone down, and walks across the spacious room to greet Fleming.

"Good afternoon, Commander Fleming," the director says, greeting Fleming with an outstretched hand to shake.

"A pleasure, sir, Admiral Godfrey said that you would introduce me to whatever transpires here, all very secure, and I'm sure, highly secretive," Fleming observes.

"Yes, indeed. Have a seat. Claire, do stay. Claire's cleared for everything here. She's also cleared for Enigma. Oxford language graduate. Somerville lady, eh, Claire?"

Claire modestly replies, "Indeed, sir."

"Speaks fluent German, like me, but didn't have to put up with fours years of being interred during the Great War, eh, Claire?"

"No indeed, sir," replies Claire in a direct and perfunctory manner.

"All right Ian, if I may, let's forget the formalities. I'm sure John's told you all about me, Oxford don and so forth, but none of what's here?"

John Cecil Masterman, Oxford don, pauses, looks directly at Fleming, and waits.

"Let's get down to business. Claire will have you sign all the security paperwork afterwards. Things you're used to. Official Secrets Act and all that, plus a lot more. I'm chairman of what's called the Twenty Committee, and called that because if you put two Roman numerals together, XX, it makes twenty, right? Schoolboy Latin. They also represent, if observed from a different angle, two crosses, in fact double crosses. Ian, I run the Double Cross System. I'm the director. Winston and his friends pulled me out of the comfort of Oxford and made me the boss here. Best job I've ever had, and ever likely to have."

They all take some tea.

"MI5 and the Special Branch rounded up, as war became imminent and then started officially, all the known German spies, agents by another name, operating here in the UK. We're confident that we got the lot of them, every man and woman. They had hidden transmitters all linked back to the Vaterland on special frequencies. The key was to ensure what I call the continuity of operations. We have done just that. Now, you'll ask, were they cooperative? No, in several cases. They were tried in secret under the best British legal practice, with all of them admitting guilt, and they were duly executed for spying. The good news is that several of them not only turned Queen's evidence, they agreed to cooperate fully rather than face the hangman."

Fleming is transfixed.

"Some of them are here, at the manor, some are elsewhere based on various radio procedures that our technical people advised us about. We weren't sure whether German direction finding would geospatially fix their location. If it all came down to this building, they would smell a rat immediately. So we do transmit from multiple locations. Bottom line, we're deceiving the Germans round the clock with our converted German double agents. Clear so far, Ian?"

"Yes, sir, very clear and very impressive."

"Claire, give the commander the details, please," Masterman requests in a consummately gentlemanly tone.

Claire is soft-spoken, but with the precise and concise touch of a well-educated Oxford modern languages graduate.

"All the people here, Commander—Ian, if I may—are not just expert German and other linguists, they understand German culture and the Nazi ideology in particular. They are the ones who are preparing the signals that we send to the various German headquarters and other centers, all with individual designated high frequencies, all encoded. The Germans send back instructions, and we are particularly diligent about all changes to encryptions. We have liaison staff here from the key Hut at Bletchley that are expert on German cryptology. We simply cannot afford to miss a beat when it comes to changing codes. It's vital. So far, so good. We have not failed."

"Extraordinary," Fleming says.

"Yes, and the real essence is what we tell the Germans, information that must be so well prepared that they do not smell deception. In return, we discover exactly what they want, what they want 'their agents', us—my colleagues and I—to tell them. Daily we're able to look into the Nazi mindset, to go behind the substance and veneer of their military operations, and see clearly where they are going, why, and how."

Fleming sits back in his chair and says very simply, "Brilliant, absolutely brilliant."

Claire then moves on, looking straight at Fleming, "Your DNI has briefed us on what you're planning in Portugal. We can help, and in the most indirect and surreptitious ways. What we can't do is ask questions that will raise alarms in Abwehr headquarters. We know how their minds work. We have to wait for them to ask us, their agents, to find answers. Let me now explain how we are deceiving them over one of the prime minister's and the war cabinet's biggest concerns at present, the possible invasion of Spain and Portugal, and in particular, either the invasion or total subversion of Salazar's Portugal to Nazi control and subjugation."

Fleming quietly comments, "And has the DNI explained my future role and planned operations?"

"Yes, indeed," replies Claire. "And we have a plan that I'll now describe."

Claire spends the next ten minutes going over how Double Cross will serve NID's purposes and provide feedback on the Abwehr's operations in particular.

"The SS, the SD, and the Gestapo are not our main concern regarding your plans. It's the Abwehr. They're going to strengthen their hand in Portugal. They're the ones to watch out for. What we can do here, together with what Bletchley is sending you and us on the Abwehr in Portugal, we can feed back cleverly designed false information that, in effect, the British do not appear to have the resources to deploy into Portugal, they are overstretched and overstressed fighting the U-boats in the North Atlantic, their army is in disarray after Dunkirk, and that they are placing all their emphasis on the war at sea against the German capital ships, the surface raiders sinking British merchant ships and leading the Royal Navy a merry dance. We can deceive them in the most subtle ways, all in keeping not just of the language style of 'our operators' but also—and this is critical—what we have assessed as the backgrounds, education, training, and frankly intelligence levels of the people that we have turned. Two are in this building at present. You'll meet them. You can practice your German, Commander."

"Are they here permanently?"

"Absolutely not. Each hitherto former German agent station, and these we never disclose, in and around London and some other odd places are operated as if it was business as usual. Each one is staffed by the best of the best linguists and communications experts. But, and this is the real *but*, the content is created here, around the corner in the adjacent rooms. Our staff lives and breathes this place. The only real benefit is that each and every member has a very nice room, private bathroom, and all the other trappings of living in a country house. We have to be in a place where we can think quietly and effectively, without pressure and harassment that could lead to fatal mistakes."

"I fully understand."

Fleming sits back, takes a deep breath, looks at Claire and then Masterman, and says, "This is golden. I can see why the DNI wanted me to visit."

"Indeed, Ian, let's go meet two interesting people, Germans. Then we'll come back here and discuss how in more detail we can frame things to meet John Godfrey's and your needs."

They climb up an impressive stairwell, shorn of family art and memorabilia, and enter an area that has been cordoned off, with armed civilian guards, clearly newly installed security doors that lead to what must be a very private bedroom area, perhaps where the lord and lady of the manor normally reside.

The rooms have been converted. In effect, they are quasi-interrogation centers where, in today's case, two of the German double agents have been brought from their normal operating areas to the manor house to work with Masterman's professionals, the "deceivers," the German-speaking experts and those immersed before the war in

German history, culture, and the Nazi edifice that Adolph Hitler and his cohorts created.

They are met by a gentleman who does not introduce himself and, clearly with Masterman's total approval, avoids any form of future recognition or direct connectivity. Fleming deduces that this must be the Lieutenant Colonel Robertson that Admiral Godfrey had mentioned. He has a military bearing, speaks "army speak" as Fleming understands how certain British Army officers tend to speak, and his manner, deportment, and gait live and breathe the British Army. They enter what is one of the bedrooms in peacetime. Sitting at a table is one of the Germans. His British handlers are moving in and out of German and English, they have maps spread out in front of them—the UK and Europe—and they have the remnants of lunch on a table nearby. They are discussing British ports and naval bases. The German, who was clearly under deep cover in the late 1930s, is most familiar with Portsmouth and Chatham, and he is explaining the significance of the latest requests that he's received on his transmitter from an Abwehr station in northern Germany. They listen for about ten minutes and then quietly leave, without a word being spoken by Masterman, Claire, or Fleming. Fleming gives a cursory nod to the indisputable Lieutenant Colonel, who returns the gesture with a smile and a wink.

On reentering Masterman's office, the director turns to Fleming.

"You have the picture, Ian. Now, let's get down to business. Please give Claire what you think that we can do, and in light of what you now know, and especially the constraints and limitations. And of course, the benefits and opportunities that we here at Double Cross can offer and hopefully make your Portuguese plans viable."

"Thank you, sir."

He turns to Claire, pen and pad in hand.

"We want them to think, primarily, that we can do very little and that the Abwehr, as a result, may have a free hand. They won't expect us to be totally inactive, that's for sure. What we could do, and I defer to you and your team here, we could give them false but credible ways that we may have weak links in our chain."

"Go on, Ian. Sounds good."

"They know that we're stretched chasing their U-boats. NID wants them to believe that, in addition to being ineffective in Portugal, we have weaknesses there that they can exploit. British merchant ships and flags of convenience in neutral Portuguese ports are potentially rife with leaky sieves, crews that can give away information. Your Double Cross people have been to Tilbury, the pool of London, Southampton, Glasgow, and Liverpool, watching and listening and picking up intelligence that they've sent back to the Abwehr, along with false naval-related intelligence. We can do the same regarding vital merchant shipping going in and out of Lisbon, a neutral port."

"Excellent," Claire comments. "I'm relieved, Commander, I was afraid that you'd ask us to give them false information that would not be credible, that no way could one of the agents that we've turned and work for us ever have access to. This is good. The dockland angle, the commercial side, the trade aspects—they work well, really well. We can send signals that goad them into wanting more information, so it always comes from them, not us. We have to respond to their instructions, but in that process, we sow seeds."

Fleming then explains his future operation. Only Masterman and Claire will be in the picture at Double Cross. No one else. He spends another ten minutes elaborating on the minutiae of how to play back false merchant ship information and how this could tie back into protecting north Atlantic convoys from the US to Britain.

"Excellent, Ian. I can see why John Godfrey brought you on board, if I may say so."

At which point, Masterman indicates that it's time for Fleming to sign the official documents that swear him to total secrecy.

He does this.

Masterman shakes Fleming firmly by the hand and tells him quite clearly, "Claire's your point of contact, Ian. No one else. Always on the secure line. Don't identify yourself to anyone else here. She has her own personal secure line. No one else can use it. Got it?"

"Yes, sir, indeed. Thank you."

Claire and Fleming leave Masterman's office. This will be the first and last time that Fleming will see Double Cross Masterman until after the war, in Oxford, at a high table dinner at Worcester College, with Fleming as Masterman's guest.

The driver has Fleming's door open. He turns to Claire, thanks her profusely, and indicates that he will be back in touch soon. She reciprocates quite formally. Fleming almost leans forward to kiss her on the cheek, but holds back. This is neither the time nor the place.

The door closes. He waves. He will not see Claire again, just serious business talk on a secure line that has to be used sparingly.

As he drives back to London, Fleming is ready for a nap before a late evening working in Room 39 and an early start in the morning. He thinks of Claire, the bright, demure, and very attractive assistant to one of the smartest men that Fleming has ever met, indeed will ever meet.

The driver has not forgotten his way, and as they drive past the Red Lion, Fleming thinks of that martini that could await him inside—shaken, not stirred—and that charming lady who could be Claire's mother.

He closes his eyes and falls into a deep sleep.

CHAPTER 10

Economic Warfare and All That

THE DNI IS a tired man as he sits in the director's chair to receive the 0800 morning briefing. He had a late night, followed by an early morning meeting with the prime minister and C to update Winston Churchill. Commander Denniston joins them at the end of their three-person-only meeting, providing the latest Bletchley intercepts, and with the cabinet secretary joining to take down and action the directives that the prime minister issued. Godfrey feels that he can almost relax after the intensity of a prime ministerial meeting. He listens patiently as the duty commander gives him the good news and the bad news about the latest submarine contacts and the successful evasion executed by the large convoy in transit from Baltimore and Boston that had joined together off Newfoundland with the help of the Royal Canadian Navy out of Halifax, Nova Scotia. Thirty minutes later, the DNI commends his operational intelligence people for a good night's work and turns to Fleming and asks him to join him in his office.

***

"I've another key meeting for you, Ian. My secretary's made the necessary arrangements. She can give you the where and when. Let me give you the why. I've great confidence in the people you'll meet. Smart as whips, a bit like the Bletchley people. Mixture of academics, business people, financiers, and traders—people that you'll relate to."

"Standing by, sir."

"MEW are the three letters that you won't forget. Ministry of Economic Warfare. Tied in with SOE, once, hopefully, it gets off the ground and does the prime minister's bidding.

"They're critical for what we have in mind for Portugal. Why? Portuguese exports to the Nazis and their war machine. Hitler needs Salazar, and he needs Nazi funds—gold, in fact, is how Hitler pays Salazar. The key ingredients, you know about. Tungsten is what I call it, but MEW refers to it by its other name, wolfram. They'll tell all you need to know. The other is iron ore. Critical for a host of German war products. They'll give you the details.

"You can see where I'm going with all this?"

"Yes, indeed, sir. The various contingencies we're drawing up for the special group fit whatever course of action Hitler orders, from the worst case to the not so worst."

"You've got it. The devil's in the detail, Ian. Go over there and soak up all that they've got. We've got to be able to stop them if we have to. The PM's relying on what I've told him, and C has backed me up. You won't have to mess with Philby and his Iberia Section people."

"Good, I'm relieved."

Godfrey smiles, frowns a little, and comments, "You really didn't like his man Philby, did you, Ian?"

"Honest answer, sir, never in a month of Sundays would I rely on that man. This is navy through and through, NID, and all that we have."

"Well, Ian, you have a green light. Get on your way. By the way, the man you're going to meet, the boss, Hugh Dalton, first-rate chap. PM thinks the world of him, hand-picked. He's cleared for Enigma, but none of our other special NID-only things. Remember that, please."

"Yes, sir."

Fleming departs the DNI's office, collects his directions from the secretary, who informs him that the staff car will be waiting in ten minutes.

Fleming quickly changes into plain clothes, and he's outside the main Admiralty entrance on time.

***

As his car wends it way to the Ministry of Economic Warfare headquarters building, Fleming starts to generate ideas for how his group will attack and disable Hitler's war materials sources in Portugal. He's doing what every good naval officer is trained to do, the *A* word: *anticipate*—see down the road, look ahead for what's coming, and be ready, well prepared, with no surprises. What he'll need from MEW are the details. Then he can form an action plan, sabotaging, disabling, and destroying all that Hitler needs from Portugal; implementing a deception plan and leading the Abwehr and the other agents of Nazi control and spy craft—the SS, the SD, and the Gestapo—down the garden path while remaining totally covert; and if and when necessary, destroying all that Hitler needs. Meanwhile he'll have to collect as much intelligence as feasible in preparation so his team is well-briefed and know the where and what. He jots down in his notebook innocuous points only intelligible to him. Most of all, he remembers at the back of his mind one key point that Admiral Godfrey had impressed on him. He could hear his words echoing in his mind: "Don't forget, Ian, we need Salazar's tungsten and iron ore too. He's feeding at our trough as well the gold Hitler pays him regularly. We need him as much as he needs our money. We can't cut off our nose to spite our face. Salazar has us between the devil and the deep blue sea. He's as slippery as an eel and as clever as a snake waiting to bite its prey."

***

He read the short note that Godfrey's secretary had prepared for him about Hugh Dalton, a Welshman, the key person that he was about to meet, the director, at least as Fleming thought, of the Ministry of Economic Warfare. It is short and to the point. Fleming got the message. Born in August 1887, so he's in his early fifties; and although a Labor Party member, he is much respected by Churchill for both his knowledge and skills as an economist but also his opposition to appeasement and support with Churchill for British rearmament in the face of growing Nazi militarization and aggression. Fleming is warming to him already. He was a King's College, Cambridge, and LSE man

(London School of Economics and Political Science), and Fleming can't quite believe what he read, because of Dalton's clear left-wing political views and affiliations, he was an Old Etonian. His father had no less been a tutor to the King's father, George V, and was a canon at Windsor. Dalton has a distinguished World War I military record. Fleming likes what he is reading. What he hadn't picked up from Godfrey in their somewhat hurried discussion is that Dalton is a member of the war cabinet; he is in fact minister of Economic Warfare, shedding a whole new light on the meeting that is minutes away. He would be meeting with one of Churchill's chosen few, Labor Party or Conservative, it doesn't matter. The prime minister clearly thinks that Hugh Dalton is the best. In a few short minutes, Fleming feels that he not only has the measure of Minister Hugh Dalton, but he is also a man for whom he has both respect and a certain amount of admiration.

***

"Welcome to MEW, Commander Fleming. John Godfrey says good things about you. Come on in and sit down. Mary, get the commander a cup of coffee, please, if you wouldn't mind, or do you prefer tea? Bit too early in the day to imbibe the navy's real elixir, eh?'

"Coffee would be perfect, sir, thank you. I'm actually not a G and T man myself or a Horse's Neck imbiber, prefer a good gin and vodka martini when the time's right and the sun is over the yardarm."

Dalton laughs. "A man after my own heart. Now let's get down to business. I've got thirty minutes before I have to get ready to go over to the Cabinet Office. My staff will take over after we've chatted."

"Thank you, sir. Sounds perfect," Fleming replies.

"Admiral Godfrey's made you aware of the Portuguese situation. I'm also heading up SOE, you're familiar with all that. But, and this is important, we're nowhere ready in SOE to do real things on the ground in Europe, least of all in Salazar's Portugal."

Fleming nods and simply listens.

"I'm worried that NID may get detected early on by the Abwehr and the other odious instruments of Hitler's that are most likely gathering in Lisbon. Any NID presence may be spotted quickly and the flame extinguished before it gets to burn fully. Maybe we should be really careful unless we see that Hitler is going to invade? That will change the dynamics, I believe?"

Dalton poses questions, not answers.

Fleming is very conscious of the DNI's instructions, indeed orders. Don't divulge all; don't give away the farm to MEW when he and C have alternative plans while the nascent SOE gets organized.

"We're team players, sir. Admiral Godfrey has made clear your thoughts and wishes."

"Good, very good, Commander. Now let me give you my take on Salazar, his war materials supply, the impact on the Portuguese economy, and most of all, the value to the Nazi war machine. And this is very important, what we need here in Britain from our neutral oldest ally, Portugal. We cannot bite off the hand that feeds us, Commander. Get the picture?"

"Yes, sir, indeed."

Fleming reverts to his most diplomatic mode, all ears, listening, not speaking unless addressed directly, and keeping a totally straight and unfathomable face.

Minister of Economic Warfare Dalton then gives Fleming ten short but exhaustive minutes on the Portuguese economy and German associations.

Fleming makes notes with Dalton's full approval.

"Remember to secure your notes, Commander, your eyes only and the right people over in NID."

"Of course, sir, always."

Dalton then says that he has to break off and hands Fleming over to his three staff members who are experts on the minutiae of the Portuguese economy and, in particular, the supply of war materials to both Germany and Britain.

They stand. Dalton proffers his hand, and they shake, with Fleming adding tactfully, "I'll ensure, sir, that we keep your people posted on all our endeavors in NID. May I request that we receive your Portuguese reports and updates as they come through?"

"Of course, already done. When you leave, we've a classified report for you and the DNI, and whoever else is cleared over in the Admiralty. It's all there, the detail. Production numbers, where, who does what, how they transport, time scales, payments, etc."

"Sir, many thanks. I know Admiral Godfrey will be most pleased."

On leaving Dalton's ministerial suite, he's met by the head of the Portuguese economic warfare section. They meet two colleagues in an office one floor up from Dalton's.

In the next two hours, Fleming learns more about the Portuguese war effort and economy than he could ever have envisaged in his city stockbroker office. He's not just impressed; he's now given the serious detail of all that he needs to plan his operations. The head of Section has spent the past six years living and working in Lisbon as the full-time Lloyds of London insurance representative. He speaks fluent Portuguese, unlike his two colleagues. He explains to Fleming in excruciating detail the shipping and trade patterns in Lisbon and Oporto—which shipping lines are involved, their cargoes, who owns what—and he opens a folder that has inside the ownership and insurance details of every ship plying in and out of Portuguese ports since September 1939. He has details on crew profiles, their captains, and flags of convenience, many with British ownership hidden inside their registration in Liberia, Panama, the Marshall Islands, and the like. He describes loading time scales and transit times between their destinations, and he spends time explaining which German ports the neutrally flagged ships visit, frequency, war materials, and other cargoes. The data is a little overwhelming at first sight, but Fleming gets the picture. The other two are from academe, one a full-blooded LSE economist who specializes in international trade and the other is an economic geographer from Cambridge who knows the Tagus and Douro Rivers and waterfronts as if he were a native Portuguese. He explains the port infrastructure, the effects of the tides and weather on arrivals and departures, the port layouts, and where the ore and wolfram are loaded. In addition, they show Fleming where these precious war materials are mined and then transported, mainly to Lisbon and the Tagus waterfront. He is told which companies are involved, how they are paid by the Germans, when, the amounts, and the comparison between German and British bills of lading. Neutral shipping is the clear name of the game, immune from attack by either the British or German navies.

They explain that given information overload, all that he is hearing is in the documents that he will take back to the Admiralty.

Fleming catches his breath, feeling a little humbled by the nature and the quality of the data, and the fact that these three men, whom he is told are supported by a larger group of analysts on the top floor, have anticipated what needs to be known about Salazar's war effort.

"Tell me, what about fishing, aren't the Portuguese seriously into fishing? We all love their sardines in addition to what comes down the Douro River and ends up as after dinner port."

James Smithers, the lead, laughs. "I thought you navy men started the whole thing, Ian."

"How come?"

"Well, Ian, Taylors and their competitors are British. You know that. They're as much part of the Porto and Douro landscape as anyone."

"Absolutely, James, they have to be a source."

James nods knowingly.

"Have been for hundreds of years. June 16, 1373, was the date we tied the knot with our Portuguese ally, but the Royal Navy passing that port bottle to the left, clockwise around the table, is it not that keeps the blood circulating between us and them?"

Fleming interjects with a smile that becomes a laugh. "We can always spot a Nazi at dinner, when they pass the port bottle across the table or, even worse, back on itself."

They all laugh.

"The Nazis don't appreciate a good bottle of Taylors!"

Fleming likes these three men. Smart, educated, cultured, traveled, and very, very knowledgeable about their subjects.

"Back to fishing for a moment, if I may," quips Fleming.

"It's all there in your package. Mainly family fishing businesses. Been doing it forever. Hate the Germans, particularly in the bars, cafés, and restaurants. Their slovenly attire and arrogant way with the local women doesn't go down well with the Tagus and Douro fishermen.

They throw their weight around, get drunk, start fights, and go back to their ships drunk out of their minds on the local hooch, evil, cheap stuff that German sailors seem to love."

Fishermen can clearly be assets, thinks Fleming. *They can be the perfect cover, and we should pay them well,* he surmises quietly to himself.

"We know the Portuguese fishing industry inside and out. Names, boats, routines, catch, exports, the lot. Refrigeration made them, like so many around the world. It's all there for you. If you need more, just ask."

Fleming is totally impressed.

"They know the rivers and the oceans around the coast and, indeed, a way out into the Atlantic. Your fishing map indicates that they go as far as their own islands, the Azores. You know that the Azores are one of our biggest nightmares. German controlled, or worse German occupied Azores, would change the whole war in the North Atlantic, a potential disaster."

Fleming's mind starts to move at a hundred miles per hour regarding Portuguese ocean fishing boats plying between the Azores and the mainland. They constitute a great source of intelligence, a way to insert and retrieve agents and saboteur teams. In the worst eventuality, if either Salazar caves into Hitler's blandishments or threats, or the Nazis simply invade, NID has to have a plan, an action plan that Churchill will approve to save the Azores from falling into Nazi hands.

At another level Fleming sees loyal, well-paid Portuguese fishermen reporting on any German naval movements, particularly U-boats on the surface at night, deploying from Bay of Biscay ports and transiting round Cape Finisterre and down the coast of Portugal.

At the same time, Fleming flashes back in his mind to his briefing in NID and at C's headquarters shortly after he joined Room 39 on Salazar's secret police, the PIDE (Policia Internacional e de Defesa do Estado). Had they infiltrated the fishing industry? *As much perhaps for internal political reasons as much as counters to German influence,* surmised Fleming. He and his new team will have to read very carefully inside Portugal. Bletchley data will be paramount in preparing insertions into Portugal. At this stage, Fleming is still unknowing of one key factor. Time will tell.

As they conclude their various briefings, including showing Fleming photographs and map locations, the Section chief presents Fleming with a double-wrapped large envelope. Inside is all the detail that Fleming and his new team will need.

He thanks them profusely, with genuine and heartfelt navy-style Bravo Zulus.

As the Section chief and Fleming descend the stairwell, Fleming cannot help but comment, "I've had more ideas in the past two hours than I've had in a long time. When I get back to the Admiralty, I'm going to talk with our one and only topographical expert, Frederick Wells. I want him to put his fine mind to all your data, especially all that wonderful material on the rivers and the infrastructure. He'll be more than grateful."

"It's what we do. We're here to try to give you whatever you need. Just call anytime, if you need anything else, anything that we've missed."

Fleming smiles, shakes his hand, and says very simply in a direct and soft-spoken voice, "Thank you, thank you very much. You're making a difference, a huge difference."

***

His driver closes the door as Fleming sits back, gripping his security pouch in which there is pure gold—not the real gold that Salazar receives for his collaboration with the Nazis, but informational gold that in the long term will be worth far more, more indeed than its weight in gold.

Fleming is exhilarated as his car draws up in front of the Admiralty. What Godfrey and C have in mind is a very different agenda. The truly patriotic and extremely capable people that Dalton leads have planned for a time in the future that may be too late if the worst case occurs. SOE is a baby, hardly out of the nursery, and Fleming is now not only convinced but dedicated to seeing his operation get off the ground in the quickest time possible. MEW has armed him with invaluable information.

CHAPTER 11

A Very Different Kind of Gnome, and Something More Than a Cuckoo Clock

I T IS A risky approach at the best of times. The weather is marginal, with low-ceiling conditions, making setting up for the final approach extremely treacherous. The outcome could be fatal if the pilot does not set up accurately for the turn to final approach into the wind, with mountains waiting to challenge the very best of pilots if they have to abandon the approach in low visibility. In such conditions, the German pilot hopes, indeed perhaps prays, if the Luftwaffe believed in prayer, that once he breaks out from the clouds, he will see the runway, adjust his course, and make a safe landing. "A wing and a prayer" is not in this pilot's mind. He is concentrating with all his energy and skill to control his aircraft. The German pilot is good, in fact as good as any Luftwaffe pilot that had been selected to fly the very top leadership of the Third Reich. He sets up his aircraft, a twin-engine Junkers 52, known as Iron Annie and Aunt Ju by Luftwaffe pilots, on final approach; he sets the airspeed and attitude appropriately and stays on course, peering throughout the windshield, waiting to break out and see the runway environment. The one thing in his favor is the wind. It is straight down the runway, on his glide path, so there is no challenging crosswind to complicate the very last stage of his landing. The pilot talks again to the control tower, informing them of his position and intentions as he informs them that he is on a "short final." He breaks out from the low cloud base and instantly sees the runway, adjusts a few degrees to starboard—to the right—raises the nose slightly, begins to pull the power back, lands his aircraft about a third of the way down the runway, and then pulls back all the way on the control wheel while applying the brakes and throttling back to idle power. He breathes a huge sigh of relief. He increases the power and taxis off the runway and heads to the terminal, a modest building with a small ground crew who are waiting to guide him into his parking position several hundred yards from the terminal. Before the pilot closes down the radio, the control tower makes one final transmission to the Junkers pilot, "Welcome to Zurich."

***

A car that is not flying the Nazi flag on its hood or has any indication of the future occupant's nationality or affiliation starts to move out toward the aircraft as the pilots chop the engines. The driver is in plain clothes, a local Swiss who is used regularly as this visitor's personal driver.

The VIP inside the aircraft goes to the cockpit and thanks the pilot for a good landing in difficult conditions. When they had left Tempelhof airport in Berlin the weather was good, and as they flew south toward the Alps, the weather deteriorated over the mountains. There is no reliable forecast of the conditions at their destination. He has safely reached his destination, Zurich, in neutral Switzerland.

The Swiss enjoy neutrality. It is almost a cultural as well as a political status. The great banking centers of Switzerland, and its global political hubs such as Geneva, Zurich, and Berne, were immune from the ravages of World War I; and now, they are to become, in World War II, centers for international political intrigue and espionage. Switzerland could harbor escapees from Nazi domination in conquered territories, and as the war progresses, allied airmen escaping either from German prisoner of war camps or managing to evade capture head to neutral Switzerland or Spain. Many have equivocated over the Swiss ability to both enjoy the benefits of neutrality, indeed profiting enormously from the use of its neutral and independent banking system for Hitler's benefit, and avoid the contagion and losses of war and having to maintain a serious military capability. However, the upside of this somewhat critical view of Swiss neutrality is that it serves all sides, and the British in particular. The same is true of Stockholm in Sweden. The main cities of Switzerland are critical locations where British intelligence can still operate with impunity, with each side watching each other and playing cat and mouse with who is perceived as the agents of each side and their international connections. The old adage that the Swiss contribution to European culture and civilization over the centuries is the cuckoo clock is still rife in Britain, but beneath this rather harsh and unfair observation lay the clear, incontestable, and discerning view that the gnomes of Zurich offers incalculable benefits to Britain, a country under severe duress and threatened in 1940 with the prospect of a Nazi invasion.

The four-star German officer steps down from the Junkers aircraft. He has no personal staff. He carries his own private attaché case and a personal bag. The crew do not deplane, waiting in the cockpit, until the car has pulled away and heads out of Zurich airport. This senior Nazi clearly wants his presence to be not known, or at least minimized.

The visitor is a regular at Zurich airport. He and his driver know the routine that they will follow. There is no personal security, no bodyguards, and no car to escort the visitor's car and its very senior occupant, indeed Hitler's most trusted intelligence chief.

Admiral Wilhelm Canaris is here to conduct the most secret business of the Third Reich, all with Hitler's full knowledge and approval. He sits back in the Mercedes and can think of one thing only, and it is not Swiss banking, the one and only reason for his secret flight from Berlin to Zurich.

The Widder hotel in Zurich is a reservation for the rich and famous, what today we call a five-star hotel, dating back so its records indicate to the twelfth century, an unbeatable record in the hospitality business. Its room rates, bars, and restaurants reflect its status that by Swiss standards, indeed European standards of the 1930s, is surpassed only by those whose locations may provide added status and ambience—the Savoy and Claridges in London and the Majestic (today the Peninsula), the Scribe, and the Vendome, to name but three of Paris's great meeting places before the Nazi occupation turned Paris into an occupied city. The Widder is not just for the moneyed of Europe; its clientele reflects a certain *Je ne Sais Quoi*, based on education, culture, taste, and upbringing. It's a veritable who's who of those who have the time and money to enjoy the pleasures of Zurich besides its chief function as banking and finance capital. The Widder accommodates many of those who visit to protect and extend their wealth, a veritable money entrepot, where good money and bad money, indeed very bad money in certain cases, are traded via sophisticated money transfer mechanisms. The Swiss are not into judgment; their neutrality predicates a functionality that is based solely on making money from financial services, not being the arbiter of good and evil. The high mountainous Swiss Cantons, untouched by war and international rivalry, know nothing of the business world in the big cities of Geneva, Zurich, Basel, and Bern. Of these, Zurich is preeminent in all regards, and the largest in size. Geneva prides intensely of being an international diplomatic center, giving its name to the code that should indeed control Nazi conduct in war, the Geneva Convention. However, the real action is here, the Finanzkapital of what will become war-torn Europe.

The Admiral's driver follows a well-understood routine, never asking questions, always being quintessentially Swiss, polite to the core, and never once uses the admiral's title, always Mein Herr. As he approaches old Zurich, Canaris begins to take deep breaths, as if he was about to run a race as a young man. Indeed, he has a race ahead, but it is against time only, not distance. The fact that he is over 800 kilometers from Berlin may fill him with confidence, but never overconfidence, the sort that leads the unwary, the careless, and the reckless into mistakes that can be fatal.

The car turns off the Bahnhofstrasse and stops outside the Widder. He is greeted as a regular customer by the head porter, who bows slightly, and his staff gathers to see if the visitor needs help with his bags. Canaris declines all help. He will keep his belongings close at hand. Inside he is greeted by the reception staff. They know him only as Herr Artur von Schodel, a Bavarian banker from Wurzburg, a man who ostensibly funds the Franconian wine industry. This is simply his cover.

While traveling on the Führer's direct orders, with secret intent, Canaris is merely employing established Abwehr trade craft. His most trusted staff member, his personal aide, a navy *kapitan*, Zur See, knows of his whereabouts. On his return, Canaris will report directly to Hitler, no one else. Himmler will not be in the loop. The Führer has no desire to know of Canaris's itinerary, merely to hear later that he has accomplished his mission. He is more than just chief of the Abwehr in Hitler's eyes; he is a man that he trusts to perform special missions in his name and with his full authority.

Canaris bathes and changes from his traveling attire to a formal business suit, the best that Berlin's tailors can provide, minus the giveaway label that he has meticulously removed for visits not just to Switzerland but other key European capitals when traveling incognito. He has over an hour before his noon meeting. He checks that a private room is ready for his meeting. The hotel front desk confirms that all is ready, and a private lunch will be delivered when Herr Schodel requires such.

Wegelin & Company is just like most other Swiss banks, hugely reliable, highly discreet, and always sensitive to its customers' needs for privacy and total security. Founded in 1741, it has not survived by making mistakes. Its record is impeccable. It is there to serve, to keep, and to transfer funds when required, for which it is paid well. Greed does not enter into its lexicon; it is all about service for a price. Located on Museum Strasse in St. Gallen, it is not Zurich-based. Canaris's visitors will have about an hour's drive from St.Gallen through Winterthur to Zurich, a very pleasant journey in the bank's chauffeur-driven Mercedes, with the junior member in the front and the two senior bank executives in the rear. The Abwehr prefers a non-Zurich-based bank, with faces that are not familiar, and connections that are less obvious than if a local Zurich bank was employed.

At noon, Canaris descends to the private meeting room, where his three banking guests are seated, with the two senior members on each side of where Canaris will sit at the head of the table. The other end of the table is laid out for lunch, with a plentiful supply of wine and cocktails on a nearby bar. Canaris greets his guests, friendly but perfunctory; they all know each other. They have met on several occasions. They know the procedure and the client's wishes. A smartly attired waiter asks if they require anything. They all decline, and Canaris says that he will call when lunch is required.

After the usual pleasantries, Canaris says, "Well, gentlemen, let's get down to business. The Führer insists that Herr Salazar is paid promptly, through the Reich's gold deposits with you, for the date certain that we have agreed. I have authorization here to transfer several million Reichsmarks to be placed on account with you to be used on demand for payment of the gold that you will transfer to Lisbon. We in Berlin have agreed with Salazar what the net value will be for the next deliveries of iron ore and Wolfram to the Reich. Here are all the details."

The three bankers share the documents that Herr Schodel has laid before them. They will require time to study.

The head of the Abwehr stands and goes to the bar, selects an unopened bottle, and with meticulous care, uses a corkscrew and pours himself a glass of Austrian wine, a very expensive Gruner Veltliner. He tastes it like a connoisseur and then eats some of the small cheeses and fruit that are on the bar.

"Take your time, gentlemen, we are in no hurry. I think you'll find everything in order. Our Reichsbank is meticulous in the extreme. Herr Walther Funk personally oversaw the paperwork. As Reich minister for Economic Affairs and president of the Reichsbank, he has personally signed all the documents."

"Yes, indeed, Mein Herr. It all looks good."

"I'll leave you for a few minutes, about fifteen to twenty, I need some air."

Canaris pours another glass of the exquisite and very expensive wine, leaves the room, and heads for the balcony overlooking the garden terrace at the rear of the Widder Hotel. He walks up and down several times, then sits in one of the armchairs, looks at his watch, and decides to give the Swiss banker about another twenty minutes to complete their survey of the documents before their signing. His mind wanders to the rest of his day and what else he must accomplish. He closes his eyes and thinks about his planned visit to, first, Madrid to call on Franco and then on to Lisbon to meet with Salazar. He has his orders from the Führer. Both leaders and their countries must do the Führer's bidding, and the Abwehr will be the critical instrument of control and oversight. He nods off, tired from the early morning flight and the turbulent last two hours flying over the Alps into Zurich. His inner alarm clock that served him so well as a junior officer at sea in the Kriegsmarine before going on watch during the night kicks in. He awakens. He looks at his watch, stands, straightens his jacket, and heads back to the meeting room.

The Swiss bankers are well satisfied. The paperwork is in order. The surrogate Von Schodel watches them sign alongside that of Walter Funk's signature. The business is complete. In just under one hour, the Third Reich has guaranteed payment for vital war materials from Portugal, agreeing to transfer Swiss gold that the Reichsbank has purchased in Reichmarks to a secret Portuguese account that the Portuguese dictator Salazar's finance people can draw down upon to support the fragile Portuguese economy.

Canaris silently breathes a sigh of relief. He calls reception and informs them that lunch can now be served.

For Canaris, the next hour is polite and tedious small talk, as the Widder waiters serve an exquisite three-course lunch, with wine pairings, followed by fine local Swiss cheeses and a fine French brandy. The conversation is measured from both sides, the bankers showing their talent for discretion and never asking anything that may approach an embarrassing question. The junior member from St.Gallen is almost mute, speaking only when spoken to by his two superiors and enjoying a lunch that is a rare treat for a young and aspiring Swiss banker, gratis the Third Reich.

The farewell inside the room is formal and polite. Both parties have accomplished what they came to do. The Swiss are masters of discretion and savoir faire. Canaris reciprocates. They have the appropriate paperwork. After shaking hands, the lead banker looks at Canaris and simply says, "Until the next time, Herr Von Schodel. We look forward to your next visit in two months." He smiles the smile of a banker who has just transacted a major international business deal.

"Auf Wiedersehen." Two parting words that say everything.

Canaris remains in the room. After five minutes and another glass of the fine wine, he leaves and heads to his suite.

The head of the Abwehr now faces a much greater challenge.

In his suite, Canaris ponders his coming actions. He walks up and down. He hesitates, and then as if totally convinced of what he needs to do, he picks up the telephone. He calls a local Zurich taxi company. The female receptionists replies and asks what she may do to help.

"I'll need a taxi please for seven tomorrow morning to take me from my hotel, the Widder, to the airport." He provides his name and then says quite demonstrably," When your driver arrives, have reception call my room, suite 307."

"Thank you, sir, seven tomorrow morning, all confirmed, and I'll tell the driver to have your room called on arrival, suite 307."

"Thank you, perfect. Auf Wiedersehen," Canaris replies in a friendly tone, with a smile on his face that only he can see, reflected in the large mirror in front of his suite's elaborate bureau with its elegant fittings and fine hotel notepaper.

Canaris looks out from his balcony window across the Bahnhofstrasse to old Zurich, picturesque and peaceful, enjoying the bliss and freedom from conflict and separate from the rest of worn torn Europe, engulfed by the Third Reich's military might. He has work to do, and he will need to change from his formal attire into something more casual and, perhaps if time permits, grab a nap before his evening begins.

The time passes quickly. He is changed and is expectant. At four o'clock precisely, there is a gentle knock on the suite's door. Canaris opens the door, and his guest enters quickly and without seemingly wishing to be noticed from outside. He closes the door promptly.

The elegant and attractive woman meets Canaris's smile with a loving and caring, "Willkommen in Zurich, Wilhelm, meine, Liebe."

They hug and kiss passionately.

Canaris breathes a deep sigh of relief. "I love your taxi service, Zurich's finest."

"We do our best, always, to please," she replies.

She is elegantly dressed, very much in keeping with a lady visitor to one of Zurich's finest hotels, and possesses of that confident air that makes every doorman and waiter immediately ready to respond to her every wish. She reciprocates with an accent and finesse that shows not just grace and breeding but a natural respect for those who do her bidding.

Canaris is enamored by his visitor.

But first, there is work to do. She knows the routine, and he knows precisely what he must do.

After further loving blandishments and personal exchanges, Canaris sits at the bureau while his visitor stretches out on the couch, her fine figure in seductive mode, with her shapely legs draped over a cushion in a relaxed and alluring mode.

"Halima, let me get down to business. The sooner we can accomplish our goal, the more time we can have for ourselves."

"My darling, I cannot wait. You do your thing, then I'll do mine. I promise not to interrupt, not even to come over there and give you some loving encouragement."

Canaris writes on the Widder's expensive note paper, using both sides. He is slow and meticulous, printing in large, bold, and clear letters. They are names, German names.

He pauses several times, pen in hand, his mind clearly working hard to recall what he will next write. There are headings, and several names under each heading.

The headings are beyond demonstrative: Abwehr, SD, SS, and Gestapo.

Below each heading is a column of names.

Madam Halina Szymanska arises from the settee. She straightens her dress and approaches Canaris sitting at the bureau. "Looks like it's my turn, my love. It will take a lot longer. Are you finished?"

Canaris looks intently at the two pieces of paper, the second only half full of his jottings.

He checks, then double-checks.

He rises from the chair, and Halina takes his place, setting her handbag down besides her, and holding a small ladies' diary that she's taken from the handbag.

The diary is something more than just her diary. Embedded in its pages are spread in random locations only intelligible to the fully initiated discreet and totally undecipherable codes. At least that is the hope of those that created them.

She goes to work, concentrating with all her being, almost not aware of Canaris's presence, who is now sitting in an armchair out of her direct view and peripheral vision, not wishing in any way to distract her from the important task that she must now accomplish.

The task requires meticulous care. She is the best. She understands the importance of what she is now encoding. The task takes almost two hours.

She closes her diary with its precious hidden encryptions, stands, kisses Canaris on the cheek, and hands him his notes.

Without a word, Canaris retires to the bathroom. Once in there, he takes out a cigarette lighter, places the papers over the lavatory, ignites the papers, and before burning his fingers, releases them into the toilet bowl. He flushes the toilet twice. The ash contents are forever gone into the Zurich sewers. Canaris breathes a sigh of relief.

He returns to Halina's embraces.

Within minutes, they are undressed and making passionate love on the large and comfortable bed. Halina Szymanska, a Polish émigré from occupied Poland, has made Switzerland her home. She has known Canaris for many years, before the German invasion of Poland, from her days in Berlin. They share something more than just physical attraction. They abhor Nazism and the creed that has destroyed the Europe that they both loved and admired. Canaris is an old-fashioned German, a believer in Germany's place in the sun, but not via violent and detestable means. He sees in Adolph Hitler the ruination not just of his beloved Germany but all that he holds dear for European culture and civilization.

Halina and he share their innermost secrets after an hour of caressing, sexual gratification, and exhausting their intimate physical energy on each other's needs and desires. They then discuss the future, their next planned meeting, and the care and trade craft that they must methodically practice. They are dedicated to ensuring that their precious, vital, and timely information reaches the right hands, while recognizing that they avoid the mortal danger of detection.

Canaris stresses to Halina his deepest, abiding fear. "Heinrich Himmler is the apotheosis of evil. We have to recognize that his spies, agents, and underlings are everywhere most of the time. He detests and hates me, pathologically jealous of my special relationship with Hitler. He'll do anything to see me gone, obliterated, career terminated, and ideally if he could have his way, conspire to have me found what you and I know in our heart of hearts I am." Canaris pauses, looks longingly into Halina's eyes, and says in a quiet stoical voice, "A traitor."

She kisses him more. "You're my hero, my wonderful, adorable, and courageous Wilhelm. We will succeed, we will endure, and mark my word, we will come through."

They both gather themselves and sit on the side of the bed.

Canaris looks at Halina, sighs a little, and says, almost as if confessing an innermost secret, "Halina, I just hope and pray for a thing, and one thing only, for the cause that you and I are staking everything."

"What is that, my love? Please, share this with me. I want to take some of the burden off your shoulders."

"C. It's that simple. I believe totally in Stuart Menzies and Winston Churchill. I trust them both implicitly. They are our lifeline. What we are giving them will change the course of the war. All I hope, indeed I pray if the God I believe in is truly looking after you and me, that they have the very best security for our information. I am assured that this is so, but one small slip on the British side, and we could be done."

"Have faith, Wilhelm, I do. C is the best. He assured me a long time ago that no one but he, and now Winston Churchill, know the source of the information we provide. We have to trust the head of MI6. Look, C knows that if anything goes wrong, we are finished, yes, gone, but he also loses his most valuable source."

"You're right. Of course you're right. It's not just me, Halina, that I'm worried about. It's you, it's that simple. If Himmler and his fiends come after me, well, that's my problem, but you, I cannot bear the thought of Himmler's thugs torturing you, and all because of me."

She strokes Canaris brow.

"We're in this together to the end, until Hitler is gone, and Europe can again breathe free."

They kiss passionately.

They both realize that it is time to bathe and change and, for Halina, to complete the next important part of her mission.

As the light fails outside and it starts to become dark, she lets Canaris know that this must be the time for parting. He is still restless, worried for her security and well-being.

She reassures him and, as she prepares to leave, gives him a passionate hug and kiss.

"Wilhelm, we will succeed. Until the next time. I will await the contact in Bern and the signal. I will be fine. You take extra care. Double, triple care. Promise me, please, my love."

"I will, I promise."

She gently opens the door, glances out along both sides of the corridor, smiles one last smile at Canaris, and pulls the door quietly closed behind her.

She glides down the hallway to the stairwell, avoiding the elevator. She looks nonchalantly in all directions as she skips down the stairwell and leaves by the Widder's rear entrance, less well used, with none of the main entrance staff parading to welcome and bid adieu to the hotel's guests. Halina must now accomplish the final key part of her visit to Zurich.

From the Bahhofstrasse, she takes two successive taxis, walking in between both and checking and double-checking that she has not been followed.

She is meticulous in arriving at the Hauptbahnhof, the main railway station. She blends in with the crowds, buys a magazine, and then leaves by a side entrance and goes two blocks, before going down a side street to a large apartment bloc.

She uses the stairwell and, checking that no one else is above or below her, heads for an apartment on the third floor.

She taps gently on the door of the apartment. A gentleman comes to the door. He greets her in Polish. She reciprocates. She pulls from her handbag the several pages that began life in her diary.

They are completely unintelligible goblledegoup. She hands them to him, bids farewell in a low voice, and disappears down the stairwell, out through the front entrance and heads for the main station, checking meticulously to ensure that she does not have company. The timing of the next fast train to Bern allows her the little luxury of a glass of wine. An hour and twenty minutes after departing Zurich, she is back in Bern and soon tucked up in her apartment, sleeping soundly, confident that she and Canaris are not only doing the very best thing that two human beings could do together, not just as lovers, but as people committed to the overthrow of the most evil despotism in modern times.

***

The Polish gentleman's night, back in Zurich, is just beginning. He leaves his apartment, carrying the day's not only local Zurich newspaper but one regarded as the Swiss newspaper of record, the *Neue Zurcher Zeitung*, and walks to the main station, checking and rechecking for those who may be interested in his movements. He enters the station café, orders a coffee, takes a seat, opens the newspaper, catches up on the news, and enjoys his espresso coffee. He glances surreptitiously at his watch. At nine o'clock, a gentleman enters and sits near to the Pole. They both know who is who. He, too, opens a newspaper, blocking the view of both. Precisely ten minutes after arriving, the Pole, to whom Halina has transferred her precious cargo, stands and goes to the men's washroom, where there are six closets. He enters one and sits down. His is the only locked closet. The others are unoccupied, and the doors are open to view. Precisely two minutes later, the other man enters and locks the adjacent closet door. The Pole coughs distinctly three times. The other man slides a copy of the *Zurcher Zeitung* under the closet dividing wall, whereby Halina's Pole places the papers in the center fold of the newspaper and slides it back under the closet divider.

The Pole flushes the toilet and heads back to his apartment.

The German-speaking British agent, recruited by Stewart Menzies, has worked in Switzerland since before the Austrian Anschluss, proceeds to the appropriate train gate, checking train times; and after further countersurveillance, he boards the last fast train of the day from Zurich to Bern.

Once in Bern, he will rendezvous with C's armed courier, not at the British embassy or anywhere remotely close, but in an apartment well hidden from the most discerning German counterintelligence agents. He has spent almost five years operating under deep cover as a merchant banker trading in gold and other precious metals from South Africa. Of South African birth, with no direct British affiliations, and being from wealthy Afrikaner stock, with anti-British and strong right-wing affiliations, he is one of Menzies' personal and finest recruits. He fits ideally into the Swiss social and financial landscape and shows from time to time the necessary pro-Nazi sympathies that have alienated him indeed from the more pro-British Swiss and adhered him to the more right-wing elements of Swiss society. He is the least likely to ever be detected as a British agent of the SIS. The courier will now travel back to Britain by the most circuitous route with a false passport and using a flag-of-convenience neutral ship that will, in due course, end its journey in the pool of London.

What he carries will make not just a difference, but a world of difference.

C and, in due course, the DNI will know not only the names of all the Abwehr agents, together with their main roles and missions, who will be dispatched shortly to Lisbon to join what at present is a modest and inexperienced Abwehr coterie, Menzies will also know who from within the competing ranks of the SD, the SS, and the Gestapo will be meddling in Canaris's rice bowl in Lisbon. The treasure inside those few pages also contained the names of current Abwehr-run Portuguese agents, paid off to provide Berlin with inside information on Salazar's regime. Moreover, in among these Portuguese nationals were those members of Salazar's secret police who have sold their souls to the Nazis and, most significantly of all, were playing in several cases, two ends off against the middle, taking money from naive MI6 agent runners, while taking payment from equally naive Abwehr agents. The head of German intelligence had provided for C the personnel list and operational blueprint for future Nazi clandestine operations in Lisbon.

C will brief the prime minister one-on-one on these latest intelligence nuggets, compounded by outstanding code breaking at Bletchley Park.

CHAPTER 12

Denouement at Bletchley Park "Action This Day" Has New Meaning

AUTUMN AT BLETCHLEY Park is no different for the code breakers than the other seasons. The routine is almost ship-like, with watches changing like naval dog watches so personnel did not keep the same watches week in, week out. Only the very senior technical staff and the daily clerical staff had the luxury of not watch-keeping at night. It was a tough round-the-clock regime. Even the most senior members would stay and work overnight when critical events are in progress. With global time changes and operations, particularly at sea, occurring on a nonstop twenty-hour basis, no one's routine can ever be nine to five. The demands on the leadership are intense.

Today is no different. The autumn leaves are falling and the nights are closing in, but the Nazi machine does not recognize the seasons. Bletchley has to keep going, no respite and no vacations, no visits to distant families except for emergencies and, worst case, the passing of loved ones. With the war at sea real, and every day a challenging and changing operational situation in the fight against the U-boats and the German surface raiders, there can be no letup and no excuses for under performing. It's maximum effort.

It is a cool and overcast day as the day's operations press on.

Hut 4 is about to become something more than its usual center of excellence for figuring out Donitz's next moves. The best and the brightest have gathered, and it's not over interpreting the latest intercepts.

Before they divert to their pressing issue, the team is evaluating the lead up to events surrounding the disastrous Norwegian campaign that ended with the German occupation of Norway and the loss, among others, of the aircraft carrier HMS *Glorious*. The occupation of Norway by the Nazis, which had commenced on April 9, 1940, bore similarities with the potential dire consequences if Portugal fell under Nazi tutelage. The Norwegian who would give his name to treachery and betrayal, Vidkun Quisling, played the dominant role as collaborator in chief with the Nazis. The SIS network in Norway was poor and Raeder's plans for the Kriegsmarine to lead the invasion had not been properly detected and evaluated by either SIS or Bletchley. Possession of Norway, similar to what may ensue if Portuguese ports fall under Kriegsmarine control, gave Raeder's navy added security to mount operations into the North Sea and beyond. The Hut 4 team is engaged intensely in learning lessons from the failed British Norwegian campaign. What else must Bletchley and Hut 4 in particular do to provide better intelligence in support of the DNI's briefings to the naval staff and the war cabinet? The young Harry Hinsley, fresh from St. John's College, Cambridge, and recruited by Commander Denniston on the recommendation of his Cambridge tutor, advises his colleagues on the similarities between Norway and Portugal and the role in particular of not just the key ports, but vital iron supplies from both countries to support the Nazi war machine. Hinsley stresses to his colleagues that the consequences and benefits to the Nazis of the seizure and control of Lisbon would not be unlike the Nazi seizure of Oslo and other main Norwegian ports.

There is total agreement. Bletchley will do all within their capabilities to support the DNI and his staff. This is a natural lead into the sensitive topic that they will now address—their own resources, code breakers, equipment, and clerical and support staff. They are understaffed, underequipped, and the pressures and work load are increasing by the day.

The older and more experienced members of the team—Alan Turing, Gordon Welchman, Stuart Milner-Barry, and Hugh Alexander—have a plan. The young Harry Hinsley listens intently to the plan that they will put very shortly to their best internal ally, the Bletchley deputy, Commander Edward Travis.

Travis enters Hut 4. His sixth sense combines with his own internal Bletchley intelligence to tell him what the best of the Bletchley brains are going to demand.

"Well, gentlemen, there's more than two of you, so it looks like a mutiny!" Travis exclaims in a nonpejorative and humorous tone. "What can I do for you? I wasn't summoned to have a pleasant chat. Tell me, what's up, what do you need, and what can I do?"

Travis pauses. He looks at them all one by one and smiles.

"We're all in this together. I have a very good idea of what you want. No holds barred. Spell it out. Gordon, why don't you be the spokesman?"

In the next three, maybe four minutes maximum, Gordon Welchman explains their deepest concerns about professional manning, support staff, and the need for instant funds for Alan Turing's technical team. Welchman is precise, concise, and spares no punches when it comes to being less than diplomatic about the director's failure to be supportive of their needs. He makes it clear to Travis that if the situation prevails, the team believes that Bletchley will, in due course, fail in its mission.

"Your solution, gentleman, tell me what you want and specifically what can I do to help."

"Here's our answer, the solution," says Turing, and he hands Commander Travis a letter that is signed by all present.

Travis reads the letter, taking less than a minute.

"Well, I'll be darned, gentlemen, you certainly know how to call a spade a spade. And may I hazard a guess? You want me to hand deliver this to you-know-who, to the man himself?"

They all stare at Travis, hanging on his next words.

"Winston, no less, the final recipient, and I'm the bearer, right, gentlemen?"

They all, as if rehearsed, but not, nod their heads with enthusiasm.

"You all do realize that Alastair will have my guts for garters if he finds out what we've all been up to?"

"Nothing ventured, nothing gained. Edward, if we don't take action, won't the PM be after our blood in any case?" Welchman declares.

"I totally agree."

A muted sigh of relief goes round the group.

"I'm not quite the dummy I sometimes make myself out to be, you know. I caught wind of all this weeks ago. Our intrepid leader, as we all know, is overworked and under great duress. He's lost sight of the woods for the trees."

"And so?" says Hugh Alexander, wanting to hear what Travis will do.

"I have a plan. Double wrap your letter please, Harry. I've anticipated what you need, and I agree one hundred percent. Let me use your secure phone."

Commander Travis calls the transport pool for a car to take him to Whitehall most urgently. He then calls his secretary and asks her to patch him through to the Cabinet Office via the secure line.

Travis talks with someone whom the group assumes is a close personal contact.

His conversation is short, to the point, and ends with the telling comment, "Yes, it's for the Cabinet secretary's eyes only, for him to hand personally to the prime minister, absolutely no one else in the loop."

There is clear agreement on the other end. He smiles, looks at the group, and says in a confident tone, "Mission accomplished."

They all thank him profusely.

Twenty minutes later, Travis carries his personal security pouch containing the letter as he enters the car for London.

Travis fulfills his objective in Whitehall.

Within less than an hour after Travis's departure back to Bletchley, the British prime minister reads the letter from the Bletchley team.

He lights a cigar, ponders the letter, and then without hesitation, takes a red pen and writes at the bottom of the letter, "Action This Day." He pauses for less than a few seconds and adds, "They are to have everything that they request, now and in the future, and more if necessary. Make it so." He simply appends "WSC." On the return journey Travis ponders what will be Denniston's reactions. Will he retaliate? He becomes more and more relaxed as the car approaches Bletchley. His person in the Cabinet Office has given him an absolute assurance of total secrecy as to the politics and issues out at Bletchley. There are no fingerprints, no traces of disloyalty, but a clear and unequivocal request for critical extra resources for what will be a continuing lifesaver for Britain.

Within a few days, Commander Denniston is informed by the DNI and the treasury that he will receive a large influx of funds to support more staff and the equipment needed by the lead code breakers.

Travis is nimble and tactful in dealing with his director, whom he encourages to take time off to nurse his painful ailment while he administers the sudden influx of funds.

A week after his visit to Whitehall, Commander Travis invites himself to a Hut 4 routine analysis meeting that is preparing the latest synopsis for the DNI.

One could hear a pin drop as Travis enters Hut 4.

The group is totally silent, in awe of their deputy director.

"Well, gentlemen, are you happy?"

There is sheer unadulterated admiration in Hut 4 for what Travis has pulled off. Without any fanfare, he gives a clear indication that he doesn't want anything from the team other than to keep pressing ahead.

"You have what you need, and more is on the way, a lot more. Now may I give you Winston's personal marching orders?"

They are all ears, totally transfixed.

"Concentrate for the next few weeks, in amongst all the U-boat and surface raider operations, on Franco and Salazar, and the Portuguese leader especially. He's the PM's target right now. Look out for anything and everything about what the Abwehr, SD, SS, and Gestapo are planning and up to in Lisbon."

"Yes, sir," retorts the duty lead analyst, Harry Hinsley.

Travis smiles. "Thank you, gentlemen, go to it."

He turns and leaves Hut 4.

As he walks back to the main building, Travis muses on the talent in Hut 4 and throughout Bletchley. He is witnessing the best of the very best working round the clock, perhaps not on the front line as such, but in many ways just as important as any ship's captain saving Britain from defeat and subjugation.

He wasn't to know it at that moment—but he would several years later—that he and his colleagues were saving, there and then, by their actions, Britain from possible defeat and certainly a much longer, bloodier, and protracted war. He wasn't to know either what fate had in store for him, paraphrasing Churchill's eminent phrase, "Now this is not the end. It is not even the beginning of the end. But it is, perhaps, the end of the beginning." Travis had a long and illustrious career ahead of him. He would come through for those he leads, and he would endure. He has the courage of his convictions and loyalty to those who mattered most. For Edward Travis, this was the end of the beginning.

CHAPTER 13

Number 30 Commando Assault Unit "Attain by Surprise" A New Beginning for British Intelligence and Commander Fleming

THE WEEKS THROUGH the end of 1940 and into January 1941 were frenetic for Fleming. Godfrey had made it clear that he wants Fleming's new operation, Number 30 Commando Assault Unit, to be ready to go into action by February 1941. The prime minister wants regular updates and is insistent that no holds be barred in accomplishing the new NID mission. Fleming works round the clock, seven days a week, moving between the special unit facility that is shrouded in secrecy and the Admiralty. Funding is no object. He is given everything that he requires via a secret treasury vote for classified programs. The DNI's accountants manage funds and acquisitions and payments to Fleming's recruits, other than those already on the payroll of the British Army and the Royal Marines. The latter are transferred seamlessly from their existing units to the new unit, with zero fanfare and no semblance of where they are headed and why. Security is uppermost, and Fleming's security chief is a veteran from the navy's own security group. He also oversees Fleming's highly classified communications section that will provide the necessary discreet, encrypted communications for the field operations with dedicated circuitry and a special NID station to manage all external communications. DNI staff will manage the interfaces with Bletchley, C, and MEW. A small cadre of NID staff is brought into interface with Fleming's unit at the headquarters end in the Admiralty. Weapons, explosives, underwater demolition charges, diving equipment, and a whole range of special European vehicles typically in use in Portugal are acquired, specially converted without any sign of their new purposes and that look as if they are just regular well-used cars, which indeed they are. They are made more robust, their bodies strengthened, and small special secret compartments built in to house weapons and explosives. They will be inserted into Lisbon by neutral flag-of-convenience ships landing other vehicular cargo.

Training is Fleming's biggest and most important task. Several of his initial recruits speak perfect Portuguese, some capable of speaking Portuguese dialects. These will comprise the first small groups to be inserted via the port of Lisbon. Each group will not know the others' missions in the event that they are captured, interrogated, and tortured. For similar reasons, each group within the overall Unit will receive limited intelligence briefing exposure except for that which they need to know.

Details of Abwehr, SD, SS, and Gestapo operations in Portugal will remain totally held in NID by just a small group. Information will be passed if and when needed by secure encrypted and coded channels. The field operatives under training standing by to deploy will have neither knowledge nor access to the most sensitive intelligence. They will be dedicated to highly specific missions. No more and no less.

Captain Stephens has provided oversight for the DNI while Fleming trains and prepares the very first units for insertion. Many others are in the training pipeline will deploy when certified ready.

It is a cold and miserable January morning when Stephens announces to Fleming a forthcoming significant change in NID.

"Sit down, Ian, please. First off, the DNI and I are most pleased with progress. Good job. You've worked tirelessly, and Admiral Godfrey has been most relieved to update the prime minister at his one-on-one meetings."

"That's most encouraging," Fleming retorts. "Our first units are almost ready, bar a few very minor technical issues, which will be accomplished within the next day or so, and then we'll be ready to embark the very first teams for insertion."

"Excellent." Stephenson paused. "I've now got some important news for you."

Fleming rose a little in his chair in expectation.

"I'm leaving, moving on, and will be relieved by a very fine fellow, Captain Ian Campbell. You'll like him a lot. First-rate chap."

Fleming is at first surprised, but then he had heard rumors that the deputy DNI might be leaving for another regular navy appointment.

"We will all miss you, Captain. Do you have a turnover date?"

"Next month, early to mid-February, with enough time to cover the waterfront, so to speak, with Captain Campbell."

"We will all miss you, sir. I don't know what I would have done without you at this end in the Admiralty while I've been working the training end."

"Well, that's what I want to chat about. I'm going to have a lot on my plate during the next few weeks. Admiral Godfrey wants me to assure him that all's set with Thirty, you've got everything in place, ready to deploy, with no unforeseen problems lurking round the corner. So to that end, I want to spend a whole day with you the day after next to review Thirty's status so that I can certify to DNI that you can deploy. Got it?"

"Yes, sir. I will have everything ready for your visit by the end of today. You have my total assurance that you will be pleased with what you see."

"One key thing that I know the DNI is concerned about is the insertion plan. I know you've been working on that, and I signed off with the security people in the Foreign Office for the false identities and passports, and our key people at Lloyds have set up everything for you via their channels with the necessary neutral flags of convenience. Our merchant shipping section is very much on the ball when it comes to clandestine insertion. I hope you're happy with their results?"

"Indeed, sir. They couldn't have been better. In fact, I feel like we'll be running a cargo business. Well, I say that, we are running a cargo business, the Grey Funnel Line, in disguise!"

Fleming's levity is giving Stephenson a break from the many concerns on his mind, way beyond just Fleming's new assault unit. He laughs. He likes Fleming's ability to see the humor in the most stressful of situations.

"That's good, Ian. Where will you be embarking the first groups?"

"Tilbury, Southampton, and Liverpool, first off. The weapons, explosives, vehicles, and all our other goodies will be mixed in with general cargo, some of which originated outside the UK. Lloyds have given us some perfect ships, Liberia registered, with South African skippers and first mates, and a mix of crews, none of whom are European, quite a few Asians, Latinos, and Central Americans."

Fleming pauses. He then adds, "The lads from the north, Scotland, and the Midlands, sergeants and petty officers—several of them—will fit in well. I'm emphasizing to the officers that they'll have to live the life of a sailor until they disembark in Lisbon. They've got the message. The nonmilitary people are a lot easier to train in this regard, less bound by rank and culture. That's why I've mixed them up. It'll work, I'm confident."

Good, very good, Ian, you know what's needed, and I'll see for myself."

"Any more questions, sir? If not, I'll get started on the arrangements. We'll give you full demonstrations. Don't be alarmed by our safe cracker from the East End, by the way. He may be a bit rough round the gills, but everyone has warmed to him. The same with some of the other civilian lads. Not exactly ready to join the Rag, but they are absolutely ready to work the waterfront in Lisbon, fit the bar scene, blend in, and work our special operation that we're setting up, one in particular we'll brief you into."

"Splendid, Ian. Let my WREN writer know the day's schedule. Plain clothes, I assume? No uniform?"

"Absolutely not, sir, with respect. Come in your oldest togs, please. Our food is good, but we're not dressed for a palace garden party."

"Got it. Thank you, Ian. I'm looking forward to getting out of Room 39 and having a breath of fresh country, air."

"I guarantee that, sir, plus the unit is different, very different, from what you've seen with C's people and the brains out at Bletchley, though there's similarities with our agents in Norway and places— tough, resilient, street smart, and ready to be resourceful in demanding situations."

Stephenson smiles at Fleming and says that he'd meet him the day after next.

The drive out the day after next is uneventful. Stephenson has brought staff paperwork to read, and Fleming occupies his time going over in his mind how to prioritize the various components of the day's visit to the training camp and the unit's operations center.

Fleming has chosen the facility wisely, with clear emphasis on anonymity and security. He has disguised the unit's headquarters as a government warehouse for emergency medical supplies. The signs indicate appropriately the function of the site and that the public are not admitted and will be arrested if trespassing. Barbed wire surrounds the area, and there are guard dogs clearly visible from the road. Most of the perimeter is covered by high hedges as well as the wire fences. The gate guards, dressed in civilian clothes, let their car through after the usual identity checks. This is the first time that Stephenson has set eyes on the camp, a series of converted farm buildings around an aged farmhouse that has seen better days, at least from the exterior view. There are multiple antennas on the main farmhouse roof and on several of the large barns and storerooms. As their car draws up in front of the farmhouse, two men appear, dressed in what appears to be a civilian version of combat gear. Both are carrying sidearms, which, to the knowledgeable, are German Luger PO8 9 mm pistols, made by Deutsche Waffen and Munitionsfabriken Mauser-Werke. Fleming and his team will explain very shortly to Stephenson that they want zero trace, and no physical footprints, of British weapons being inserted into Portugal in the event of compromise. They will want Salazar's secret police and undercover agents to associate any uncovered clandestine activities and hardware to be associated with the Nazis. Fleming will explain an elaborate and achievable deception plan in the event of the worst contingencies occurring. Fleming, however, comments that there is one modified British weapon that they consider essential.

Captain Stephenson has been briefed by Fleming that the unit does not observe the usual military civilities and marks of respect, such as saluting. He has reassured him, however, that discipline is not only strict, it is an implicit part of the training, while at the same time, the small teams of special operatives, acting as if they are just any other Portuguese civilians going about their business, will behave in ways that may appear at odds with conventional military relationships.

"Welcome to 30 Commando Assault Unit, I'm Dunstan Curtis, and this is Quentin Riley," says the very fit-looking thirty-year-old Curtis. Unbeknown to Stephenson, the man who has greeted him is an Old Etonian, like Fleming, and a Trinity College, Oxford graduate, a solicitor in civilian life and now a commander, Royal Naval Volunteer Reserve.

"Quentin and I are going to show you around, explain our training in support of our operational objectives and those focused right now on Portugal. If we have time, we'll give you our ideas for making life difficult for Donitz's submarine force that's set up shop in St. Nazaire and other places we don't care for."

"Sounds good, Dunstan. Quentin, good to meet you." Stephenson holds out his hand, and Quentin Riley gives the Captain a welcoming hand shake.

"We've some interesting things to show you," Quentin adds. The thirty-five-year-old Riley's name rings a bell in Stephenson's memory bank, and he suddenly realizes that without saying anything, the man in front of him is the well-known Polar explorer.

They go inside, with Fleming explaining before they reach the main farmhouse dining-cum-sitting room, a spacious area that is now completely converted to a military-style operations center, that Curtis and Riley are the two section heads with lead responsibilities for the planned initial operations.

Fleming lets the section heads make introductions to the others gathered to greet Stephenson, explaining that the main body of 30

Assault Unit personnel will be met when they tour the training areas, the armory, and the special warfare facility.

Stephenson is impressed with the gathering. Four of them will stay in his memory long after his departure and change of appointment. Charles Wheeler, a journalist before the war, shines as someone with imagination, inventiveness, and personal strength; Patrick Dalzel-Job is a specialist naval intelligence operative, a commander, with lots of hands on experience and deep knowledge of the Nazis. Ralph Izzard, whom he assesses is about thirty years old, is another journalist, and he remembers reading his columns in the *Daily Mail*. They all have considerable language skills, with Izzard speaking absolutely perfect German that would confound any SS or Gestapo agent. He was a Cambridge man, Queen's College, and had a grasp of what the unit is up against in Lisbon with the worst of the worst Portuguese collaborators with the Nazis and a patchwork of rival and competing Nazi groups from the Abwehr, the SD, the SS, and the Gestapo. One of the last people to step forward to greet Stephenson is a man who looks a little more disheveled and not quite as accomplished based on outward appearances as the others that he'd met so far.

"I'm Johnny, Johnny Ramensky, glad to meet you. Welcome to our unsavory group. Ian roped me into this hive of very interesting people, gents that I wouldn't normally socialize with, but whom I'm warming to every day that we work together."

"Oh, sounds interesting." Stephenson pauses. "Johnny," he says with a certain lilt and almost trepidation in his voice.

"Well, Johnny is one of our most accomplished unit members," Fleming interjects. "His remarkable skill set and experience will stand the unit in good stead."

"I'm intrigued," comments Stephenson.

"I've been caught only a very few times, and that was only because my accomplices were plain incompetent. I've seen the inside of His Majesty's prisons, and not as a warden, I hasten to add."

"Johnny's the best," chimes in Fleming, almost nonchalantly. "He's the best safe blower in the realm, the very best to crack any Nazi safe, and absolutely the master of small lightweight charges to get us in anywhere the unit will want to go. Right, Johnny?"

"Yes, sir, Mr. Fleming. I'm your man. I'm here to do my bit for King and country. I hate those Nazi bastards. Can't wait to blow my first hole in Lisbon."

"We're all very proud of Johnny, so glad to have him on the unit," chimes in Fleming.

"Here, here," echo the others, almost in unison.

Curtis and Riley take turns to explain the training in support of their key missions, clandestine intelligence collection, sabotage, and assassinations; collaboration with only the most trusted resistance groups and individuals; the disruption of the flow of Nazi war materials; attacks on critical command, control, and communications nodes; demolition and penetration of Nazi and Portuguese Secret Police intelligence and clandestine operations; and the destruction of their infrastructure and leadership, together with undercover Nazi field operatives who pose special threats and their Portuguese collaborators.

Stephenson is well pleased with what he hears.

"Before we start the tour, Captain, I want you to hear our deception plans. It's absolutely crucial that we confuse and deceive the Abwehr and the others, by which I mean the SA, the SS, and the Gestapo, but it's the Abwehr who we have to watch out for most. We know that they're the main threat to us and to British interests. We know well how the Portuguese Secret Police operate and who of Salazar's people—they're mainly very wealthy and influential people, plus some of the Portuguese foot soldiers who are poor and ready to take Nazi bribes to improve their lot in life—are all up to."

"To avoid suspicion and ensure that Salazar's people and the Nazis have zero inkling of our covert and clandestine operations, let alone even our presence in Portugal," comments Riley, who picks up a cue from Fleming to continue the briefing on deception, "we're making sure that our disinformation campaign is getting through, that both Salazar and his underlings, plus the Abweht, think that we've got our hands full with the Atlantic and the U-boat threat to mess with Portugal, and Lisbon especially."

Fleming looks at Stephenson, anticipating that he's likely to have questions streaming through that astute mind of his.

"Captain, questions, sir?"

"The big one for me is what worries Admiral Godfrey most of all."

They all stiffen, hanging on Stephenson's next words.

"Compromise, that's our biggest fear. We know a lot about what the Nazis and Salazar's people are all about. It's our own people we're worried about, not traitors, or anything like that, but bungling failures by less than careful MI6, SOE, and MEW operatives inside Portugal, or their people back here communicating with them. The DNI and I are most concerned that with too many people in the loop outside of the unit here and the small number cleared back in NID and Room 39. There's a serious risk of compromise. Please ensure that we don't tell the others much, if anything at all. MI6 and SOE don't need to know. The DNI knows how to work with C himself, no one else, least of all that Iberian Section that Philby heads up. We need MEW badly. They're good, really good, because they've got the information that you need on the what, where, and when of iron ore and tungsten shipments from Portugal to the Third Reich. But even they don't need to know how we are using their information and, least of all, your planned movements into Portugal."

Fleming reassures Stephenson, with the others pleased that he's taken up the mantle and is addressing the key issues.

"We're naturally one hundred percent in total agreement with the DNI's concerns. There will be zero contact by the unit with any of these entities. We have separate safe houses planned in Lisbon, short-stay seamen's rentals that we can be in and out of, depending on the changing situation, and to not arouse suspicion from locals who are in the pocket of Salazar's hoods. Our communications are absolutely watertight, with no connectivity outside the unit's special network, each part of which is separate and not interconnected for clear security reasons. Any information that we may need from MI6 or even possibly SOE at some point in the future will be via subterfuge, without reference to any in country operation. SOE have nothing to offer at present. They're a babe-in-arms outfit, just getting off the ground. However, we'll have to watch very closely once they do get into gear. We don't want them treading on our toes or, worst case, getting detected by the Nazis and wrecking the whole show. I don't trust the man Kim Philby, the MI6 section chief in charge. I'm informed of training SOE recruits on how to conduct operations in the peninsular. That fills me with trepidation. He has zero credentials in any kind of covert operations work and was recruited into 6 by one of his Cambridge friends, whom I gather is another weak link."

Fleming pauses to see if Stephenson has more questions.

Stephenson nods with approval and then says, "And the worst case plans? Are you there? Are they in place and ready to go?"

"Yes, sir, if Hitler invades, worst case, or if Salazar flips completely, breaks hundreds of years of close alliance with Britain, and tries to kick us out of Portugal for good, with iron ore and tungsten trade terminated, we will execute Plan Alpha on the prime minister's direct command."

"Got it, and the Azores, his other big worry?"

"We're in there too. We'll not only destroy and disrupt all trade out of Lisbon and Oporto and take down their critical port infrastructure, we'll move into the Azores immediately and seize control of all their port facilities, particularly Punta Delgada, on Sao Miguel Island, and of course Lajes too. We will seize the airfield and the other air strips that the Germans could land aircraft from France. We have a detailed plan, equipment at the ready, and the means of rapid insertion. No one knows of these plans other than this unit, the DNI, you, and the prime minister and his most trusted inner circle."

"Good, and Frederick?" questions Stephenson. He is referring to Frederick Wells, the Oxford don in Room 39 running all topographical intelligence.

"He's here today. I told him to be ready to brief you. He's over in the shed working with the Lisbon and Azores teams, providing all the data on the Tagus and Douro Rivers and valleys, the port topography, tides, weather, the lot, and the same for the Azores. His material is absolutely essential. Without Fred's material, we'd have one arm tied behind our backs. He's incredible. The men love Fred Wells."

"Good, I'll look forward to seeing Fred."

"He's taken all the MEW data, plus what the Bletchley people have, and distilled all this with his own topographical intelligence into a fine composite intelligence picture of all the targets, with all the problems and issues about location, and how terrain and even underwater factors will affect our operations."

Fleming pauses to see if Stephenson has anything on his mind. He seems to be content so far.

"Before we begin the tour, we've some coffee to keep you going, sir. Coffee for the Captain, please."

They all pitch in. No stewards to do the serving in this briefing room. The galley and staff for feeding and ensuring the unit is well-housed are separate, away from the main house and the other sheds and barns that have been converted to the unit's various operational purposes. The galley and makeshift wardroom-cum-mess is an old former rental property near to the main house where probably the farm manager or foreman lived with his family. This is now the galley, wardroom, bar, and one place where the unit can relax, eat, and drink, with a simple rule: zero discussion of any unit-related matters or personal matters at any time within earshot of the galley and wardroom stewards, all handpicked naval cooks and stewards with perfect records and security cleared. There is even a wine steward, a chief petty officer who was head steward at the Royal Naval College, Greenwich, just as war broke out. He's now serving wines, spirits, beer, and ports to a very different kind of wardroom than Greenwich. He loves the job, and although he's not sure what they're all about, he has his ideas and keeps them totally to himself.

"I needed that coffee, Ian. OK, let's get on with the tour. I am very pleased, gentlemen, with all that I've heard so far."

"Thank you, sir. We'll go systematically from one section to another. They're each in different converted barns and out buildings. We've erected one special building for the vehicles, where we've done the conversion work. I should have mentioned that in this building where we are now, in the main farmhouse, we've got my small headquarters staff, operational planning section, special communications planning group, the security and deception group, the people who do all the false passport and forged document work, language training, and a very small personnel section from NID that does personnel work, pay, travel, and so on and so forth."

"That's fine, let's move on to the barns. Thank you, Ian."

The group as a whole then accompanies Captain Stephenson on about a two-hour tour of each of the operational training sections. He meets the men that Fleming has recruited from multiple military and civilian organizations. They comprise men from the Royal Marines, the Parachute Regiment, the Royal Engineers, and several from the infantry and guards regiments. They are all handpicked with outstanding service records. The civilians do not have formal military training and experience. However, they are an accomplished group of yachtsmen and sportsmen, fit and strong, with many possessing the necessary language skills—German, Portuguese, and Spanish. They are all well-traveled and know pre-war Europe as well as any diplomat or military attaché.

Stephenson moves from one barn or shed to another, separated by functionality. He is fascinated by the weapons and explosives center that houses not only the best range that he has seen in his career but also an armory for all the various German weapons that will be imported to Portugal. He meets the explosives and demolition instructors and the operatives-to-be. The instructors will deploy. In a hangar type of building with a very high roof, what must have been a large barn with a loft at one stage, now converted by Fleming's civil engineers, he meets someone that he has not seen for a while, Paymaster Lieutenant Commander Norman "Ned" Denning, who is a Room 39 person, one of the DNI's staff whom he uses for special missions in and around Whitehall. With his supply officer background, Fleming has employed Denning with the DNI's full knowledge and total approval to be the unit's quartermaster—Q for short.

"Ned, I didn't realize that you were working out here. You're a perfect fit."

"I do my best, sir," Denning replies. "As Q, I get to put together a lot of the good stuff, including the special vehicles at the rear of this building and all the weaponry, explosives, and anything that the unit decides it will need in the field."

"Are you funded completely to your satisfaction?"

"I have everything that we've requested, all through the special vote. All the equipment you'll see has been delivered as quickly as anything I've ever seen in my service career."

"Good, very good. What's next?"

After seeing the group of converted special vehicles, they move, with Commander Denning accompanying them, to the barn with all the underwater demolition equipment, diving gear, and mock-ups of the Lisbon and Tagus River waterfront facilities, a model as good as anyone could have created, with the help of Fred Wells and his Room 39 group. Around the walls are enlarged photos of the approaches to the Tagus and Douro Rivers, the streets, and the port facilities in and around the Lisbon and Porto waterfronts. There are photos of many of the recent merchant ships that are known to have visited Lisbon in particular. Several of the photos are of the iron ore and tungsten loading docks and cranes.

Denning introduces Stephenson to the next to last barn, converted into what Fleming describes as the assassination barn, where a small group of doctors recruited from the Army Medical Corps work with civilian pharmacists to create a range of poisons and delivery devices that can be used to end the worst of the Abwehr, Gestapo, SA, and SS if and when required. In addition, a small group of three men are designing, and have already built in some cases, lightweight explosive charges that can be concealed in brief cases and a series of small pistols with limited ranges enclosed in innocuous-looking spectacle and sunglass cases; and one device is a fountain pen that shoots a poisonous, deadly dart several feet without deviating.

Before the last stop, they watch for a few minutes the outdoor range where one group of four are practicing with small arms against standard targets and another group is some distance away firing specially modified Sten guns, with a 100 m effective range. Some of the Stens have had their lengths modified from the conventional thirty inches to be less obtrusive and fit in handheld cases. The marksmanship is of a high order. In another area, beyond the buildings and not in sight, Fleming and Denning explain respectively that there is a large pit used for high explosives training and testing, and a large, deep lake used for diver and underwater demolition training. Denning explains that he arranged through Room 39 to have the underwater teams deploy to Liverpool to practice their demolition and sabotage skills on real merchant ships and harbor facilities by day and, by night, in all weather and tidal conditions.

The last stop is the special communications barn where Q has assembled a group of specialist communicators to manage and organized the supply and training of all the unit's various radios from VHF to HF. Denning explains before entering that he regards this as the most sensitive site at the complex, emphasizing that secure, encrypted, reliable, and versatile communications are essential for operational success. Inside they see a range of the latest and best radio technology that British brains and technology can produce. Denning makes a salient point, "We know from World War I onwards that secure communications practice is essential, as well as good equipment. Handling these radios absolutely one hundred percent securely is, in my opinion, more vital than handling a Sten gun. Poor communications security can unravel all that Ian has set up here. Enough said."

Denning asks for a test demonstration, and one of the specialist civilian communicators sends a short burst encrypted and coded message to a special station within the Whitehall wireless complex controlled exclusively by the DNI. A message is returned within minutes.

Stephenson is well pleased and says so.

Back in the main building, the farmhouse, they all imbibe coffee, and Fleming invites everyone to take a seat. Once settled, he begins what is the most sensitive part of the visit, the initial deployment plan into Portugal and the port of Lisbon. He starts by recapping what the prime minister has ordered, as an imperative, emphasizing one key factor that Churchill has made clear to the DNI: "That we must be inserted and ready to take appropriate action as the situation develops—in other words, be ready for any and all possible contingencies."

Stephenson nods and says simply, "Absolutely, we have the tasking. You're all right on the ball. Go ahead, Ian, don't let me interrupt."

Fleming describes how very small groups, comprising two to three operatives, will be inserted shortly. Once inserted and several safe houses are secure, a routine has been achieved, and there is confidence that A1 security has been accomplished, he will deploy to Lisbon to make a final assessment before he issues the final code word for full insertion of the unit's wide-ranging capabilities. The latter will require all the safe sites to be totally secure, with zero possibility for compromise. Fleming describes the highly classified insertion plan and schedule based on various neutral flags-of-convenience merchant ship sailing from several UK ports. All the personnel deception tools are in place, with all the necessary false passports and identity histories in place, with all operatives daily practicing and being tested on their individual false histories, based in some cases on people known to be deceased but not in the records of foreign countries. Everyone will know their own documentation as if their lives depend on it, as indeed they do.

Stephenson has no questions. He stands and faces the group.

"It would be churlish of me even to offer any comments or suggestions. You are all experts in your own domains, and you have, as a fine team, put together a most accomplished capability. What I find most impressive is the collective strength of how you all work together, without a hard rank structure, yes, but with clear, dedicated respect for each other's particular talents. I find that, simply, gentlemen, most impressive. Discipline is self-evident. You're working seamlessly as a team. Gentlemen, Ian, my heartiest congratulations, and most of all, good luck in the operations that you are about to undertake. In the morning, I will have nothing to say to the DNI other than one simple statement, "They're the best, Admiral, and I'm totally one hundred percent pleased to report that they're ready to go."

"Thank you, Captain," comments Fleming. They all stand, shake hands with Captain Stephenson, and he and Fleming depart.

Waiting for them in the car are sandwiches and a flask of coffee. There hasn't been time for a meal in the mess-cum-wardroom. Time is of the essence, and both Stephenson and Fleming need to be back in

London for a major final meeting with the DNI early in the morning, before Fleming launches his operation. They sit back, relax for the first time all day, and enjoy their roast beef sandwiches and coffee.

After they've eaten, Stephenson turns to Fleming and asks him a simple question.

"Ian, I didn't want to ask you in front of your team in case there was some sensitivity. I also did not want to embarrass you if you haven't got there yet. But what is the codename for your operation? Do you have one?"

"Yes, indeed, sir, I do. It's very simple. Golden Eye, Operation Golden Eye."

CHAPTER 14

Fleming Receives the DNI's Blessing The Palacio Beckons

J OHN GODFREY HAS a twinkle in his eyes and a slight smile on his face as Captain Stephenson provides him with a short and succinct fifteen-minute synopsis of his day with Fleming and the 30 Assault Unit. The others in the room listen intently. They are almost rigid with concentration, absorbing both the operational detail and implications for the Room 39 team. Every word from the captain's mouth breathes life into what will become a hallmark operation, the model that SOE will follow.

Fleming is anxious, but also confident in himself, not out of a sense of false modesty, but rather knowing that his people are the best of the best, and that they have not only trained hard and effectively, but they have also explored every unforeseen possibility, everything that could and may go wrong, with backup plans to the backup plans. Many fine and experienced minds have been brought to bear on Golden Eye. Fleming has done his utmost to ensure that no stone has been left unturned, including every likely aspect and contingency regarding the Abwehr, the other odious instruments of Nazi tyranny, Salazar's internal secret police, and the likelihood of a nest of double agents in Lisbon playing off both sides. Security has been their watchword. Fleming is confident that there have been zero leaks.

"Comments, gentlemen?" the admiral says to his key staff, all cleared for Golden Eye.

He turns from his deputy and looks at Ewen Montagu, Patrick Beesley, Frederick Wells, and Commander Roger Winn, and awaits their responses.

Somewhat surprisingly, it is not Commander Winn who is the first to comment, but the Oxford don, Frederick Wells.

"Superb, Admiral, simply superb, if I may say so. What I like from my side is the way the unit, if I may call them that, has integrated all the topographical, weather, and economic intelligence into their operational plan. They know the terrain, the environment, the likely weather conditions, the tides—everything—down to the last detail. Plus all the information about the supply chain from MEW. One word, sir: impressive."

"Well, Frederick, thank you for that vote of confidence."

Godfrey pauses.

"Sir, they've hit every nail on the head," comments Commander Winn.

"I think, sir, that maybe we should discuss the implications of what you've called recently since the prime minister's directive, the Salazar factor. It could be crucial. Plus the other aspect that you and I discussed yesterday while Captain Stephenson was out in the country with Commander Fleming, those whom we all hope are with us, but also whom we may have to watch out for."

Fleming internally winced when he heard this from one of Room 39's most capable and most knowledgeable leaders. Did he know something that Fleming didn't and maybe should? His body language gave nothing away, but he inwardly was one hundred percent on the edge, in anticipation of what would come next.

"This is a very good time for me to say several things, gentlemen, some of which is going to be new to one or two of you, including you, Ian. They don't change anything, in fact they may very well enhance what we've heard, but first, let me make some important observations, reminders perhaps—things that the prime minister never wants us to forget."

Fleming is both relieved and also totally intrigued. *He is clearly one of whoever else in the room is not aware of whatever the DNI is about to say, has up his sleeve,* Fleming silently thinks to himself.

"1373, gentlemen, you all know the significance of that date."

Everyone quickly processes its significance in anticipation of Godfrey's next words.

"Our oldest ally, Portugal, has been with us through thick and thin. Yes, Salazar is neutral, sitting on the fence, but frankly as we all know, for some very good reasons, he's also a bad boy. We know that. But he's not that bad. Compare and contrast with Franco, he's not in the same league. We need Salazar, and we need to help him preserve his neutrality while we move forward with our plans for the Azores and, worst case, prepare for the likelihood that Hitler may wake up one morning and issue the order to invade Portugal."

Godfrey takes a sip of water. All gazes at him intently.

"We have to most secretly execute Golden Eye without any risk, absolutely zero risk of compromise. If the worst happens, and the Nazis march in, then the game changes, completely and utterly. Now to some sensitive diplomatic matters. Our current ambassador in Lisbon, Sir Walford Selby, is a weak reed, totally ineffective. He and several of my colleagues on the JIC want him out."

The Room 39 team perks up. Selby had not been on anyone's agenda, never a factor in planning.

"We're pushing hard with the foreign secretary to get a stronger, more capable person in the hot seat in Lisbon. Selby's way past his usefulness. Out of his depth and is being outmaneuvered by both his Nazi opposite numbers and the Salazar pro-Nazi group, feeding off the Abwehr trough. Sir Anthony Eden has his number, thank goodness. He's a short-timer. But, and this is an important but, I want you to ensure, Ian, that you avoid him like the plague. We're not sure how far the Abwehr are into our embassy in terms of locally recruited Portuguese staff working there and also how far the lower end of the British staff are monitored and tracked both by the Abwehr and also Salazar's secret police. Whatever you do, don't go anywhere near the embassy or any of its people. Understand, gentlemen?"

"Yes, sir," comes back a universal affirmative.

"However, there's good news in Lisbon as well as not so good."

Fleming is all ears. What did the DNI have in mind?

"Eccles is his name, David Eccles. None of you know him. First-rate chap. Sharp as needles and hugely capable. He's MEW's top man in Lisbon. Ostensibly, he belongs to SOE, but frankly, gentlemen, between us, until SOE gets his act together, I treat him as MEW. Ah, I've just remembered, Frederick knows him well, right, Frederick?"

"Yes, indeed, Admiral. First-class man. I've worked with him on how the supply chain of Nazi war materials out of Lisbon in particular fits in with all our topographical intelligence here in NID. He's invaluable. We've tied together the overland routes through Spain as well as out of Lisbon and Oporto. Vital for what Ian and his people are doing."

"Exactly right, Frederick. Ian, work with Frederick and his people, and get the very latest before you leave for Lisbon."

"Yes, sir," quips Fleming

"We're very much up to speed with all of the MEW material, and Frederick and his team have been terrific in keeping us abreast of the Nazi war material supply chain and how it all fits together with the topographical aspects."

"Good, excellent," comments Godfrey. "My concern is this, Ian, for you personally, as I see no need for any of the unit to have contact with not just the Embassy people but also any of the MEW people, including Eccles. We know that Salazar's secret police are on to Eccles. So he's being watched, probably tracked. They'll likely know where he goes socially and what he's watching in his day job."

"Understand, sir," Fleming retorts.

"Well, this is my real concern, and C's." Godfrey pauses.

"We know that several of Salazar's henchmen are in the pay of the Abwehr. In fact, we know that a few of them are sucking out both tits, pardoning my language, gentlemen."

The group smiles almost to a man at the DNI's metaphor.

"We're paying some of them, while the boys in Berlin are doing the same. Now to the real point. Eccles uses two safe houses in Lisbon. He doesn't go to either himself. Dead give away. Too risky. Just two of his own people use them, as if they are flats, apartments. There's a transmitter in just one. It sends out local music and nondescript news items, sports, and the like. Tough to DF. There's a lot of radio clutter in the area. The site was chosen very carefully. All coded, over multiple transmissions. It's only used for most urgent alerts. If anything changes, Ian, that we need to tell you urgently, one of his two people will contact you indirectly. Remind me where you're staying, please?"

"The Palacio, it's an old-fashioned hotel outside Lisbon, in Estoril. We know more about the inmates-cum-guests than they know about themselves, sir. We've the very latest on the guest list and who's who, including the German contingent, mainly undercover Abwehr people."

"Very good, Ian, tell the others the cover we've set up for you."

Fleming turns to the others and gives a short synopsis, almost staccato-like, in short bursts.

"Trading on my years of miss-spent youth in Switzerland. Fluent German, Hoch Deutsch, and all that. Swiss businessman. Cashing in on the war, Swiss-style. Just another gnome making money out of others misery."

There's a chuckle among the group, and the Admiral smiles.

"False identity, with excellent credentials if the Abwehr start to poke around. Passport is top-notch. Made by the best!"

Everyone laughs, including Godfrey.

"My business credentials are second to turn. They all check out if I'm checked out. I can use my fluent French to effect too, and I'll use my Russian to fool any of the snoopers from the German Embassy who party and wine and dine at the Palacio. It's a haven for intrigue. Where it all happens. Makes Claridges and the Savoy look like modest venues by comparison. The Nazis and their sycophantic Portuguese hangers-on and toadies in their pay waste Adolph's Reichmarks in the Casino, where it all happens—and goes wrong, evidently, for the faint of heart and those not skilled in the arts of black jack."

"I trust, Ian, that you will be relieving some of them of *Ihr Gold*," says Commander Winn, imitating a passable German accent.

"Absolutely, *Mein Freund*," retorts Fleming.

They all laugh.

"I think I'm in good shape. Black jack will have new meaning. The casino is where I hope I'll figure out the lineup of the Abwehr and their Portuguese friends and associates."

"Any more questions of Ian, gentlemen? If you think of anything, please ensure you update him before he leaves for his ship in the morning."

Fleming relaxes. He feels that he's said his piece.

"Before we break, I want to bring you up to speed on a couple of important developments, both of which not only affect you all, but also impact Commander Fleming's departure for Lisbon."

The group stiffens with attentiveness to what the DNI will say next.

"The prime minister and the foreign secretary and the best people that the FO has on Iberian Peninsula affairs are reasonably confident that the Treaty of Friendship and Non Aggression Pact that Salazar signed for Portugal and Franco for Spain last July is not only real but is sticking. There were concerns at first, but they seem to have gone away, so the upshot of this is that the PM and Eden both agree that it's less likely that they'll be any falling out, with Franco gravitating to the Nazis and repaying some of his debts to Adolph Hitler. It looks like both dictators see self-preservation for themselves and their regimes in mutual self-promotion. All the better for us, as it most probably means that Hitler will be less and less inclined to touch Portugal directly so long as his war supplies keep coming. So the balancing act goes on, gentlemen. We may be supping with the devil, but Salazar is the devil we know, and we have to play a deft game while having Golden Eye in our back pocket if things get out of kilter."

Godfrey waits for just a few seconds to see if there is a reaction from his top people.

They just wait for his next point, to which he had alluded.

"My next piece of news is also positive. The prime minister is getting increasingly close to, and dare I say cozy, with President Roosevelt. The American people are still delusional about the impact Nazism will have on the US, in spite of the reports of our great American friend here in London, Edward Murrow, doing a great job telling the American people the daily facts of life. Franklin Roosevelt, with Winston's help, is slowly but surely coaching his people. But secretly—and I stress secretly, gentlemen—the PM and the president are preparing for the worst. From our end, we know where the Japanese are headed. Roosevelt is totally on the same page. So stand by for cooperation with the Americans. Any questions, gentlemen, before we adjourn?"

There are none.

"Remember where we are at, gentlemen, a key junction in our survival. We have to defeat the U-boats. They alone can be the downfall of our islands, as the prime minister has so eloquently articulated. We have to defeat the U-boat threat. Raeder and Donitz are public enemies numbers one and two. In fact, as far as I am concerned, as I said to Winston and C only yesterday, Karl Donitz is in my opinion public enemy number one. His submarines can do us in. So we need to keep Portugal free from Nazi occupation, and we need to ensure that the Azores do not become a haven as the next U-boat base."

There is a still in the room, a pregnant pause no less. The group silently weighs the seriousness of Admiral Godfrey's comments. He then relieves the tension.

"Very well. Thank you all. Good job, everyone. Go to it."

The group leaves the DNI's office, and as Fleming is the last to leave, Godfrey beckons him, "Ian, I need a quick word, please. Close the door."

The others depart, and Godfrey invites Fleming to take a seat.

"Ian, I'm not keeping things from our other colleagues, but I do need to share an additional piece of information with you, as it pertains indirectly to 30 Assault Unit."

Fleming is intrigued. "Yes, sir?"

"Things are a little more developed with Roosevelt than I indicated, and what I'm about to tell you is highly sensitive. If it got to the wrong part of the American press, the paper's less inclined to Franklin Roosevelt, the PM will be apoplectic. The president knows that war is coming, both with Hitler and the Japanese. It's just a matter of time, the how and when will become clearer as the clock ticks. Meanwhile, he wants to create a special clandestine group, separate from ONI. Being a navy man, he thinks the world of the navy and their naval intelligence people. But he also recognizes that, at some point, they're going to have to get into the undercover clandestine business. He's found the right man to run the American show. It's all very hush-hush at this stage. No one other than a select few knows, Roosevelt's very closets advisors and confidants. The man is a person called William Donovan, he's evidently know as Wild Bill because of his past glories. Quite a chap evidently, and very smart as well as audacious."

"This is good news, sir," chimes in Fleming.

"Yes, indeed, and it will involve you. Here's how. The prime minister likes what you've set up with 30 Assault Group. He's told C and me that we're to be the interfaces with the president's man, with Bill Donovan. He wants us to make the connection soon, in the United States. He wants us to meet secretly, with no fanfare, zero knowledge by anyone other than Donovan, the president's insiders, and our very small in-the-know group here in London. Understand, Ian?"

"Yes, sir, totally. May I ask where and when?"

"You've anticipated my next points. We've got to proceed totally undercover. The plan is to meet in New York City, well away from the Washington, DC, spotlight and the press. I'm working with C on the exact location. Now this leads to you and your schedule. I want you to get the Lisbon operation off the ground immediately. You're off to Lisbon tomorrow. It will take a few more weeks before things are ready in the US. The prime minister and the president are taking no chances on premature action leading to discovery by the wrong people on the other side of the pond."

"I fully understand, sir. So you want me back in London as soon as I've got Golden Eye underway?"

"Yes, exactly. Don't rush things though, Ian. You have time. I don't want any mishaps. Caution's paramount once you get settled into the Lisbon environment. Be wary constantly."

"I will, sir, please be assured. The whole team is running on the most well-thought-through, best operational practice. To say it's watertight is inviting fate. However, we've done everything possible as a team to ensure not just secrecy, but protecting the operation from just about every foreseeable contingency known to NID."

"I know, Ian, I have total confidence in you and the rest of your people. You know where I'm coming from. I have to reassure Winston that nothing's been left to fate or some unforeseen event."

"You have my assurance, sir."

"Thank you, Ian, now for something else. This is equally sensitive, but you need to be completely in the picture before you embark in the morning."

Fleming straightened in one of the DNI's most comfortable armchairs. He took a deep breath as if just about to perform a major athletic move.

"Three people you need to know about, two with code names— Garbo is one, and Tricycle is the other. They're not going to cross your path with Golden Eye. C and I have agreed that you need to know, complete the picture of who's who in the rogues' gallery of SIS-Abwehr double agents. It's intrigue at its best, or worst, Ian, depending on your view of the world and human nature. Garbo is in Madrid and is ostensibly controlled by the Abwehr, or at least that's what they think, if you take my point. Part of Double Cross. Garbo is a man whose real name is Juan Pujol Garcia, a valuable asset, a Spanish double, recruited in Lisbon by the Nazis and also recruited by us. He's playing both sides, but the good news is that he's really with us, and we know this, guaranteed. Similarly with Tricycle. He's a Serbian named Dusan Popov, a very unusual man to say the least, a triple agent, first of a kind I think, but he's the real thing. He's a lawyer, very wealthy, smart, knows how to play the game and fool the opposition. He's got a brother, Ivan Popov, code name Dreadnought. They're both serious assets. Before you leave, read this file. It tells you all that you need to know about them, C's latest assessment and their current value and risk. Tricycle is controlled by the Lisbon Abwehr. You'll need to keep an eye open. No more though, Ian, understand? Do nothing."

"Yes, sir, absolutely."

"You're seeing all this in case you pick up some further vibrations, particularly about Tricycle since he's in Lisbon, on your doorstep. Now to the person I really want you to watch out for. This man is possibly dangerous. Be extremely careful. Who is he? Man called Paul Fidrumuc.

We know a lot about him. Born in Moravia, 1898 if I recall. It's in the file. Read every word carefully. He moved to Hamburg in 1934 and became a freelance Abwehr agent for want of a better description. In '38, he moved to Copenhagen where he was the correspondent on Danish affairs for the *Deutsche Allgemeine Zeitung*."

Fleming momentarily interrupts, "Very prestigious newspaper, sir."

"Yes, indeed. He was arrested by the Danes for spying for the Germans, which he was, and was later released as part of a prisoner exchange. Well, our man is now in Lisbon and frequents the casino in Estoril. You'll read in the report how he set up an import-export business in Lisbon, and the Abwehr trust him as a loyal agent so much that he has the privileged code name of Ostro. Well, our friend Ostro, a.k.a. Fidrumuc, is literally making hay out of his friends in Abwehr headquarters in Berlin. He's feeding them fiction and getting paid very well for what is, in effect, a pack of lies. However, he's dressing it all up very well, most convincingly as far as the Abwehr recipients are concerned. He's claiming agents in the US, South Africa, and here in Britain. Quite the accomplished liar. You'll read how we know all this. Very, very sensitive, Ian. Your eyes only. Bletchley reads the Abwehr codes as you know. Well, they hear all about Herr Paul Fidrumuc as a result. Be on the look out for him. There was a time when one or two people close to C wanted him gone, but C and I said absolutely not. Killing him would likely alert Berlin to the fact that we're reading their codes. In any case, I argued that he's an asset, indirectly, feeding the Nazis bad information, living off their largesse, and they're none the wiser for it. Pointless, killing him. Also, and here's the part that will get your attention, Ian. We know more about Herr Fidrumuc than he knows about himself. C's running a Czech female agent in Lisbon. She's a born seductress. Not sophisticated in terms of providing hardcore vital intelligence, but very good at providing pillow talk from a man who doesn't know when to keep his mouth shut in bed."

"She sounds effective, nonetheless, sir, if I may say so."

"Absolutely, Ian. He's got very expensive tastes, and she's one of them. However, C's funds are more alluring than Fidrmuc's romantic dalliances. We're paying her well!"

"So I need to look out for this pair of love birds, sir?"

"Only if you run into them at the casino. C and I want you to know who they are and what's what. Take no action at all. You need to know and be aware. We don't want you stumbling across Fidrmuc without knowing that we're already on to him and his paymasters in Berlin. You'll see her SIS code name in the file. If I recall, it's Ecclesiastic, quite a good cover for the ultimate seductress, I think!"

"Indeed, sir. I'll be on the lookout for them. Are there photos of them, sir?"

"Yes, indeed. They're all in the file. Fidrmuc in his different roles. You won't mistake either of them, alone or together. It's quite a collection. C's people did a good job at assembling a Fidrmuc album, so to speak."

They both laugh.

"Very well, Ian, I've got another meeting to go to. Sit and read the files and tell my secretary to secure them in my safe as soon as you've read them. She's not aware of the contents. Third safe on the left, the one with the top drawer open. In fact, I want you to secure the files and then spin the combination."

"Very good, sir. Will do."

"Good luck, Ian. Be careful, watch your back. You know who the bad boys are. But there's always the chance there's someone who we either don't know about or they're playing both sides. You're not there as a collector. Remember your primary mission. To survey the scene. Make absolutely sure that you're satisfied for Golden Eye to commence. That's all we need. Take no unnecessary risks, and watch your back the whole time."

"Yes, sir, will do."

"Goodbye, Ian."

"Thank you, sir."

Admiral Godfrey shakes Fleming's hand and leaves his office while Fleming settles down to read the highly classified files.

Little does Fleming know that the next time he will see the DNI will be in the most unusual and critical circumstances.

CHAPTER 15

The Hotel Palacio, Estoril
Let the Battle of a Different
Color Commence

THE RUA PARTICULAR in Estoril is an attractive street in one of the great gems of Portugal, Estoril. The focal point on a street, which has not experienced the violence inflicted by the Luftwaffe on London and the other great cities of Britain, is a fine hotel, one of the most glamorous and emblematic—not just in Portugal but in the whole of Europe. It is located in a perfect position on the Lisbon Coast near to the picturesque towns of Cascais and Sintra, themselves magical spots away from the turmoil of occupied and Nazi-controlled Europe. However, it has a darker side. All that glitters is not gold. This is the Palacio Hotel, haunt of royalty and those who can afford its opulence and its casino. Around its lush gardens roam a mixture of people from all walks of life, caught up in one way or another of the European tragedy precipitated by Adolph Hitler and his odious regime. Many are wealthy émigrés seeking a new life away from the strife, depositing large fortunes in many cases in the Lisbon banking system, renting expensive suites in the Palacio's most prestigious quarter, and others simply regular visitors to the hotel from nearby high-quality homes and apartments, or downtown Lisbon, purchased from the sales of other homes distant from the relative quietude of Estoril. There is one group that tends to stand out, not just because of language and ethnicity, because the Palacio is filled regularly with a quintessentially diverse and multilingual cross-section of Europe, but because of their disposition. The latter, on close observation reveals, tension, nervousness, and awareness that things are not normal, that they may be being watched. They are in anticipation, not of staying and enjoying the good life of Estoril, but leaving, departing for a life beyond the shores of Portugal and war-torn Europe. This group is a diverse mixture of European Jews escaping from the grip of Nazi anti-Semitism, which has torn them from their homes, their businesses, and their professions, from all that is near and dear to them. Their way of life has been emasculated by a tyranny that will know no bounds, culminating in the most atrocious crime against humanity in history, the Holocaust. Many of the Jewish people strolling the gardens, taking a swim, eating and drinking in small groups, and attempting to maintain a sense of both dignity and proportion are made of sterner stuff than Hitler's evildoers. They plan to escape to the United States, a country that they perceive to be—and hope will become for them—exactly what one of that country's key national anthem lines embodies: "The land of the free, and the home of the brave." Many await the news of a sea passage to New York from Lisbon, and the very wealthy are in anticipation of a flight from the Tagus River on the Pan America Clipper flying boat, a long twenty-two-hour flight that stops to refuel in the Azores, Portuguese Islands in the eastern Atlantic. Transferring their financial assets has been a major challenge for most, ensuring that they can survive until a new life beckons in what indeed will be the New World in every sense.

The hotel is full of others less well disposed to these would-be immigrants to the United States. These people are the apotheosis of goodwill to stricken escapees. These are the people who precipitated their cultural, social, and financial demise in their countries of origin in Nazi-occupied Europe, particularly the Fatherland itself, the Third Reich. Commander Fleming is about to arrive in a veritable nest of strife, intrigues, espionage, and intense political-diplomatic interaction. He is entering a microcosm of Hitler's Reich in the very heart of Portugal's most elite gathering place, the Palacio Hotel in Estoril.

The taxicab that delivers Fleming to the main entrance is greeted by a bevy of porters and elegantly dressed hotel staff, with the head porter bedecked as if greeting royalty. He scans the scene, taking in the opulence and the clear presence of wealth. Instead of going straight to his suite after check-in, Fleming walks slowly around the hotel, getting the lay of the land, and after surveying the main interior lounges and dining areas, he strolls casually into the gardens and inspects the outdoor eating and drinking areas. The Palacio is alive with diplomats of all types and judging by their accents from all those unoccupied countries still able to send diplomatic representation to Portugal. This is clearly where it all happens, just as he was briefed back in London. He spots the one location that he's been particularly seeking, the famous casino. There it is, right before his eyes. He does a quick and cursory look inside, quiet now before the evening's gambling ensues.

On his way to his suite, Fleming sees and hears what he has anticipated all along, not just German voices and several accents from the Third Reich, but clearly pro-Nazi representatives of what he correctly surmises are a mixture of the German Foreign Ministry and, most of all, the Abwehr. He spots them a mile away, to quote his own internal assessment of what he hears, sees, and observes the body language of the arrogant and those who believe that they are indeed the "master race." Fleming silently notes that he plans to change all that.

He heads to his suite, where he finds that the staff have already unpacked his large suitcase and hung his attire in the various palatial wardrobes, dressing tables, and drawers. He deliberately kept hold of his briefcase while walking the hotel and insisted at reception that he would keep his passport. He opens the safe, places his passport inside together with a very large number of high-value Escudos, resets the combination, and then places a hair across the safe with saliva.

He bathes and decides to take a short nap before calling for a taxi to take him into Lisbon, where he plans to walk and establish the location of the key bank where he will purportedly be doing business.

Herr Fritz Freitag looks the perfect Swiss banker—elegant, accomplished, wealthy, and ready to do business.

The Caixa Geral de Depositos is arguably Lisbon's oldest bank, founded in 1876. Fleming's cover operation back in Zurich has been dealing with this scion of Portuguese finance for some time. The trail is totally watertight, and there are no footprints, fingerprints, or other apparent signs of those behind the various business deals that Fleming is about to execute. Stuart Menzies's deeply buried SIS operation that wheels and deals, as if the perfect Swiss banking machine, with all the polished accoutrements of Swiss high finance, is about to be at the service of a visiting Swiss banker to the Caixa Geral de Depositos.

Fleming's lack of Portuguese is compensated for by the two senior bank officials' rather mediocre but passable German, more than sufficient for Fleming to conduct his business.

The two officials greet Herr Fritz Freitag as if they have known him forever, almost fawning with servitude, all in anticipation of further deposits from Fleming's bank in Zurich. Their servile attitude is matched by Fleming's clever portrayal of the somewhat obsequious and patronizing Swiss banker, extending his largesse, in the form of funds, to the banking community of Lisbon. It works like a charm.

The two bankers have invited to their meeting a high-end real estate broker who is managing the various real estate deals that Fleming will execute over a rather indifferent cup of coffee. His German is poor, and he is clearly interested only in one thing: the consummation of the various deals on the large table in the manager's office. Fleming is buying several properties. Two are high-end houses, and three are apartment buildings. One of the latter is the lowest priced of the five that he signs off for and on behalf of the Zurich bank. It is located very close to the Lisbon waterfront near the seedy and red-light district. It's a three-story apartment building, quite large, old; and of the three apartments, it is the only one that is a self-contained building, one block from the Tagus River and the dockyard.

"We have more properties for you, sir, if you are interested?"

Fleming prevaricates in perfect Hoch Deutsch.

"I'm going to do my own surveying. Get the lie of the land. Then I'll invest further. The bank wants me to be thorough in my evaluation."

Fleming knows what he knows. Each of the five properties had been chosen with enormous care by London, with logistics, and Frederick Wells's and MEW's information paramount in both location and facilities. One of the very expensive houses by Lisbon standards will be a genuine let. The customer will be a wealthy renter from Nazi Germany, a Jewish man and wife who will stay in Lisbon and hope to see the war out in what is already their old age. They have no plans to immigrate to the United States. The high rent is easily affordable. The real estate agent is blossoming with the thought of the commission for his first renter. They have paid a handsome deposit and the first six months' rent fully in advance, almost unprecedented, reports the real estate agent.

After further pleasantries, Fleming executes all the sales documents and the first rental agreement, insisting that he approves all future rental agreements personally and says in a perfectly cultured and rather pompous German accent, "I want to ensure that we have the right kind of people living in our properties. No one with the wrong pedigree or poor financial credentials. You do understand?"

They all nod approvingly, thinking of only one thing: the funds that Fleming is paying into the bank.

"If all goes well, and I am sure it will, we will be sending further funds to you."

"Sir, thank you, we very much appreciate your business."

Fleming then plays literally his card.

"I have a pension for cards, always have. I hate to lose. As a Freitag, we never lose, I'm sure you understand?"

They all agree in a most insincere and groveling way.

"Of course, sir, we want Herr Freitag to be a winner while with us here in our wonderful Lisbon. How much would you like us to place on account for you with the casino at the Palacio?"

"It's already transferred from Zurich. You should have it in my name."

"Ah yes, sir," quips the junior banker. "We have it already. Whatever you need, Herr Freitag. We can transfer to the Palacio. We'll do all that you request, naturally."

"Thank you. You are absolutely first rate. I will report accordingly back to Zurich."

Fleming is at his most duplicitous best, a star no less.

"Oh, that is so kind, and we look forward to further business."

After further pleasantries and even more obsequiousness on all sides, the gathering ends, and Fleming is pleased to breathe the fresh Lisbon air and heads to the waterfront. He needs the exercise, having been cooped up on board a ship from the London docks in a neutrally flagged Liberian-registered merchantman with a South African skipper and mixed South African and Asian crew that docks in Barcelona, where he transferred to a modest Portuguese-registered passenger liner that docked in Lisbon. His Swiss credentials and perfect German accent ensure undetected and uninterrupted passages.

Over the next two days, Fleming lies low. He reconnoiters Lisbon methodically, piecing together the waterfront area and main downtown area. It all fits together like a jigsaw puzzle, and his fine memory for the detail provided back in Room 39 and at the unit's training base now interlock leading to several key decisions that he needs to make over the next two weeks in preparation for his team to slowly and surely infiltrate Lisbon.

The property deals are consummated. Fleming ensures that the real estate agent is both paid and then off the scene as far as the other properties are concerned. He makes that clear to him in his office on the Rua da Adica, which Fleming likes to frequent because it is in the authentic and elegant Alfama neighborhood, with fountains and a relaxed atmosphere. He has another important reason. He takes cabs and walks in totally random ways. He ensures that he is not being followed.

Fleming visits all the bank's properties.

The real estate agent does a final walk-around with him, transfers the deeds after all funds have been transferred, and Fleming informs him that his bank will handle the rest. His guarantee of no further meddling by the agent is the promise of further lucrative business. Fleming expresses in no uncertain terms that he does not want the waters muddied. Funds will be coming the real estate agent's way, just be respectful of his wishes. Fleming says on final parting in a direct way that leaves no misunderstanding, "We like to do things the Swiss way, you know, total privacy and respect for the customer. I'm sure you understand. We also like to reward well those who work well for us. You've been excellent. We look forward to doing more business with you."

The donkey takes the carrot.

Thirty Assault Unit's Lisbon cover facilities are now in the hands of a reputable Swiss bank with impeccable credentials. Fleming's youth spent in Switzerland has paid off, coupled to his firsthand knowledge and experience of the London and international banking scene, and especially wheeling and dealing with the Swiss banks. John Godfrey, he surmises, should be well pleased with his recruit.

Fleming now feels that it's time to test his black jack skills. He's honed his skills over the years, winning far more than losing. For the unknowledgeable, black jack, sometimes known as twenty-one, is played clockwise, usually between several players and the dealer, with each player competing against the dealer. At the Palacio Casino, Fleming has observed that the typical number of players at one of several tables is seven. He has been meticulous in observing the who's who at the casino tables. He knows the lineup. The latter reflects a combination of both the hotel guests and the nightly visitors. It is the visitors in whom Fleming has most interest and concern. In among the bevy of assorted diplomats and high-flying local residents with serious bank accounts are the suspects that concern him most. They are as far as Fleming, Herr Freiberg, observes clear and obvious members of the Reich's Abwehr, with the possible Gestapo and SD agent thrown in for good measure. He assumes that the Gestapo and SD are there to keep an eye in their own people, the counterintelligence and undercover people sent to make sure that the Abwehr are not selling themselves to the Portuguese Secret Police or, worse still, to the British Secret Service. By the beginning of his second week, he's feeling comfortable in playing the odds. He has been meticulous in not making himself known, in case he catches the attention of the wrong people.

After an excellent Palacio dinner with an older and wealthy mix bag of residents whose company he's thoroughly enjoyed, he regales them with his youthful skiing experiences in Switzerland and Austria. He's delighted them with his stories of his times in the fashionable resort of Kitzbuhel east of Innsbruck, in the Austrian province of Tyrol, and his many Swiss escapades and dalliances in his "native" Zermatt, Verbier, St. Moritz, and Davos. The older crowd, particularly the men, love his stories. The Swiss banker has made his mark. Time to gamble.

On night one at the tables, Fleming stands out for his skill and tenacity. He banks a profit and, in so doing, gains a certain attention, particularly from those who lose, and notably the Germans. The languages at the tables are diverse. He speaks in German first and foremost, and French second. He never speaks in English. Whenever the dealer or others speak in English, he protests politely, "Please, German or maybe even French," in his best Hoch Deutsch. He's convincing.

He deliberately lies low some nights and, on his third night at the tables, deliberately overstretches his hand, losing to a German who is Abwehr through and through. He congratulates him for his fine skill and tenacity. The German agent is vain and conceited and rises to the bait with consummate predictability. Fleming's panache and flamboyant style pleases the local wealthy set, and he is soon one of the locals.

At the end of his third week at the Palacio, and with all his "business" complete, Fleming is at the tables for a long night of what he feels will be a winning streak.

His luck is about to acquire a different dimension.

An attractive Portuguese lady, probably in her early thirties, makes herself known to Fleming in a way that he instinctively knows is planned. This is not a coincidental meeting. He has noticed her looking at him, and he has been attentive to the fact that she's not only a fine-looking lady, she also can flip from her native Portuguese to German. Fleming wonders to himself if she is also an English speaker. However, he's not about to test her English language skills.

"I'm Maria Santos, and who do I have the pleasure of meeting, may I ask," she says in reasonably good German with a passable accent. She smokes too, waving a German Nil cigarette between her elegant right-hand fingers. Fleming knows the brand well, popular with more sophisticated Germans and Austrians, known as the Austria Tabak. This endears her to Fleming, who enjoys the nicotine stimulant and inhales profusely. She proffers a cigarette to Fleming, producing the distinctive packet consisting of a blue rectangle with white capital letters surrounded by a white eagle, under which is the name Regie. Fleming thanks her and responds, "My name's Freitag, Fritz Freitag."

"Very nice to meet you, Herr Freitag, perhaps you will permit me to call you Fritz?" she says in a very warm and friendly voice that Fleming picks up on through her German pronunciation.

"You certainly may," responds Fleming. "Call me Fritz, please, delighted."

They enjoy their first smoke together at the casino bar and exchange a series of pleasantries, and Fleming notices that she is in no hurry to establish both Fleming's credentials or origins. She deftly and, to a certain extent, graciously allows all the basic personal details to emerge.

Fleming makes his signature drink offer to the lady, one that he has used on so many occasions in many different social settings and with ladies to whom he is instantly attracted. This is a vivacious, sexually attractive woman who is exhibiting her female wares in no uncertain terms. Her long and elegant legs nestle close to Fleming, and he feels her vibrations.

"What is to be, *Fraulein Maria?*" he says in impeccable Hoch Deutsch.

Her German response is not polished, but good enough.

"Whatever you have, *meine Liebe*, I'm yours."

Fleming announces to the barman, "Two martinis please."

"And how do you like them, sir?"

"Vodka and gin mixed, three ounces of gin to one ounce of vodka, with half an ounce of dry Vermouth, and garnish them both please with a lemon peel. And"—Fleming pauses, with both the barman and the Portuguese beauty all ears—"shaken, not stirred."

Fleming deduces and correctly anticipates that his favorite drink, which Maria is clearly not used to imbibing, will loosen her tongue.

The drink works, and she talks.

Fleming establishes the one key answer to a question that he poses in a very subtle and indirect way without actually saying, "Well, Maria, what do you?"

He is tactful and circumspect, and also respectful.

"You must lead a busy life in such a beautiful city, with so much going on. My banking business has really shown me what a wonderfully vibrant and exciting place you live in, Maria."

Maria gives Fleming a more than direct response. It's blunt, to the point of lacking any restraint or sophistication. The first martini has not only loosened her tongue, it has exposed slight vulnerabilities.

"Fritz, let me be totally honest with you. I'm a hostess. I accompany businessmen like yourself so that you enjoy your time here. I'm an escort, here to keep a man like yourself happy and content while doing business all day. I rest during the day and enjoy the night life with charming and successful men."

Fleming reassures her that she is fulfilling an important service. He comments in a low, dulcet voice, wishing to both reassure her while knowing that she has other paymasters other than those who reward her for whatever services she provides.

"I think that's a wonderful thing to be doing, and I already feel that you are excellent company." Fleming inwardly chokes on his hypocrisy and knows that he has to play the game, just as he knows that she, too, has to play her game; and it is more than just hostessing.

Fleming both entices and indulges Maria, plying her with a second martini. The barman is an accomplished observer of men, both reacting to and then luring the Palacio's hostesses, adding more than the usual combination of vodka and gin.

After two martinis and what becomes profusely stilted conversation about both something and nothing, with considerable sexual innuendo from Mario, Fleming has quickly deduced that she's an Abwehr stooge sent to check him out, to make sure that he's the real thing, the Zurich banker with lots of funds and most adept at the tables. He decides that he needs to play along, to guarantee that pillow talk will end up being reported in the Lisbon Abwehr office, whose location is well-known to both Room 39 and C. He knows that she needs the money, German money, to pay her way and live a life beyond that of an otherwise modest but extremely attractive and seductive Lisbon woman with little to offer life beyond her physical attributes. She will also anticipate expensive gifts and financial rewards much in excess of what madams in the local whorehouses receive. Money will be handled in a way that will demean neither party, given as a "gift," not as payment for services rendered. The aura of respectability is added to the otherwise patently clear services rendered part of her work.

They adjourn to his suite.

Fleming is not only the perfect lover; he is also the perfect gentleman. In his suite, he treats her with consummate attention and flattery, with every move and every word reinforcing just one thing, his Swiss banking background, credentials, and desire to make money in Lisbon out of the misfortunes of the many wealthy émigrés. In between their lovemaking, he subtly leaves one critical impression on someone he perceives to be a relatively simple though glamorous lady: that he is exploiting the Jewish community and how he abhors, as a good German-speaking Swiss, the wealthy Jews and how he supports the Nazi anti-Semitic philosophy. Fleming chokes inwardly on his hypocrisy and web of lies and planted deceit, but he has to do it. He knows that in the morning, she will play back in Abwehr headquarters his web of deceit. He also surmises that if she is playing both ends, the Abwehr and Salazar's Secret Police, then he has covered all his bases.

Fleming relaxes with her lying in his bed, naked and purring for more pleasure. He orders two more martinis from room service, and these are soon in their hands, sitting side by side on the large, opulent bed, with the finest sheets and covers spread back now in a disheveled array of postsexual coitus.

Just as Fleming both anticipated and planned, the third martini sends his companion out for the night, asleep in a combination of alcoholic and sexual haze.

In the morning, he orders breakfast for them both in his suite. She bathes and eats a healthy breakfast, consuming more coffee than he's seen in some time. For Fleming, the good news is that she insists that she has to leave for a nine o'clock appointment that she cannot miss. Fleming does not ask, quite deliberately, where she is going and why. He never offers her money. He feels that such an offer will degrade their relationship because it is obvious that she wants to see him again. He wants to continue the pretence, to guarantee that whoever is paying her receives the necessary feedback. He makes a pointed comment in a way that brings a smile, "I'm looking forward very much to treating you to all that you desire and providing you with whatever gifts you may like. My pleasure. The best that a Zurich banker can provide for a wonderful lady." Fleming's words work like a charm. Maria beams and almost lunges at Fleming.

They kiss and embrace. He explains that he has a lot of banking business to do and has to entertain several of the Lisbon bankers with whom he's associated. She seems perfectly content, and they agree to meet a few days later.

Fleming feels that he's sowed the right deception seeds. She is not pressing for immediate further engagement, a good sign that she is convinced of his Swiss bona fides.

Over the next three days, Fleming is convinced that he is safe; his cover is not blown.

He visits the properties, and once he has accomplished all the necessary legal aspects of the real estate transactions, he takes what he considers his first real risks.

He visits men's clothing stores, purchases various low-end working attire that will make him look more like a dock worker than a banker, including three different hats. He keeps these in a haversack that temporarily is kept inside a shopping bag from a Lisbon Department Store, El Corte Ingles, in keeping with his Swiss banker status.

Fleming has found the perfect café, large and with a rear exit. He changes there in the men's room in a cubicle and exchanges the use of the store bag for the haversack, now slung over his shoulder with his regular clothes inside, and exits unobtrusively from the back exit down several side streets, checking and rechecking possible surveillance, and heads for the river and the wharfs. He is wearing dark glasses, and today he is unshaven.

Fleming checks out the waterfront where the merchant traffic load and unload a variety of goods, and based on MEW data, he locates where the Portuguese load the wolfram and iron ore. He feels confident after two days of careful and unobtrusive observations in different attire each day he has left in the SOE safe house, which will be the site for his next main risk-taking event. C's people recruited at the time of the Spanish Civil War, and have paid extremely well, a local Portuguese agent. Fleming is scheduled to meet him on the day in question and the time agreed back in London between NID and MEW. This is the only contact that the DNI and Fleming would agree to with the nascent SOE, who are totally unknowledgeable of Golden Eye. Fleming has always seen this as a risk in case the agent is a double or is being followed or if Fleming is being followed, will lead them both into a possible Abwehr or Secret Police trap.

However, both Godfrey and Fleming assess that the risk is minimal to nonexistent.

The reason is simple: Canaris.

The DNI and C know that the Portuguese agent is reliable, untouched, and that the Abwehr do not have him in their sights in Lisbon.

The meeting is uneventful in the safe house. Fleming does only one thing. He listens. He tells the agent nothing. What he learns though gives him reason for concern. The agent, whose name he never learns, tells him of the latest plans that David Eccles and his SOE leadership back in London have for their Operation Panicle. The latter is to prevent Lisbon becoming a German U-boat and naval base, should that contingency look like occurring. While he was in transit from London to Barcelona and then Lisbon, and during the weeks that he has been at the Palacio, Fleming learns that SOE has drawn up plans to destroy oil and gas installations along the Tagus River by blowing up cranes in the event of a Nazi occupation. However, what he learns is that this is all on paper, concepts, with no physical execution. He concludes that what he hears is in effect conceptual. He is relieved. He wants zero conflict with Golden Eye. He parts company with the agent who, in a short, less-than-two-hour meeting, he came to like. Fleming will never see him again. He concludes that there is no added value in another meeting.

Fleming exits the safe house via a rear entrance, checks and double-checks for possible surveillance and, after about an hour of criss crossing Lisbon's working class quarter, heads back to Lisbon's center and a second large café where he changes and executes a critical task of his Lisbon deployment.

While Fleming was in his transit to Barcelona and then Lisbon and enjoying the fruits of the Palacio, the vanguard of 30 Assault Group, in small teams of three to four, deploys via different neutral merchant vessels into Lisbon and Oporto and are now in situ, including several other towns close to where the Portuguese supply the Nazis with wolfram and iron ore. Each of the lead groups have Portuguese and Spanish speakers in their ranks.

Fleming walks down the Avenida da Republica, checking one final time for surveillance. He is adroit at entering Lisbon's iconic café Versailles, French in name but very Portuguese in terms of its fine cuisine and splendid art nouveau. He is most surreptitious, and after enjoying outstanding pastry with coffee, he adjourns to the men's room. He enters a predesignated closet, relieved that at the time he enters, it is unoccupied, perhaps because it is at the far end of what is any standards an opulent men's room. The closet adjoins the far wall, with no other closet on one side. He enters the closet, changes from his walking attire into his business clothes and shoes, and then climbs onto the lavatory seat within the totally enclosed closet and places a coded message in German behind the cistern, adhered with sticking tape, "Gute Jagd. Heil Hitler."

This is the go signal for 30 Assault Group's designated operative to spread the word to commence the first stages, largely logistical, of Operation Golden Eye. Fleming will never see the person designated to retrieve his coded message, but he knows exactly who it is and that today is the day, at this time.

He scans the large café. The assembled crowd is noisy and all enjoying the sumptuous Versailles dishes and drinks. No one notices Fleming. He leaves by the rear entrance, and after several minutes of watching the movements at the back of the Versailles, he locates the so named Lixeiras, or trash bins. He checks and double-checks and, without appearing suspicious, deposits the haversack and clothes into the largest bin that is full of garbage. He retains the posh-looking shopping bag and heads back round to the Avenida da Republica, walks several blocks, then goes down a narrow side street; and at the end, he hails the first taxi to take him back to the Palacio.

Within five days of Fleming's coded signal in Café Versailles, 30 Assault Group will have implanted in multiple covert locations in Lisbon and Oporto, and several other towns, with war materials production, hidden caches of explosives, weapons, radios, frogmen's gear, special nighttime clothing, and a whole assortment of disguises.

Golden Eye is set.

Fleming returns to the Palacio, tired and ready for rest. He now has to turn his attention after two days of inactivity, other than two visits on consecutive days to the bank, to his next key operational task. There awaits Commander Fleming a challenge that may have always been possible, predictable, but no one could fully anticipate with certainty. Meanwhile Golden Eye begins a life of its own, and in one part of Lisbon, which is not for the reputable and respectable.

CHAPTER 16

The Oldest Profession in the World Has New Meaning

THE WATERFRONT AT Lisbon is a bustling place with fishing boats going to and returning from the Atlantic fishing grounds, some as far as the Azores, ferry boats, passenger liners, and a large international merchant shipping industry with every flag from across the world. The latter includes a sizeable fleet of neutral flag-of-convenience vessels, registered in distant parts in countries with few claims to being maritime powers. These countries make a serious living from registering and technically owning such ships. However, the nature of real ownership is very different from legal registration. Most are owned, managed, and operated by companies now either occupied by Nazi Germany or, in the case of Britain and its imperial allies—such as Canada, India, Australia, New Zealand, and many Dominions and colonies that comprise too long a list to name, such as Hong King, Malaya, and South Africa—are at war with Germany. Such neutrally flagged vessels have to be insured, and Lloyds of London continues to insure many of these ships, protected under the accepted rules of war and the Geneva Conventions. There is no such thing as a law of the sea and technically no protection should the Nazis decide to change the rules. So far, neutral shipping plies the sea lanes of the world. The reason is simple. Hitler and his henchmen need neutral merchant shipping as much as Britain. They need war supplies and oil. In the case of Portugal, the Berlin leadership needs wolfram and iron ore to stoke its war machine. Portuguese merchant vessels can transport such vital materials without fear of being sunk by the Royal Navy.

Lisbon also has a significant ship repair and maintenance capability. It employs a sizeable workforce of skilled, semi-skilled, and unskilled workers, with tax income for Salazar's government's coffers. At the same time, crews and passengers staying for short periods while in transit through Lisbon, or longer periods while in various stages of repair and maintenance, need food, beverages, rest, and recreation. The crews represent the world's populations, recruited by the neutrally flagged shipping companies from just about every ocean-going country in the world. Many of the crews have endured long sea passengers with weeks in transit in many cases.

Of particular interests to the Abwehr are ships crossing the Atlantic, particularly from the United States and Canada, and those ships that are either neutrals or—and these are the vessels of most interest—British flagships that are running the gauntlet of Atlantic crossings in the face of Donitz's underwater menace, the U-boats, the UnterSeeBooten.

The Abwehr wants to know as much as possible about sailing dates, actual navigational transits, ports of both embarkation and arrival, and their cargoes, together with the vital differentiating factor of whether neutral or British flagged.

Sailors the world over tend to have a common need, perhaps a weakness depending on one's worldview. They need sex. After weeks of often unrequited abstinence, their natural impulses get the better of them. They need women, both for the pleasure of their company and also for the pleasure of their bodies. Whorehouses—brothels by another name—provide such services, at a price. The market, supply and demand, drives the cost. Religion, morality, ethics, social etiquette, and well-being do not enter the economic equation of customers' demands being met at market prices.

Lisbon has a thriving underworld of dockland brothels, and away from the more seedy areas are more up-market facilities, not just for the ships' officers who can afford a so-called more sophisticated lady of the night, but also for wealthier local men who feel the need for whatever reason to meet their basic desires. These latter clubs and private venues are a few blocks from the waterfront, within walking distance of where ships tie up.

Along with the sins of the flesh and the desires of the body come the usual array of medical problems that keep the private clinics and doctors' surgeries busy treating gonorrhea and syphilis, and other variants. The prostitution business is not just prevalent on the Tagus waterfront; it is an industry, and it is also something equally sinister and worrisome to British Naval Intelligence.

The Abwehr have insidiously inserted into the prostitution mix a significant group of trained ladies of the night, primed to entice their customers into revealing details of shipping movements. The latter's priority list include any ships, and especially convoys, leaving the United States for Europe, and in particular those whose final destination is Britain. Times of departure and simple questions, posed after intercourse and during alluring sexual activity, include "Where will you be sailing from next, and when, so that I can look forward to seeing you, and taking care of you?" The questions are well-rehearsed, in English. The Abwehr have taken great pains to recruit and train only either existing prostitutes with English language skills or specially trained Portuguese young women who are somewhat ignorantly prepared to run the risk of venereal disease in return for what is significantly more income than they could ever earn in regular Lisbon employment.

Furthermore, these Portuguese women are controlled by two Abwehr female agents, the worst of the worst, totally bereft of any guilt or conscience, and all in the service of the Third Reich and the pursuit of power for the master race, the *HerrenVolk*. The ideology that disenfranchises any deviations or ethnic variations from its creed is now insidiously inserting itself into the oldest profession in the world. The poor, wretched, unknowing, and financially motivated Portuguese women have, in effect, not just sold themselves to the devil, who has ensnared a generation of otherwise fine young Lisbon women, but they are also now threatening the survival of the one nation that stands between Hitler and western domination, Britain.

Fleming's 30 Assault Group is diverse in the extreme, ready for any task, anywhere, anytime. Dealing with a group of Nazi-trained whores enticing sailors to give away vital information requires different skill sets than the usual kinetic solutions that they have in mind in the event of either a Nazi take over of Portugal or Salazar and his regime decide to flip completely to the Nazi way of life.

Fleming leaves the Palacio and takes a taxi a few blocks from the waterfront area where he knows that certain key bordellos are located. He is circumspect, checking and double-checking for possible surveillance. He walks the rest of the way to his destination. He has invested in one such building three blocks from the waterfront, now rented out as a gentlemen's club, whose new manager looks very much like one of Fleming's finest. The contract was signed between Fleming's Zurich bank's Lisbon real estate company and a Portuguese-registered company that has been in business since the early 1930s specializing in tourism and is 100 percent Portuguese owned. There are no SIS or NID fingerprints anywhere. However, the truth is another matter.

Fleming was assiduous in ensuring that one of his best Portuguese-speaking recruits with years of working in and out of Lisbon is now running the new business. He speaks Portuguese like a native and holds a Portuguese passport. He is indistinguishable from the locals. He has also scored a major success. He has recruited to the club's employment two young German women who are known Abwehr-trained prostitutes, along with at least three more who he suspects are definitely on the Abwehr's payroll based on observation and the vital information provided by the one woman that he totally trusts, his girlfriend of seven years who has infiltrated the inner sanctum of the Abwehr's whores' malevolent coterie. Both Fleming and he have privately mused on the thought that he must be the most accomplished pimp in the history of NID.

Added to Fleming's business initiative is a very small group of his unit who have been briefed and given explicit instructions on how to behave as customers at Fleming's own house of ill repute and the other waterfront brothels. The one issue for all seven men is how to avoid contracting venereal disease, something that none of them naturally want to contract while on His Majesty's Secret Service, the NID. They need a combination of both excuses for avoiding sexual intercourse with the Abwehr's planted whores or, if willing to take risks, use latex condoms provided through the good offices of NID's medical naval services. The British military had begun issuing mass-produced latex condoms to its armed forces for use worldwide. Fleming's men are therefore no exception.

The coordination of false information trails, deception by another name, to the Abwehr's whores is non trivial. NID becomes expert at feeding "accurate" information to the Abwehr ladies of the night in Lisbon based on what Bletchley intercepts, which show Donitz's U-boat operational staff have gleaned sufficient accurate intelligence through their own sources, some of which are German agents in the United States and Canada, that British Naval Intelligence is not giving away possibly damaging intelligence to the enemy. The good information is played in parallel with the bad. As a result, the Abwehr deduce that their sources in Lisbon are not just reliable but worth every Reichmark paid to their prostitutes. The real secret, the essence of NID's operation, lies therefore in the information that is planted that is in fact false.

Fleming and his team will not witness the end game, the outcome of their deceptions, planted in the bedrooms of Lisbon whorehouses with women who are the unwitting but nonetheless evil purveyors not just of illicit sex but life-threatening information that may cause the sinking of critical British convoys.

The benefit to NID is considerable, and the consequences for protecting convoys are prodigious. How can this be? Fleming and his very tightly and highly trusted group of secure operatives know how Donitz's headquarters operate, gratis the brilliance of Bletchley Park. The latter deciphers how Donitz's staff react to both the false and the accurate planted information. The Hut 4 team listen as the U-boats deploy, heading across the North Sea, around the north of Scotland, and out into the Atlantic onto a great circle route to intercept actual and false convoys. NID deftly handles the Bletchley gold and feeds sufficient information to both the navy command in Liverpool and to the headquarters of Royal Air Force Coastal Command. Donitz's wolf packs deploy on their hunting missions. Their most likely courses, speed of advance from their north German and French Bay of Biscay bases, allowing for both underwater and surfaced transits, are calculated; and together with further Bletchley intercepts married to the calculations of Patrick Maynard Blackett's operational research mathematicians, the U-boats are heading into well-conceived and executed ambushes in the North Atlantic. This is the Battle of the Atlantic at its most sensitive and most secret, with the lifeblood of Britain at stake.

As Fleming heads back to the Palacio, his mind dwells on one thing, and one thing only: the lives that will be saved and the British sailors who will be spared the harsh vagaries of the cruel sea if their merchant ships are torpedoed by German U-boats, either dying quickly from explosive forces, or drowning in the pitiless Atlantic, unless fortunate enough to be rescued by one of the Royal Navy escorts. His sense of commitment and determination is unrelenting. Fleming wants to make his contribution vital, along with the DNI, the Room 39 team, the Bletchley people, Patrick Blackett's number crunchers, SIS and SOE, and most of all, those on the front line at sea, facing the harsh realities of the war at sea. He thinks momentarily of his late father, killed in action in World War II, and wants him to be proud of what his son is now doing. He will go on, to the end if need be, whatever that may be.

As he checks and double-checks for surveillance, his sharp and intuitive intellect dwells on what else he can do to help his country escape and defeat the merciless tyranny that grips Europe and threatens the very survival of his beloved Britain.

He climbs into a taxi and, in German, instructs the driver, "Zum Palacio, Schnell, Bitte."

As the taxi speeds to the Palacio, unknown challenges await Fleming that will test all his skills, his intellect, his ingenuity, his courage, and his endurance.

As he climbs out of the taxi and the head porter greets "Herr Freitag," Fleming dwells on the coterie of Abwehr and undercover Salazar agents inside this hotspot of espionage, perfidy, and treachery.

As he enters the main foyer, he notices two PVDE undercover agents, Salazar's finest, hovering in one corner, smoking and talking in low tones. As he collects his suite keys, he notices several Abwehr agents mustered in the inner lounge area. Something is afoot. What exactly, Fleming knows not. He will bathe, change, and return to the fray.

CHAPTER 17

Salazar at the Hotel Palacio A Night to Remember

FLEMING ENTERS HIS suite and immediately lifts the telephone and calls the reception.

"I'd like to make a call to my bank in Zurich, Switzerland, please. I know it's late, but I want to leave a message. How long will it take to get through, please?"

"About ten minutes, sir. I'll call you back as soon as our switchboard makes the connection to Switzerland. Please bear with us, sir, it takes a while to make the connections across Europe."

"I understand, no problem, I'll await your callback."

Fleming knows one very important thing. Others will be listening, not only the Palacio switchboard operator, but also the PVDE, Salazar's secret police, and in addition, as a result, whoever in the PVDE is in the pay of the Abwehr. His call therefore has to be as businesslike and seemingly correct as possible. Fleming has his words primed. His message is not about business, but the code that Operation Golden Eye is now in place. He will be telling London via the Zurich bank that all his initial key people are in place, and that they are secure and free from any counterintelligence operations. In addition, his simple message will signal that the first batch of weapons, explosives, communications equipment, underwater devices (limpet mines), and frogmen's gear is hidden successfully in the various safe houses now operating under the control of the lead assault unit operatives. He has passed operational command and control to his very best and most trusted small group of leaders. They are on their own, effectively in enemy territory, surrounded by the PVDE and German Abwehr agents.

The telephone rings.

"Herr Freitag, sir, your call to Zurich is connected."

"Thank you."

There is a momentary pause as the European telephone switching system clicks into gear.

Then Fleming hears the magic words that he has expected with anticipation.

"Good evening, this is Lena, the night service concierge, how may I help you?" came a friendly and warm-sounding female voice with a discernible *Zurituutsch* Swiss German dialect, local to the Swiss canton of Zurich.

"This is Herr Freitag with a message for the finance director on his arrival in the office in the morning."

"Yes, sir, Herr Freitag," replies Fraulein Lena. "Go ahead, sir, I'll write a note for the director and leave it on his desk."

"Tell him all the initial housing deals are complete. Please send the additional funds we've discussed for further purchases to the Caixa Geral de Depositos in Lisbon."

Lena repeats the message, and Fleming concurs.

"I have it written down, Herr Freitag. I'll ensure that he has it first thing in the morning."

"Thank you."

Fleming hangs up, knowing full well that every word was intercepted.

He is greatly relieved and breathes a huge sigh of relief.

The word will be passed to London and Room 39, and only Menzies himself in SIS will know soon enough that the pump is primed in Lisbon. Operation Golden Eye is activated.

The prime minister will be briefed accordingly.

Fleming shaves and takes a bath. He dons a very expensive Palacio bathrobe, calls reception, and asks for a light dinner of lobster salad to be delivered to his room at nine o'clock. He does not order wine. He plans to save his alcoholic needs until later, when concentrating on his black jack cards, surrounded by the usual suspects from the Third Reich and the other multinational, multicultural, and multiracial mix of wealthy gamblers. He sprawls across the suite's luxurious bed and takes a nap until he hears the doorbell ring at nine o'clock and the delivery of his sustenance for the evening.

Several floors below, a major event has been underway in the select VIP dining area. When Fleming observed the extra security people on his return to the Palacio, and what clearly were Policia International e de Defesa do Estado, the dreaded PVDE if you happen to be a Portuguese national on the wrong side of the Salazar regime, there was a very good reason. The Abwehr were also clearly present in force.

No less than the dictator himself, Dr. Antonio De Oliveira Salazar, is dining with a very select group. This is no casual gathering, no personal relaxing dinner for the head of state. This is a serious business and diplomatic event. The guests of the dictator are the giveaway. They signal everything.

Salazar is accompanied by one of his foreign policy advisors and, like Salazar, a distinguished University of Coimbra graduate, Jose Caeiro da Mata. Salazar trusts Jose implicitly, more so than several of his staff whom Salazar somewhat pathologically and irrationally believes may be in the pay of the Nazis. He may be correct in this regard, but his own PVDE has so far not ferreted out any traitors to the Salazar cause. The dictator has two important guests, both critical for his and Portugal's well-being. The first is the British ambassador, Sir Ronald Campbell, who has replaced the ineffectual Sir Walford Selby. The DNI and several of the top advisors to the British Foreign Secretary, Sir Anthony Eden, had lobbied successfully for placing Sir Ronald in the Lisbon hot seat. Campbell is not only an experienced and accomplished diplomat of the old school, he is recognized by Eden for his astute and perceptive grasp of the intricate interplay of Portuguese-German-British policies and objectives. Campbell has already endeared himself to both Salazar and Caeiro da Mata as not just a straight shooter who does not bandy diplomatic niceties but someone who acknowledges the harsh realities facing Portugal as a nation and Salazar as its leader. Campbell is a realist, and he knows how to frame and articulate British policy with Portugal. The other significant guest at Salazar's table is the German ambassador, Herr Hoyningen Huene, who has been in place since the war began and who will remain in place to the demise of the Third

Reich. Huene likes Portugal for many reasons. One is very much a personal secret. He's Hitler's man in Lisbon, and he knows how to keep Berlin happy and off his diplomatic back. His boss back in the Third Reich is no less than Ulrich Friedrich Wilhelm Joachim von Ribbentrop, who is better known by his ambassadorial staff as simply Joachim von Ribbentrop, Hitler's foreign minister. Little does Huene realize that the best thing that he can do is stay the course in Lisbon and never return to Berlin. Over this significant dinner, no one at the table could foresee the fate that will finally await von Ribbentrop on October 16, 1946, in Nuremberg. Tonight, the German ambassador is playing the role of the representative of the master race, Hitler's man to a tee. English is the chosen language for the dinner. Salazar has insisted that English is to be the diplomatic language in Lisbon, itself a positive sign so far as Sir Ronald and the British Foreign Office are concerned. Salazar is a gourmet and so is da Mata. They are both equally proud of Portuguese cuisine and enjoy showing off their knowledge as each dish is delivered with consummate decorum by the Palacio's finest wait staff. The Caldo Verde is served first, a soup of dark green cabbage, potato puree, sausage, and olive oil. As the soup is served Salazar makes a significant comment, and one that does not seem to flex Hitler's man.

"I want us to use English because I feel honored by the honorary degree recently conferred on me by Oxford University, a doctor of civil law, no less." He turns to Huene and comments that he hopes that the German ambassador will understand. Huene responds in a tactful and pleasing tone.

"I quite understand, Prime Minister. May I be reminded, sir, when Oxford conferred this honor upon you so deservedly?"

"May 1940. Splendid occasion. I love Oxford. Jose and I are both Coimbra graduates and very proud indeed of our heritage, but I have to confess that there is something very special about Oxford. It's quite unbeatable, unless of course you are a Cambridge graduate!"

The dinner table erupts with genuine laughter. Salazar has endeared his guests.

Salazar could not know this at this moment in time, but both of his ambassadorial guests will be with him until the end of World War II. They are both to be diplomatic survivors in Lisbon for the long haul.

The German ambassador is quite gracious and mentions that Britain is Portugal's oldest ally.

"Prime Minister, I fully understand. I only have one regret, and that is simply that I wish my English could aspire to that of your Oxford accent."

They all laugh.

There is clearly no animosity between Campbell and Huene. Salazar and his advisor feel comfortable in their presence. The prime minister seems to be bracing himself for a statement when the second course is served, Bacalhau, an iconic traditional Portuguese dish of salted codfish with potatoes, onions, hard-boiled eggs, and lots of olive oil. Salazar introduces the dish with relish, and his guests express their delight as a selection of Portuguese fine wines are offered to accompany the fish course.

The four men savor the cod.

"Exquisite!" exclaims His Majesty's ambassador.

"Superb," pronounces the Führer's plenipotentiary.

"Thank you, gentlemen, I love people who enjoy good food and wine. We are so blessed in Portugal with both."

There is a pause as fine food and wine are enjoyed.

Salazar chooses the "Le Moment Juste," to steal a French phrase that epitomizes the atmosphere over the dinner table.

"I have several reasons for inviting you both to dinner. I want to take the opportunity in a more relax and convivial atmosphere to explain my position, our position, my ministers and I, on several important issues."

Campbell and Huene both lower their utensils and look directly at Salazar.

"I want both Prime Minister Churchill and Reich's Führer Hitler to understand one cardinal point, gentlemen, that Portugal will remain neutral for the duration, however long that may be."

There is a pause, a pin could drop.

Both ambassadors are transfixed.

"My government and I want to make it absolutely clear that Portugal will trade freely, as a neutral, with whomever it chooses. The *Estado Novo*, of which I am the emblem, is Portugal's aspiring new state, what I hope will be a thriving economy that will improve the living standards of our people."

Salazar is at his altruistic and patriotic best.

Both ambassadors nod sagely and concur in unwavering terms.

One after the other, first Campbell, then Huene, show total support for the Portuguese view of the world and Salazar's wishes.

The timing of the third course could not have been better if planned to the minute.

"Porco Preto!" exclaims Salazar.

"One of my all-time favorites, gentlemen. I hope that you enjoy."

The Portuguese cured ham from the Alentejo region of Portugal is served, exquisitely cooked and served to perfection. The flavorful black pork is crisp on the outside and juicy on the inside, served with small potatoes and freshly cut parsley.

There is total silence, and each man savors the delights of the pork.

Fresh wines are offered, from different regions of Portugal, and Salazar, the genial host, does not presume to tell or advise his guests which wine goes well. In fact, all the wines have been specially selected by the Palacio's top sommelier.

At an appropriate point in the eating, Salazar addresses his guests with what is clearly to be another policy statement. This though also has the spirit of a request.

"Gentlemen, I need to address with you that age-old subject of money, dare I say what the English literati call, I believe, filthy dross. Well, Portugal needs, very badly, funds."

Salazar then expounds lucidly on Portugal's urgent need to be paid promptly for the import by both Britain and Germany of materials, such as wolfram and iron ore from Portugal. He says that Portugal is not a bank offering extended credit.

"We understand in Berlin," comments the Reich's ambassador.

ANTHONY WELLS

Salazar looks at Sir Ronald and says very directly, "Please do let your prime minister know, Sir Ronald, that we cannot afford to bankroll British imports from Portugal."

Sir Ronald then promises to pass on this message. At this point, Campbell decides to change the tempo of the meeting and thanks Salazar profusely for the support he gave refugees from Gibraltar, finding a temporary home in Madeira, and he somewhat jokingly says that if he had to choose a place to be a refugees, Madeira would be it.

All four men respond to Campbell's humor, and the German ambassador laughs.

As they imbibe more wine, tell pleasantries, and relate family matters, the German ambassador says that he has to pass on a couple of messages from the Führer, and he feels that this is the best time. Campbell bristles slightly, and this is noticed by Salazar's advisor.

He says that Hitler is concerned about the number of Jewish refugees fleeing to Lisbon. Oswald Hoyningen-Huene makes this highly sensitive statement in an officious and less-than-delicate way that clearly annoys Salazar. "Your borders, Prime Minister, and ports such as here in Lisbon and Oporto seem to be porous."

The choice of the word *porous* grates on the other three, and Salazar is not amused.

Salazar hits back.

"Portugal, Ambassador, is a neutral country," and then says to Hoyningen Huene as a pronouncement, "My good ambassador, should you ever find the need to stay here with us in Portugal, you will always be welcome. I regard you as a friend and good person. We welcome many to Portugal as long as they respect our traditions, history, culture, way of life, and laws. I am sure you understand."

The German ambassador winces, totally taken aback by this personal comment that on the surface seems out of context, but clearly was not. Maybe Salazar and his people know something very personal about Huene and his views of the Third Reich?

There is a quiet that all four men fully understands. For several seconds, no one says a word.

Huene thanks Salazar for his graciousness, and then says that he is compelled to pass on a second message from the Reich chancellery intelligence leadership.

Salazar is now rising in his seat, and Campbell knows instinctively that although Huene is merely doing his Nazi master's bidding, this is about to become tense and potentially a showstopper.

"The Führer and his intelligence staff are concerned about how the Portuguese consulate in Bordeaux in France seems to have become a safe haven for Jews escaping from Europe, and likely trying to head for the United States."

Salazar is about to interrupt von Ribbentrop's mouthpiece when Huene just keeps rolling, almost oblivious to the fallout and clear consternation of the other three.

He mentions the consul by name, "Aristides de Sousa Mendes, he's your man, Prime Minister, a great friend of the escaping Jews. The Führer does not like such people," Salazar interrupts.

He is definitive.

Sir Ronald Campbell is keeping totally quiet and seemingly unperplexed. Internally he is cheering.

Salazar is adamant.

He says that he will hear no more of this. He says that Portugal is neutral and, "That is that, and enough is enough. I hope that my message is clear, Ambassador."

To lower the temperature, Sir Ronald talks about Salazar's economic achievements and how his people seem to be happy. He rhapsodizes about Salazar's sense of what's right for the Portuguese people and then deftly shifts to Portugal's fine food and wines that they are enjoying over dinner. Salazar looks at Campbell, smiling. Campbell then says in a clear and robust voice, "May I add to the prime minister's statement and also stress the importance of the freedom of the seas, and particularly for a neutral country."

There is a pause.

"I hope that you agree, Ambassador?" states Campbell, turning and looking Huene directly in the eye.

Huene is caught off guard, almost stutters, and momentarily reverts to German, "Ja, Ja," followed by, "Of course, of course."

Salazar himself then breaks the ice.

"Dessert, gentlemen, Portuguese style."

The wait staff bring on Pastel de Nata, dessert pastries made from flour, butter, eggs, and cinnamon.

Salazar says that," You don't have to drink it now, gentlemen, but it's traditional to have a Portuguese coffee with the Pastel de Nata. Here in Lisbon, we have a special coffee with our Pastel de Nata, called Bica. Try it. It's OK if you say no. I won't be offended."

All four men enjoy a cup of Bica.

Neither ambassador is that tactless.

By the time the port arrives, a fine-aged Jackson from Porto and the Douro Valley, Salazar says that he wants to make another important point for transmission to London and Berlin.

"Gentlemen, I don't have to say this clearly enough, but I want to make it explicit. The Azores are sacrosanct Portuguese territory, and I do not wish to see any encroachments."

Salazar is playing to a Nazi audience in Berlin.

Campbell takes a breath and, knowingly in his mind, thinks of the ongoing secret talks to have Lajes in the Azores become a leased airfield for use by the Royal Air Force and a base for the Royal Navy, to be shared jointly in due course with the Americans. Salazar is being extraordinarily deft in front of Hitler's emissary.

Huene is respectful.

"I will pass on both your wishes and your concerns, Prime Minister. I fully understand."

The port bottle is passed a second time by the sommelier, to the left, British style.

Pleasant banter ensues, with good humor and personal epithets and minor adventures relayed about the good times enjoyed being with the Portuguese people. There is laughter and smiles, and no sense of ill will or unrewarded goals for the evening.

Before they arise, Salazar says that he has one very important request to be passed to both governments.

This takes both ambassadors by surprise after an interlude of low key, almost jocular exchanges.

"Gentlemen, please give me your assurance that neither London nor Berlin will undermine my government. That is critical for our relationships."

Salazar pauses, and then says, "If your various intelligence agencies want to spar with one another here in Lisbon, that's your business, as long as it does not affect my government and my people. I hope you understand. My PVDE is everywhere. I receive regular updates. There's nothing we don't know, gentlemen."

Both ambassadors acknowledge Salazar's wishes.

There is little to be said to such a definitive statement, indeed an order.

Salazar smiles, looks at them both, and says in the most disarming way, "Now let's relax and have a good time."

The British ambassador says to himself, *If only you really knew.*

Sir Ronald proposes a toast to Portugal's finest leader. They drink heartily, and Salazar suggests that they adjourn to the lounge for an after dinner drink. He looks at Campbell and suggests that, with a name like his, "Maybe a single malt for you, Sir Ronald, with your Scots ancestry?"

They adjourn to a private and secure lounge area to enjoy their after-dinner drinks and further pleasant banter.

Campbell is pleased.

The Third Reich's ambassador gives nothing away. However, the British know that Huene is no loyal Nazi, no epitome of the master race, no fawning and servile toady to von Ribbentrop's every whim, a man who knows a sense of decency and also knows full well that at some point the Third Reich will crumble like a pack of cards. He genuinely loves Portugal and the Portuguese, and he will stay on when the end comes, so very glad that he maintained his sense of place and perspective in the darkest days of the Nazi tyranny.

***

It is nearing 2300.

As the ambassadorial cars take the two ambassadors to their residences and Salazar's security detail escort him to the prime minister's residence, another pack of cards is about to be played.

Herr Fritz Freitag enters the casino. This is going to be a night to remember.

CHAPTER 18

Casino Royale
Fleming's Finest Hour

FLEMING IS AT his most sartorial and suave best. His made-to-measure Savile Row dinner jacket has been freshly laundered, and his bow tie is perfectly tied. His shoes are not simply shiny, they gleam a mirror of perfection. His cuff links have been well-chosen, emblems of his Zurich bank, an advertisement that he wants observed as his cuffs protrude from his jacket's sleeves.

As he surveys the casino, he takes in who's who. He is in no hurry. He has all night as far as he is concerned, or at least until he feels that he's had enough. Fleming does not lack stamina. He is feeling both mentally and physically strong.

He heads to the table where his skill and persistence have endured.

The croupier instantly recognizes him and gives him a rousing salutation. "Welcome back, Herr Freitag. Zurich's finest has returned. So nice to see you again, sir."

"Thank you, it's nice to be back."

The maître d' welcomes Fleming and asks if he would like his usual.

Fleming is explicit, "Yes, thank you, shaken, not stirred."

Fleming now sits down in the casino for a night of black jack, gratis His Majesty's treasury. He senses a winning streak. His sixth sense is in overdrive.

He surveys the assembled players.

Opposite him at the card table is Lieutenant Colonel Hans Rudolph. Fleming knows precisely who he is and more about him than Rudolph probably knows himself. He's German Abwehr, 100 percent. To Fleming's surprise, but not distain, and lurking near the

Nazi colonel, is the lady with whom Fleming shared sexual pleasures just a few days earlier, Maria Santos. Fleming vividly recalls. How could he forget her? She's definitely different, a Portuguese national who speaks German, and a rare commodity in wartime Portugal. Now she's back on the scene, and with whom, and why? She is looking as attractive and seductive as ever. Fleming tells himself to concentrate, and he does so with every fiber of his card-playing being.

Another player that Fleming notes with considerable interest is a man with whom he has made himself very familiar among the regular hardcore players over the previous nights that Fleming has been either observing or playing in the casino. This is Paul Fidrumc. Fleming is well-informed about Herr Fidrumc, feeding at the Abwehr trough and not concerned about what he tells his paymasters as long as the funds keep heading his way. Fleming has observed over several nights that Fidrumc and the Nazi colonel have several things in common, not least their propensity for late-night drinks together, heavy at times, smoking in a cloistered area off the main lounges created for private and discrete conversations. Fleming has observed who else of Rudolph's underlings have joined them from time to time, almost as if ordered by the Abwehr colonel to take notes and presumably take follow-up actions based on whatever the man from Czechia is providing. Fidrumc is very sociable, ingratiating himself with the wealthiest of the Palacio's guests and card players. Fleming figures that he's in his early forties, well-dressed and groomed, and clearly loves the good life at the Palacio. Fleming thinks to himself, *He who pays the piper calls the tune.* But what is Rudolph asking Fidrumc to provide? What sort of piper is he? Fleming surmises. What tunes is he playing for the Nazi Reichsmarks that are feeding his lifestyle? Fleming has shared several short exchanges with him, all social chit-chat of little consequence, with Fleming always playing a consistent tune from his chords of the wealthy Zurich banker interested in making money for his bank out of the political-social-moneyed entrepot that is Lisbon. Fleming has Paul Fidrumc well-marked. He notices without giving away his subtle observations that Rudolph and Fidrumc make regular eye contact during the card games.

The croupier commences.

The game ensues.

Time passes, and the tension rises.

Fleming is winning.

Fleming orders a second drink, "A martini, my usual—shaken, not stirred. Thank you," as he smiles at the attractive young waitress.

He glances at Maria, and she turns her cheek in a coy expression of both wanting to acknowledge Fleming while also ignoring him.

Fleming sips his martini.

He looks at her a second time, almost tempted to ask if she would like a martini.

He controls himself. *The night is young. There's time,* he surmises.

He also remembers exactly who she most likely works for. Her boss is likely right there, feet away from her.

The waiter returns, and Fleming raises his glass to his fellow card players, and he looks Rudolph directly between his intense, unfriendly eyes and taught face. Fleming has quickly deciphered his various medal ribbons and insignias, all reminiscent of the Third Reich's rewards to those who show total and undivided fealty and loyalty, to die for the Führer and the Nazi cause.

The rounds are intense.

Fleming is on a roll.

The British treasury's funds have been well-invested.

They take a break, and Fleming adjourns to the bar, taking his drink with him to slowly enjoy his second martini.

He is followed by an American player and one of the two wealthy German Jewish players, who is an émigré awaiting a flight to New York on the Pan Am Clipper.

The American, James Bell, introduces himself and announces that he is a New York businessman with Wall Street connections. He's representing several US interests investing in Portuguese iron ore and wolfram (tungsten) expansion as the wartime demand increases, and they are teaming with Portuguese business interests as both partners and bankers. He asks Herr Freiberg about his interests, and after he hears about Fleming's banking connections, he suggests that they meet the following day. Fleming concurs. The aged Jewish man, Werner

Wegstein, says that he welcomes connecting with Bell's office in New York City regarding his financial assets and investments in the United States. The three exchange pleasantries and then the maître d' calls the players back to the tables.

By 1:00 a.m., Fleming has amassed considerable winnings. Colonel Rudolph is on a losing streak, and his exasperation and anger are clear. His dislike of Fleming has grown. He senses that the Swiss banker is too good for his liking. He is glaring at Fleming; and Rudolph's lady, Fleming's one-night stand, Maria Santos, has consistently placed her long-gloved hands on his shoulders in a soothing manner, offering consolation for his losses. She whispers sweet nothings in his ear, but Rudolph's arrogance and sense of his own self-importance outweigh any blandishments. He's building an aversion to the man from Zurich.

The games go on. Fleming does well, very well. Maria Santos coyly avoids any eye contact with Fleming, indeed any evidence of prior association.

By 2:00 a.m., the group cash in their chips, and those, like Rudolph, now know the bitter end to a three-hour series of games of wits.

As Fleming heads to the cashier to hand in his winnings, which he will have on account for transfer to his Swiss bank, he is accosted by Rudolph, who congratulates him in grudging German and then invites him for a late-night drink in his penthouse suite.

Fleming instantly has to decide. In a split second, he decides that maybe there's more to gain than lose. Fleming accepts, and after bidding goodnight to the other players, Fleming follows Rudolph and his lady to the elevator and then to the Abwehr colonel's suite.

In Rudolph's suite, Fleming is invited to sit in one of the comfortable and large arm chairs. There is a series of polite exchanges about the Palacio's facilities and the mixture of different people from all over Europe. When the Nazi lowers the tone of the conversation with various anti-Semitic comments about some of the hotel's guests, Fleming does his best to play along, though very grudgingly. Then without any preamble or warning of a change in his approach, Rudolph cuts to the chase after more flattery of Fleming's card skills and suddenly goes for the verbal jugular. He becomes the Abwehr interrogator. He asks one question after another about Fleming's Austrian youth, schools, and parents, how he began a banking career, and so on. What did Fleming think of the Anschluss? Rudolph compares Switzerland and the Swiss with Austria and the Austrians, pointedly stating that the Swiss play the neutral gain to their financial benefit. Fleming does his very best to keep cool and not raise the temperature, but Rudolph is heading in one direction that Fleming now realizes is not good. The colonel pauses, glares at Fleming, then pointedly asks, really demands of Fleming, in a high-pitched, guttural voice, "Are you underneath that thin veneer of Swiss noblesse, a loyal Nazi, like every good Swiss should be?" Fleming without a pause, stood up, and said in good Austrian German, "Heil Hitler," giving the Nazi salute. Fleming sits, and Rudolph says without hesitation, in prefect English, "Maybe you speak fine German with an English accent." Fleming, without a hesitation or wince, responds in prefect German, "Ich verstehe nicht. Was meinen Sie?" Rudolph retorts back in German this time, "You have a very different accent from my Zurich friends." Quick as a flash, Fleming responds, "Your Dortmunder accent, Colonel, does you little justice. My *hochdeutsch* is 'Das Beste vom Besten.'"

At this point, Rudolph is inflamed. He accuses Fleming of lying, and he wants to know what he is really doing in Lisbon, "Von den Reichen stehlen," including, he says in the most vile, low German, "Those vile Jews whom you seem to befriend, the enemies of the Reich. Who are you really?"

Rudolph comes right up to Fleming in his armchair, pulls his Luger, the famous Pistole Parabellum, from his holster and points it directly at Fleming's face. "Now who are you? You'll notice that I have a silencer on this fine German-killing machine."

Fleming, without batting an eyelid, says quite nonchalantly, "My dear colonel, you've forgotten one thing. The safety catch is still on." Rudolph momentarily looks down. Fleming raises his right leg and kicks the gun from Rudolph's right hand.

A split second later, Rudolph slumps forward and all but falls in Fleming's lap, with Fleming quickly leaning forward and springing to his feet.

Rudolph collapses face down, with a long stiletto blade firmly implanted between his shoulder blades, through to his heart. He gurgles, and then expires with one breath.

Maria Santos steps forward and says in English, "Mr. Fleming. Welcome to Lisbon."

Fleming retorts, "Whose side are you on?"

"Yours, on His Majesty's Secret Service, Mr. Fleming."

Fleming takes a deep breath. "Menzies never told me about you."

"I know, nor did your admiral, Godfrey. I was recruited after Franco came to power in Spain and he tied his future to Adolph Hitler. I'm a Coimbra modern languages graduate with high honors. MI6 recruited me the summer that I graduated, in London. I play all sides, but am loyal to only one. I know most of the undercover Secret Police too."

Maria checks Rudolph's pulse in his neck, and then removes the stiletto from Rudolph and goes to the bathroom to clean it. She returns and picks up the telephone. She speaks in Portuguese. Fleming realizes that although he cannot understand what she is saying, she is clearly not calling the hotel's reception.

She requests room service as soon as possible for clean bed linen and a full service. She asks that the concierge be contacted to arrange an early morning fishing trip for the house guest. She says that she expects service as soon as possible.

While they wait, Maria gives Fleming a very brief description of her work and says that in the interest of security, neither of them should divulge anything further. She adds that here in Lisbon, the Gestapo "have their ways and means."

She then informs Fleming that they must leave on the first Pan Am Clipper out of Lisbon in the morning for New York. She will ensure that their departure is guaranteed. They must leave Lisbon as soon as possible, no later than the next twenty-four hours, but in the morning, if things can be worked satisfactorily.

Fleming is not flabbergasted, but certainly caught off guard. This is not how he planned the evening or his departure from Lisbon.

Maria has not mentioned how she will leave, her means of escape, just that she, too, will depart Lisbon.

All becomes crystal clear immediately.

Maria looks at Fleming and says quite demonstrably, "I will be accompanying you." Fleming winces slightly. He is again taken aback.

London says, "Things are just too dangerous for me to stay. My disappearance with Rudolph's disappearance will create a host of speculation. London will create the right disinformation. Something to the effect, perhaps, that Rudolph and I have sailed for a new life in Brazil at an unspecified location, all for love, with the gold that Rudolph has been amassing from the bribes he's been taking in the iron ore and wolfram trade with Germany and his winnings on the tables here, until of course, he met the master! His name will be mud back in Berlin.

"We'll have a letter signed by Rudolph, resigning his commission in the Abwehr and bidding the Third Reich farewell for the benefits of life in South America. I know how to forge his signature on his letterhead. I have some. The letter will be just as he would write it, believe me."

Fleming is both impressed and still reeling from the impact of what has transpired, with the dead Nazi colonel lying at his feet.

"What about Rudolph's body?"

"By morning, the cleaning crew will have him joining the fish beyond the 100 fathom curve, in the deep water off the Continental Shelf. He deserves no less, *Bastardo Desprezivel*," she utters painfully in Portuguese.

Fleming is quickly assimilating all that she has said and done. For once, Fleming is actually totally nonplussed. He does not know what to say to Maria. He looks down at Rudolph's corpse and says the first thing that comes into his mind.

"I wouldn't mind his luger for a souvenir. Admiral Godfrey will appreciate."

"No," Maria says. "You must be kidding."

"Oh well, it was worth the try. Can I offer you my—I hope, our—favorite drink to celebrate the demise of this evil man and our future survival?"

Maria comes back with an instant retort, "Commander Fleming, you do have the right answer for every occasion. Why the hell not? We both need a drink."

He mixes two martinis—shaken, not stirred—and they await the cleaning crew. They talk about New York City, where she has never been. Fleming explains that Godfrey and C will ensure that she will be well taken care of, and maybe she'll eventually come over to London and work for NID.

Maria is quick to respond that she's always had an escape plan if discovered or something like Fleming's situation arose.

"C has always said that he would take care of me. He will. I know."

There is a knock at the door.

She tells Fleming to hide in the bathroom.

Maria answers the door in Portuguese.

Two men with a large laundry cart enter the suite, saying absolutely nothing. Maria inspects Rudolph's body and removes certain items. She then gives the men the go-ahead. They place Rudolph's body in a canvas bag that is loaded with what must be boulders or rocks. They cover the bag with linen so that the cart is full to the top. Without saying a word, they depart. Maria locks the door.

She summons Fleming, smiles, and comments, "Mission accomplished, Commander."

Fleming is relieved, impressed, and more than grateful.

He hands her the unfinished martini, raising his glass to cheer their success.

The phone rings. Maria answers in Portuguese. It is a short conversation, seconds in length. She says nothing, just listens. She replaces the telephone.

"All is well. New York City beckons. First flight at first light. We have a few hours."

Fleming says, "Well done, Maria, you're the best."

Maria makes a further call, one which she regards as significantly risky.

She adroitly informs her contact to prepare, "A letter of resignation for the Colonel." She adds that, "He wishes to sign it first thing in the morning."

Fleming is astounded when she explains what she just said in Portuguese.

They finish their drinks, and without much encouragement, Fleming says that if they are to leave in just a few hours time, they should enjoy their last night in Lisbon.

"We won't be back until the war is over, Commander Fleming."

Maria is smiling with anticipation.

Fleming hugs and kisses her. "Yes," he says, "Let's end our time together in Lisbon the way we started."

"Ian, you're incorrigible, as you British say, but I do love you."

They leave Rudolph's suite, locking the door, and use the stairwell to go one floor below to Fleming's suite.

They enter the bedroom and begin a final Lisbon fling.

CHAPTER 19

This Is Not the Cutty Sark
A Different Kind of Clipper

WHILE MARIA DRESSES, Fleming calls reception to announce that he will be leaving early because of urgent business back in Zurich. He gives various instructions about payment of his bill from his running account that the Palacio had established, allowing unfettered access to the hotel's facilities. He gives instructions for the transfer of what is a significant positive balance on his account, his casino account offsetting his other Palacio debts. His casino winnings have more than paid for his stay. The funds are to be transferred to his Zurich bank. Fleming opens the room safe and withdraws his Swiss passport and a large amount of escudos. He plans to reward well Maria's "friends." The latter calls from the Palacio lobby, and Maria answers. The "taxi service" to the waterfront awaits them. He hands Maria a large roll of escudos, a thank-you for the men who have disposed of Rudolph's body and are now not only making their escape possible but also covering their traces in ways that Fleming can only surmise. Maria leaves first, carrying what in effect will be her sole belongings until she reaches New York. She travels in a separate taxi, with Fleming following less than five minutes later after biding farewell to the reception desk staff that he has come to know well and like. They wish him safe travels back to Switzerland. Fleming looks around surreptitiously. It is very early, and most of the guests are still asleep or arising. None of the usual suspects are around, just a hotel security person who is chatting with one of the doormen. Fleming departs unobtrusively, with no mention of his destination in Lisbon. His driver heads to the Pan American Airways flying boat waterfront terminal. Once inside the terminal, he begins to appreciate the quick and efficient work performed by Maria's people to make this flight possible. The Boeing 314 Clipper, built in 1938 and introduced into service in 1939, was sitting at its moorings at the Cabo Ruivo Seaplane Base. Today it will carry Fleming and Maria, plus sixty-six other passengers, to New York, with a refueling stop in the Azores. Its four Wright Twin Cyclone fourteen-cylinder air-cooled radial piston engines will cruise their Clipper at 188 miles per hour. They will have a crew of eleven to take them across the Atlantic. Fleming does not know this until they are airborne, and in the United States aircraft over international waters, Maria tells him that two passengers were urgently displaced to allow them to travel. Fleming was relieved that there were no outward signs of PVDE presence at the terminal and the passport check was relatively perfunctory, Maria explaining that only the chosen few could afford to fly on the Pan Am Clipper, so in effect all passengers were treated as VIPs and no one was scrutinized.

The flight is long but not as tedious as it otherwise would have been but for Maria's company. They learned more about each other in the twenty-two hours between Lisbon and New York than they ever had time for earlier. They had a free and frank discussion about their lives in intricate detail, from their early childhood beginnings until the present. They warm to each other in a way that has no sexual connotations. By the time the East Coast of the United States appears and the flight attendants prepare the passengers for arrival, Fleming and Maria feel very much at home with each other.

The Pan Am Clipper descends from 6,000 feet to make its approach to landing on the Hudson River in New York City. They both squeeze each others hands. Fleming leans over and kisses Maria. As the giant flying boat touches down and taxies across to its mooring, they both breathe a sigh of relief.

The chief steward proudly announces, "Ladies and gentlemen, welcome to the United States."

On arrival, they are met on first disembarking by a person who appears to be a British consular staff member who provides them with new British passports. It becomes clear very quickly that secret handshakes have been made between London and Washington, DC.

The apparent consular official announces that he works in the "New York office." Fleming realizes that this is not the time to ask questions. They are escorted through a VIP area with no others present, other than Maria, Fleming, and the man from New York, to a special reserved area out of public sight where they clear US immigration. The US official asks no questions and, in a quiet and friendly voice, looks Fleming in the eye and repeats the fine words of the Pan Am flight attendant, "Welcome to the United States. Enjoy your stay." Fleming is much relieved to say, "We will, thank you very much." The official smiles and, in a broad Brooklyn accent, adds, "Have a nice day." They proceed to US Customs, which becomes a formality, and on departing the customs area without any kind of questions or inspection, they are met by two men, one clearly a driver. The other is a well-dressed and very sharp-looking man who says quite clearly, "Commander Fleming and Miss Santos, I presume?"

They both reply in unison, "Yes."

"Allow me to introduce myself, my name is William Stephenson, I'm Mr. Churchill's private emissary here in the United States, nothing to do with Lord Halifax and his people in the embassy in Washington. I work closely with the people you know. Admiral Godfrey awaits you in the Waldorf Astoria. I'm sure you're tired after the long flight. Let's go."

Fleming inhales visibly. Admiral Godfrey has, yet again, in Fleming's estimation, scored yet another first. Who really is William Stephenson, Prime Minister Churchill's trusted and clearly highly secretive man, under cover here in the United States? He rapidly deduces that all is with the full knowledge and approval of President Franklin Roosevelt and that all this is highly classified. Stephenson is a gentleman of the old school, charm itself, and underneath the exterior politeness, Fleming detects both nerves of steel and a sharp, discerning intellect. Stephenson appeals immediately to every iota of Fleming's being, a man after his own mission in life.

"You must be in need of a good meal, I'm sure a good drink," Stephenson comments.

"I believe a martini in your case, Commander Fleming, and then some rest and relaxation. Maybe the good commander's introduced you too, Maria, to his favorite beverage, as the Americans tend to say?"

"He has indeed, sir, quite incorrigible, but I'm glad to always enjoy Ian's finest drink."

Stephenson laughs and also picks up on the first-name usage and that Maria clearly likes Commander Fleming.

"You'll both be able to enjoy the rest of the day and then have a good night's sleep before tomorrow's important meeting. Both of you are required. It's the beginning of what Winston wants to be not just a special relationship but something beyond that, highly secret indeed," Stephenson says no more. He clams up, as if he's given them all that they need to know at this stage, their very first meeting with the man who, many years later, will be known to history as the man called Intrepid. Indeed, Intrepid is Stephenson's operational, highly classified codename.

Without saying a word, or making eye contact with each other, Fleming and Maria instantly realize that the DNI has significant events in store for them.

Both are wondering what the following day will bring as their car wends its way through the crowded New York streets to their home for the next few weeks, the Waldorf Astoria hotel on Park Avenue, one of the fashionable areas of Manhattan. Stephenson is quiet, recognizing that both his guests are quite exhausted and relieved to be safe and sound in New York. He casually points out various landmarks and gives them a pleasant and low-key tour. Fleming is pleased that he does not have to ask questions, because clearly that's not appropriate at this stage.

However, as they near the Waldorf Astoria, a matter of a few blocks from their destination, William Stephenson changes from New York tour guide to special emissary.

"I'm sure you're both wondering, speculating, 'Who has John Godfrey lined up for us?'"

Fleming politely responds, "I'm sure Maria feels the same way as me, sir, not ours to ask. Wait and be told, all will become clear."

Stephenson then makes a definitive statement.

"Admiral Godfrey, yourselves, and me are scheduled to meet tomorrow with President Roosevelt's handpicked man to head a new and highly secret special agency. He is totally undercover and only the president's closest and most trusted advisors are in the know. In fact, be aware that I had a direct hand in advising President Roosevelt to appoint this person. The president has full knowledge of, and fully approves, of our meeting and agenda. He and Mr. Churchill have agreed what we need to achieve. His name, and please, you're not to repeat this outside our immediate confines, is Mr. William Donovan, and he has a well-earned nickname, Wild Bill. He's the president's handpicked man to head up what is likely to be called, if my sources are accurate, the Office of Strategic Services, an American version of your 30 Assault Unit, Commander. It will be quite a large operation, but more of this after you've had food and rest."

Fleming and Maria say nothing, realizing that this was neither the time nor place to ask questions or discuss further.

Just as their car nears the front entrance of the Waldorf Astoria, Maria turns to Fleming.

She opens her handbag and says to Fleming, "Ian, I have a gift for you, a little memory for you of your time in Lisbon".

Stephenson politely pretends that he's neither listening nor looking. This is a personal moment.

Fleming is tired, looks at her, and says, "A good small bottle of port, I'm sure?"

Maria laughs.

William Stephenson glances away as she retrieves from the bottom of her fine leather handbag the Luger that belonged to the erstwhile Rudolph.

Maria hands the Luger to Fleming.

Fleming is amazed, smiles the broadest smile that he's ever made, and looks at her in stunned amazement.

"Ian, my dear, from Lisbon with love."

He instantly kisses her.

The head porter opens their car door, "Welcome to the Waldorf Astoria, sir, madam, we're here to make your stay comfortable and memorable."

CHAPTER 20

The Big Apple Hides Its Secrets
Mission Accomplished

NEW YORK IS totally unlike war-torn London. The Waldorf Astoria is humming as if the world is still a normal place. Fleming and Maria discuss over a late dinner, after a long sleep through the afternoon into the early evening, how could the American people be so oblivious to what is happening in Europe. They are cognizant of the need to keep their conversation low key and avoid mentioning Stephenson, Donovan, and whatever it is that the DNI has in store for them tomorrow. Fleming tells Maria that Godfrey has left a handwritten note for him, instructing them both to meet him for breakfast at 0800 in the morning in the main breakfast area. The admiral's plan is for a relaxing breakfast, followed by a meeting in his suite, and then departing for a meeting in central New York. That's all the note states, reports Fleming. It's clear that the DNI wants total discretion and no giveaway comments over breakfast.

Maria is refreshed. Fleming cannot help but notice that she seems to blossom in the new and nonstressful atmosphere of the Waldorf, away from the Lisbon strife and pressure. They enjoy a long and relaxed dinner, with New England oysters and the best of American beef from the Midwest and Idaho potatoes. They adjourn to the bar where they share the inevitable second martinis of the evening after their predinner aperitifs, "shaken, not stirred." As they gaze at each other, their minds are thinking the same thing, "To sleep together, or not?"

"Ian, I don't know where the admiral's suite is, I guess we can find out easily enough, but I'm pretty sure he's in another part, on another floor, from both of us. What do you think?" Maria pauses and then adds in a low, dulcet tone, "My love."

"Life's too short, we're lucky to be alive and well, and more than lucky to be here in this splendid hotel, away from all that bad stuff you and I know so well. Sweetheart, we've earned our time together. Let's finish these splendid drinks and adjourn to my place."

Maria smiles, learns over, and kisses Fleming.

Fleming tips the barman handsomely, commenting as they depart the bar, "They were the best martinis we've had in a very long time. Thank you."

"You're most welcome, sir, have a great evening."

The night is theirs. The moment is theirs, for in the morning, the director of British Naval Intelligence has a challenge for this hugely brave and dedicated couple.

Fleming and Santos are on parade before 0800 the next morning, dressed in smart business attire and waiting at a table that Godfrey has reserved in a quiet part of the hotel's breakfast area. They are enjoying their first coffee of the day when the admiral appears, looking as spry as ever.

They stand.

The admiral is his usual charming self. "Please sit, it's wonderful to see you both, Miss Santos—Maria, if I may—and, Ian, good to see that you're as fit looking as ever."

The conversation does not reflect the dire circumstances from which both Fleming and Maria have escaped. Godfrey is well aware, but this is all for later, not over breakfast in a public place.

They chat about New York and what to enjoy in the city. Fleming mentions Wall Street and how his city background in London would fit well with the American stock market. The conversation becomes almost businesslike, with the three of them reflecting on the current value of the pound against the dollar and US imports to Britain.

They adjourn.

Godfrey tells them both his suite number and to meet him there at nine. He comments that he has one call to make.

Maria and Fleming wait in the main foyer, sitting and relaxing in armchairs, observing life go by, and watching the body language of a vibrant American culture, so different from London, the Blitz, and the struggle to survive.

The time goes quickly, and soon they are standing outside the DNI's suite, expectant, refreshed, well-fed, and ready for whatever he will demand of them.

They both sit side by side on a sofa while Godfrey sits opposite them in a comfortable armchair.

The DNI pronounces.

"I want to congratulate you both on an outstanding job in Lisbon, and I'm naturally relieved that we're sitting here and that you're both alive and well. Well done. I'm very proud of you both and what you've accomplished."

Fleming and Maria both smile a discreet and modest "thank you" smile, recognizing that the DNI has more to say, and indeed he does.

"BSC, Ian and Maria. BSC. Never heard of it? Well, it will become ingrained in your minds from today onwards. It stands for British Security Coordination, and it's highly secret, based here in New York City, in fact not that far from where we're sitting. Listen carefully and please never repeat what I'm about to tell you to another human being."

Fleming and Maria are transfixed.

"It's run by the man you drove with from the seaplane terminal to the hotel, William Stephenson, handpicked by the prime minister for the job, with the total approval of President Roosevelt. He is, in my opinion, the single most important person in our war with Hitler and the Third Reich. I am not exaggerating, far more important than the likes of me, the First Sea Lord, or any of our other military leaders. It will become very clear why this is so over the next few days and particularly after the meeting that we will have later this morning."

Godfrey pauses.

"Stephenson supported Winston in the darkest hours of appeasement, feeding him valuable intelligence on Nazi Germany when Chamberlain, Halifax, and the other hangers-on were playing Hitler's tune at Munich. He's hugely successful, wealthy, and by the way, refuses to be paid for his services, the ultimate patriot. He also has an incredible World War I military record—MC and DFC, extraordinary flying record, an ace. He has personal and direct access to the president. Roosevelt listens to him. So the man who you met at the airport is our most valuable asset. His code name is Intrepid."

Fleming and Santos simply listen, amazed at what they are hearing.

"The cover operation for British Security Coordination is Passport Control Office, that's what it says on the main office door entrance. It's located in Rockefeller Center. I know the room number like we all know Room 39. It's room 3603. Remember that number. You'll not forget it. We're headed there after I've given you more background on what BSC is doing to help save the day for Britain and what the prime minister, the president, and I want you both to do in conjunction with William."

Fleming and Santos now become aware for the first time that they will play a role, that New York City is more than the Big Apple and that they have been inducted into Britain's most closely guarded secret.

"You both need to know a couple of highly sensitive aspects. The prime minister uses Intrepid to pass Ultra-intercepts from Bletchley Park to the president. Stephenson personally briefs the president on actual content. Second, you need to know that Stewart Menzies did not want Stephenson to have this privileged position. He opposed his appointment and lost. He's been told to shut up and not disclose any of this within SIS. Stewart and I are friends, and he gets it, that this is what Winston wants, and what he wants, he gets. By the way, I'm a total advocate and personal supporter of Stephenson. He's an extraordinary human being, the best of the best, and frankly, Menzies and the whole SIS crowd have no knowledge of what he does most of the time. Some of the time, yes, but not all of the time. We'll be going over things at our meeting. All will become transparently clear.

It becomes self-evident to Fleming and Santos that questions are not in order. The DNI has told them all that they need to know at this moment.

Godfrey informs them that Stephenson's personal driver will be waiting at the main entrance and that they should leave.

The DNI removes some papers from the wall safe and places them in his briefcase.

They take the elevator to the main lobby and, without fanfare, are greeted by Stephenson's Canadian driver. Stephenson has bought for BSC the best of American sedans, a large and luxurious Lincoln Continental. As the DNI indicated, Intrepid has paid for this car, his driver, and just about everything else that makes BSC operate around the clock from his personal finances. He is the ultimate patriot. The SIS has no clue what this man is doing to preserve and protect not just Britain but the free world's way of life and survival.

Room 3606 in Rockefeller Center lives up to Fleming's and Santos's expectations.

The DNI leads their entrance. They pass through an area that looks like and acts like any overseas British Consular Office handling day-to-day bureaucratic matters for British citizens or, as in this case, answering Americans questions about visiting war-torn Britain.

Is this just another day in the Passport Control Office?

Perhaps only for those Americans who have questions about where to go and not go in Britain in 1941.

After leaving the working office area, Godfrey heads directly through a security door, having entered a four-digit code, and they then find themselves in more palatial surroundings with the many comforts of an expensive Manhattan office suite. A very small staff of three people, who greet the visitors with clear Canadian accents, smile and indicate that their boss awaits them. At the rear is Stephenson's office, large, imposing, and with a view of downtown bustling New York City.

Stephenson is the master of graciousness, putting his guests at ease.

Coffee is served, and after short pleasantries, with Godfrey clearly deferring to Stephenson, the man called Intrepid holds forth in a melodic voice, without any sense of formality, pomposity, or rank consciousness. His very voice puts them at ease. Both Fleming and Maria instantly relate, as at their first meeting the day before, to Stephenson. He is not only their kind of man; he is very different, altruistic at one level and down to earth, strong-minded, and clearly determined and resolute at another.

Intrepid provides Fleming and Maria with some background on his upbringing near Winnipeg, Canada, back in 1897, how he moved on from very humble beginnings and a complex parenting situation, through war service in World War I, to making money in the 1920s and 1930s, through a series of inventions and successful business ventures. What captivates most of all is his description of how he has become Churchill's head of Security Coordination in the United States, and he details how he coordinates the exchange of secrets between Prime Minister Churchill and President Roosevelt. Fleming is mesmerized by Stephenson's modest description of what are unbelievable achievements, and internally he is mentally setting up Stephenson in an almost Godlike position, his personal hero, and also alter ego. Fleming will never forget the words that Stephenson utters, the past achievements and the present challenges. He becomes Fleming's newfound role model. Maria senses this, and although she too has warmed enormously to Stephenson in a short space of time after the previous day's drive from the seaplane terminal to the Waldorf, she admires all that he is doing for Britain and instinctively knows that her man, her lover, Commander Fleming, is seeing in Stephenson a hugely one-of-a-kind human being that he cannot possibly emulate. For the first time, Maria feels that she not only loves Fleming but adores him now for his humility and inner strength in front of a man who is changing for Prime Minister Winston Churchill in the most positive ways possible the very dynamics of the war against Hitler.

(Author's Note: Ian Fleming modeled James Bond on William Stephenson. He wrote, "James Bond is a highly romanticized version of a true spy. The real thing is … William Stephenson." William Stephenson died on January 31, 1989 (aged 92) on the Goldeneye Estate, in Tucker's Town, Bermuda.)

Stephenson quietly explains that the Prime Minister wants full cooperation between Stephenson's office and President Franklin Roosevelt's chosen man, William Donovan. He then says something that is music to Fleming's ears.

"What you've been doing, Commander, with 30 Assault Group is a role model for Wild Bill, the name we all privately call him. When you meet him shortly, he'll appear as an accomplished US attorney. Don't be fooled, I'm sure that you won't, but underneath that polished exterior is a man of iron, ready to take on the Nazis as much as you and your colleagues in Naval Intelligence. He's tough, very tough, and an American hero. Roosevelt thinks the world of him. Rightly so. Personally, I find him the very best American that I've been privileged to know and work with. He and I get along like a house on fire. He cannot wait to get at Hitler and his bully boys."

Stephenson pauses to see if there are any questions or reactions.

The three visitors are listening intensely.

He continues in a low-pitched voice.

"This is all top secret, need-to-know. Only the president's inner few know what we're all about. Now you know. You're members of the most closely guarded and secret club in the world."

Stephenson takes a breath, pauses, and continues. "The new outfit that Bill—that's what I call him by the way, you'll see how we get along in about fifteen minutes."

Stephenson looks at the clock on his large desk.

"He'll be here shortly."

Fleming and Maria both smile instantly. They are going to meet Donovan within minutes.

"The organization that he is going to set up will likely be called the Office of Strategic Services, OSS for short. It's going to need all your help. Admiral Godfrey is in the picture completely. What we both want, the DNI and me, is for you two to help him structure the nascent OSS. Give him ideas and pointers, and most of all, I would like you to host him over in Britain and show him your training center and how you do business. I hope that will work?"

Fleming is beyond pleased with these last words from Intrepid.

"Of course, sir, we'll do all and everything to work with Mr. Donovan. We'll make him not only welcome and show him everything that we have, perhaps I may say that we'll look forward to full operational coordination and cooperation when the time's ripe."

"Commander, perfect, thank you. This leads me to a highly sensitive point. We're planning on the most secret meeting of all time in just a few short months, probably August if things works out. This will be between Winston and Franklin, at sea, probably off Newfoundland, in Placentia Bay, is what the British and US Navy leadership have recommended. This will be totally secret. The public will never know. Winston will sail across the Atlantic in the utmost secrecy and with a significant escort to protect his ship, the battleship HMS *Prince of Wales*. Given the state of things in the Congress, President Roosevelt wants to ensure that there are no leaks. He is very worried about the rumor mill in Washington and parts of the press that are less than friendly to him jumping to the wrong conclusions, that he may be planning on entering the war without Congress being informed. None of this is true, of course, but perception is reality in Washington, DC, so he wants no one to know when he quietly slips out of Washington on USS *Augusta*, the designated US warship, to transport him northwards to meet Winston. This will be a strategic planning meeting, with a clear-cut agenda. The president knows that war is inevitable at both ends of the globe, in Europe and with the Japanese. He just has to be very cautious how he informs the American public that peace will not be theirs for much longer, given the threat from Japan. He and Winston, through this small office here in New York City, need to coordinate a way ahead and not be caught short and unprepared once the inevitable happens. I'm sure that you understand?"

The DNI looks at Fleming and Santos for their concurrence.

"We're with you, sir, to the end. Rest assured. We'll do everything to support you and BSC and Mr. Donovan."

"Excellent, thank you, Ian. Thank you, Maria. John, you've two very fine people working for you. Before Bill arrives, I've one other important piece of information for you. I'm the prime minister's means to convey Bletchley material to President Roosevelt. I brief the president personally on material that deals with Hitler's plans as well as current operations. John, your fine DNI, knows all this. The link with the US Office of Naval Intelligence, ONI for short, is crucial in my opinion. The PM and John are well aware. We're forging links with the navy people in ONI in Washington and also with what the Americans call Station Hypo in Hawaii. They're listening to the Japanese. One of the most closely guarded agenda items for the August rendezvous off Newfoundland is the exchange of intelligence. Only a very small number of the president's inner sanctum and top military and navy people are in on this. Winston sees this as crucial for Britain's survival. He wants to build a special relationship with Franklin Roosevelt. The fact that his mother was American helps a lot. Half American, half British."

Stephenson pauses and looks at each of them, slowly and individually, and then smiles.

"I hope that this is all very encouraging."

"Yes, indeed, sir, Maria and I will do whatever you and Admiral Godfrey require."

"Thank you. Now before Donovan arrives, any questions? He'll be arriving any minute. He's very punctual, always spot on time."

Godfrey takes charge of the response.

"No, William, thank you. You've been more than explicit."

"All right. Our guest should be here momentarily. One quick, final thing. John may have told you that Stuart Menzies was not exactly favorable to me being in this position, and BSC operating here in New York City. He actually voiced opposition with Winston. It's not because of this prior situation with SIS, but please be aware that we don't include SIS in almost everything that BSC does. It's based only on one simple and crucial criterion, called security. Menzies and his people don't need to know what we're doing here in BSC. The prime minister fully approves, in fact ordered that SIS are not involved and knowledgeable, with only his very closest people in London in the know about BSC and my role. Any kind of compromise—or worst case, the possibility of internal treachery in SIS—could be fatal for all that we're doing. I'm sure that you understand?"

"Yes, sir, absolutely," Fleming replies.

"No question, sir, our lips are sealed," responds Maria.

"Thank you," Stephenson says in a low-key voice.

As if by clockwork, Stephenson's right-hand man knocks on his door, enters, and announces, "Mr. Donovan is here to see you, sir."

"Thank you, please do show him in."

They all stand.

William Donovan, President Franklin Roosevelt's chosen man, enters the suite without fanfare and shakes hands with everyone.

William "Wild Bill" Donovan meets all Fleming's and Maria's expectations.

He is attired to perfection and has a sharp image and determined, unmistakable, glint in his eyes. He greets Fleming and Maria with a smile.

"My pleasure, Commander, Maria. Your wonderful DNI has told me a lot about you both. May I congratulate you on your operation in Lisbon. I want to learn as much as I can from you about how we can set up a similar organization to 30 Assault Group and how you do business. We have a lot to catch up on here in the United States. When the worst happens, which it will, we need to be ready and not get caught with our pants down, as we Americans tend to say."

Fleming and Maria smile.

"We're standing by, sir, to do all and everything that you and Mr. Stephenson require. We here to serve you and do whatever Mr. Churchill and President Roosevelt order."

Thank you, Ian, thank you, Maria."

Intrepid breaks the ice a little further as coffee is poured.

"Bill, maybe you could give a few words on your background. You saw the note that I gave you on Commander Fleming's and Maria's past. It will give them both a little context perhaps."

"Well, I don't want to go on an ego trip, William, but here's a little about myself."

Donovan's natural modesty about his past achievements becomes evident as he chats in a low-key way about his antecedents.

In a very unassuming manner, Donovan talks about his upbringing in Buffalo, New York. Born in January 1883, he started life as an attorney after graduating from Columbia Law School, and he then went through army service, fighting in World War I and became, in due course, a major general. What Donovan does not mention is that he is the only person to have received all four of the United States' highest awards: the Medal of Honor, the Distinguished Service Cross, the Distinguished Service Medal, and the National Security Medal.

Such is Donovan's wish to not appear arrogant, conceited, or any way immodest. He then comes to his main point after just a few minutes of personal history.

He explains that President Roosevelt has signed an order, making him coordinator of information. He stresses to his Canadian and three British hosts that the US has no spy agency similar to the British. He will, in reality, be it. He then makes one thing abundantly clear.

"I need all your help to set up what you already have in Britain. I've got a right-hand man, my most trusted friend and advisor to assist in all this and help me make things happen as quickly as possible. His name is Allen Dulles. You'll meet him shortly. Great guy. He has a brother, John Foster Dulles, hugely influential in foreign policy matters. With William's approval, I'd like to discuss, please, a way ahead."

"Of course, Bill, that's the idea. We're here to do all and everything to help you and make sure our leaders' wishes are fulfilled to the letter, particularly with the August meeting off Newfoundland not far away.

"Absolutely. Can we make plans than, please?"

"John, over to you, please," says Stephenson.

During the next hour and a half, before they adjourn for lunch, Fleming provides Donovan with a complete background on 30 Assault Group, their current operations, and how they are set up and operating in Portugal, and Lisbon in particular. He describes Operation Golden Eye in fine detail, the Nazi presence in Portugal, how the British circumvent Salazar's secret police operations. All the various operations are outlined in graphic terms by Fleming—the planned sabotage; collaboration with Portuguese nationals loyal to the British; who will be assassinated of the Abwehr, SS, SD, and Gestapo; who will be revealed to Salazar as those Portuguese on the Nazi payroll; the details of wrecking the port infrastructure in Lisbon and Porto, including all the underwater demolition plans; and the plans in place for the disruption of all wolfram and iron ore exports to Germany, particularly those exports going the overland route through Spain. At the end of this lengthy briefing, Fleming details his final twenty-four hours in Lisbon and how Maria saved his life and kept British covert operations secure and in tact as a result. He is explicit, in graphic detail, about the demise of the

Abwehr colonel. Donovan remains totally transfixed as Fleming goes into how 30 Assault Group entered Portugal and began operations. He hands over to Maria to explain her role in Portugal. She is brilliant in describing what she achieved undercover since war began in September 1939 and her past relations with SIS. Donovan has much to absorb.

The DNI breaks the intense discussion on current covert NID and 30 Assault Group operations with an aside about British naval history and prior operations in the Iberian peninsular. He tells Donovan that back during the Napoleonic Wars, the Royal Navy had to take instant action after France and Spain invaded Portugal, Britain's oldest ally, in May 1801, leading to the Treaty of Badajoz that required Portugal to close all its ports to Britain. Godfrey says with a certain amount of pride that the Royal Navy occupied the Portuguese island of Madeira to prevent the French from interrupting Britain's trade routes, not dissimilar, he notes, to the current threat from the Germans, with the possibility of either a German occupation of Portugal or Salazar capitulating to Hitler's demands to keep the British out of Lisbon and providing tungsten to Britain. He goes on to tell Donovan that later, in October 1807, the French returned again and succeeded in occupying Lisbon in November 1807 and demanded that the Portuguese quarantine all British trade, with the goal of undermining the British economy and therefore its war effort against Napoleon's regime. With some fanfare, Admiral Godfrey delights in describing how the British Navy launched Sir Arthur Wellesley's army onto the Iberian Peninsular that led to France's defeat in what became known as the Peninsular War. He goes on to comment that Wellesley was later the victor at Waterloo and became the Duke of Wellington. Godfrey ends his fascinating piece of naval history with the comment that all this is highly relevant for the current situation in Portugal.

Donovan says how much he loves the admiral's naval history lesson. He then says something that surprises even William Stephenson.

"We can't do much to help right now, Admiral, Ian, Maria, but we've made a small start, in Portugal, very small compared with your great achievements."

What are they about to hear?

Even Stephenson's ears prick up. He's heard none of this before.

"Ian, you never did get to meet my man, James Bell, again, after yours and Maria's encounter with that evil son-of-a-bitch Abwehr colonel. He's my man in Madrid. Wall Street guy. Told me all about your skill at the tables, outwitting the very best. He was planning on meeting with you the following day, I gather, but things changed, to put it mildly! It's my very modest way of trying to let Salazar know where America stands through one thing, the American dollar. By buying up Portuguese tungsten and iron ore and shipping to Britain in US and other flags of convenience, we can help the war effort for Britain and keep the flow to Germany down. A small contribution perhaps, but every little bit counts. James is our man to do all this. Smart as a whip."

Fleming is exuberant, as is the DNI.

"Herr Freitag, you had a friend in James Bell. He thinks you're not just the best, but the best of the best."

They are collectively amazed.

"James told me that he personally would have liked to have shot that Nazi bastard, Rudolph, but I guess Maria beat him to it. Oh, and by the way, if you and the admiral ever need quick extraction for any of your people out of Portugal, just let William know. We'll have them on the Clipper to New York City ASAP. Pan Am and me are on the same page, if you know what I mean, when it comes to who gets seats on the Clipper."

Fleming and Maria beamed.

They realized there and then one simple, inexorable fact: William Donovan is more than just special. He will make a huge difference in the war against Hitler once the United States is on board.

"Sir, 30 Assault Group is at your disposal. We await your visit with great anticipation."

Fleming says no more, not wishing to get ahead of himself with the DNI sitting there, who now very clearly wishes to come back into the discussion.

Admiral Godfrey suggests a time table for Donavan's visit to London, a meeting with Winston Churchill, and a visit to both Room 39 and 30 Assault Group's training center. Donovan concurs fully, and

Godfrey then raises the August Churchill-Roosevelt secret meeting off Newfoundland. The group shares their thoughts on the intelligence sharing item on the two leaders' agenda. They come up with agreed practices and procedures for intelligence exchange, critical security protocols, who should and shouldn't know what, with total emphasis on navy-to-navy intelligence sharing, NID to ONI, and how Station Hypo in Hawaii and NID's operations in Asia can further cooperate.

The five of them have achieved an enormous amount in a short space of time.

Donovan is clearly enervated, energized by the discussion and his first meeting with Ian Flaming and Maria Santos.

"Time for lunch, Maria, gentlemen," Stephenson announces, with his guests clearly ready for a change of subject and tempo.

"Let's all go and enjoy some fine food at Delmonico's, one of my favorite restaurant's based on French and, especially for Ian's past, Swiss cuisine!"

The group laughs.

"I have two cars awaiting us. Perhaps Ian and Maria can enjoy each other's company while the older members share a ride? I hope that works."

"Perfect," says Admiral Godfrey.

William Donovan interjects one final comment before they head out of Stephenson's suite. He turns to Ian Fleming and says in a direct and sincere way a comment that Fleming will not forget.

"Before we all leave, may I just say one short thing, please?"

He looks at Ian Fleming. "Commander Fleming, you may not realize this, but I am extremely grateful to you, as will be my president. You have just given me the blueprint for the Office of Strategic Services. Thank you, on behalf of the United States."

Outside on the sidewalk in front of Rockefeller Center, the three senior members—Stephenson, Donovan, and Godfrey—climb into Intrepid's personal limousine. Fleming holds the door open of the second car for Maria. They are both relieved to be together, alone, after the most exhilarating morning.

The car pulls away.

Maria looks at Fleming, touches him lightly, and says in a low, calming voice, "Ian, today's May 28. I looked in your passport. It's your birthday. Thirty-three, and you don't look a day older. Happy Birthday, Ian, my love."

"Ever the most wonderful Maria. I adore you."

"Let's celebrate tonight. A special treat from me, your lady in Lisbon, forever Ian's."

(Author's Note: The Office of Strategic Services, OSS, was the forerunner to the Central Intelligence Agency, CIA, established in 1947.)

The End

EPILOGUE

THE CAST OF characters are remarkable for many varied reasons. Ian Fleming touched all their lives, either directly or indirectly. The Nazi leadership that he helped to undermine, and contributed to their downfall, never knew him. In our story, the complex relationships of those that he did touch reveal the very nature of Ian Fleming's extraordinary World War II career and the inspiration for his later books. It is fitting that the epilogue provides readers with the details about the lives and careers of the main characters, together with other aspects that will complete the picture of events that transpired after the story's finale in New York City. They are not in non-alphabetical order.

Commander Edward Travis, Royal Navy

Commander Edward Travis, later Sir Edward Travis, KCMG, CBE, became the head of Bletchley Park in February 1942, and later, he would become the director of GCHQ (Government Communications Headquarters, the British electronic spy agency).

Vice Admiral John Henry Godfrey, CB

Vice Admiral John Godfrey, July 10, 1888–August 29, 1970, was initially a Royal Navy navigation specialist, later commanding His Majesty's ships *Kent*, *Suffolk*, and *Repulse*.

Vice Admiral John Godfrey became director of Naval Intelligence (DNI) 1939–1942 and then went to India to be the head of the Indian Navy, 1943–1946, promoted to admiral on the Royal

Navy retired list in 1945.He was succeeded as DNI by Rear Admiral Edmund Rushbrooke from 1942–1946. The author was the first person to be given access to Admiral Godfrey's more private papers by his widow as a result of a request from Sir Harry Hinsley and Professor Bryan Ranft. These papers were different from the memoirs that he had donated to Churchill College, Cambridge, 1966–1967. Ian Fleming based James Bond's boss, M, on John Godfrey. As well as being made a companion of the Order of the Bath in 1939, he was also awarded the Order of the Nile of Egypt and made a Chevalier of the French Legion D'Honneur.

Captain William Stephenson, Royal Navy

Captain William Stephenson, the Deputy DNI, was succeeded in February 1941 by Captain Charles Campbell, who was succeeded in April 1942 by Captain Charles Nichols.

Baron Patrick Maynard Stuart Blackett, OM, CH, FRS

Lord Blackett (November 18, 1897–July 13, 1974) was the father of operations research in the United Kingdom and led major contributions during World War II that contributed significantly to the Allied victory. He was trained initially as a naval officer, initially for two years at the Royal Naval College Osborne, on the Isle of Wight, before moving on to Britannia Royal Naval College, Dartmouth. In 1914, as a midshipman, he was appointed to sea-going duties and saw considerable action, including the Battle of Jutland on board HMS *Barham*. While on board *Barham*, Blackett was the coinventor of a gunnery device that the admiralty patented. After the war ended in 1918, the admiralty sent Blackett to Magdalene College,

Cambridge. He left the Royal Navy and began studying mathematics and physics, graduating from Magdalene College in 1921. In 1923, he became a fellow of King's College, Cambridge, a position he held until 1933. His academic advisor was Ernest Rutherford, and Blackett became immersed in research at the Cavendish laboratory. Before World War II, he worked at Birkbeck College, University of London, and from 1937, he was at Manchester University as the Langworthy professor. In 1953, he became head of the Physics Department at Imperial College, University of London, and retired in July 1963. In 1940, he was awarded the Royal Medal of the Royal Society, having been elected a fellow of the Royal Society (FRS) in 1933; in 1948, the Nobel Prize in Physics; and the Copley Medal in 1956. During World War II, Blackett was director of operational research at the Admiralty, working with E. J. Williams on ways to best ensure the survival of convoys. Blackett argued forcefully, based on sound scientific reasoning, for greater resources to be employed in countering the U-boats versus the heavy British investment in resources and manpower for the nighttime area bomber offensive of the Royal Air Force's Bomber Command. He did not win the arguments that ensued. However, after World War II, the Allied Strategic Bombing Survey proved Lord Blackett correct. His contribution to the Battle of the Atlantic was outstanding. He remains a giant in the field of military and specifically naval operations research.

The Azores

On August 18, 1943, the Azores became officially used by the British, using the original 1373 Treaty between Portugal and Britain as the basis for the agreement.

Admiral Wilhelm Canaris

Admiral Canaris continued to meet British agents in Spain who entered Spain from Gibraltar. He passed on vital intelligence to the British. He survived until 1944 as head of the Abwehr until Heinrich Himmler grew suspicious of him as a possible double agent. Hitler dismissed him in February 1944 and abolished the Abwehr. Himmler accused Canaris of treason, and he was imprisoned without trial. On April 9, 1945, Canaris, at the age of fifty-eight, was summarily executed in Flossenburg concentration camp, just days before the German surrender. While in prison, Canaris made claims about war crimes committed by his fellow countrymen, including General Keitel, who was subsequently tried and found guilty by the International Military Tribunal at Nuremburg, and executed. In the 1976 film, *The Eagle Has Landed*, Admiral Canaris is played by the British actor Anthony Quayle.

Admiral Canaris was likely the most unsung hero of World War II, never fully recognized for how he helped the British and Allied cause.

Operation Torch, Salazar, and Nazi Gold Payments

Operation Torch took place November 8–16, 1942, and Portugal was no longer vulnerable to Nazi invasion and the continuing influence of the German intelligence services. However, Salazar needed German gold from wolfram and ion ore purchases to keep his economy alive, and he traded access to the Azores, enabling him to keep the Nazis' gold payments. Salazar continued to publicly support Franco in Spain, with weapons imported through Lisbon for Spain. Portugal also continued to export wolfram to the UK and the US. The British and the Americans continued to turn a blind eye to Salazar's trade with the Third Reich until it imploded.

Grand Admiral (Gross Admiral) Karl Donitz

Admiral Karl Donitz (1891–1980) briefly succeeded Hitler as the president of the Third Reich (German head of state), from April 30, 1945, to May 23, 1945. He succeeded Admiral Erich Raeder as supreme commander of the German Navy, the Kriegsmarine, on January 30, 1943, until May 1, 1945. He died in Aumuhle, Schleswig-Holstein, West Germany on December 24, 1980 (aged 89). As head of the Kriegsmarine's submarine service, Donitz was a constant target for British Naval Intelligence. Donitz's plans, policies, and operations were the subject of round-the-clock intelligence collection and analysis by Room 39 and Bletchley Park. On May 7, 1945, Donitz ordered General Alfred Jodl, chief of the operations staff of the Oberkommando der Wehrmacht, (OKW), the high command of the Nazi armed forces, the Wehrmacht, to sign the German Instruments of Surrender in Rheims, France. Donitz remained head of the Flensburg government as it became known until it was dissolved by the Allied Powers on May 23, 1945. Donitz, a dedicated Nazi and anti-Semite, was indicted as a major war criminal at the Nuremberg War Crimes Trials. He was found not guilty of committing crimes against humanity. He was found guilty of committing crimes against peace and war crimes against the laws of war. He was sentenced to ten years in Spandau prison in Berlin. He served the full sentence. After his release on October 1, 1956, Donitz remained unrepentant about his role in the Nazi party and World War II.

Spandau Prison, Berlin

Spandau prison was located in the borough of Spandau in West Berlin. It was demolished in August 1987 after the death of its last Nazi prisoner, Rudolf Hess, who died from a suspected suicide at aged ninety-three, to prevent Spandau from becoming a neo-Nazi shrine. It later became a shopping center for British forces located in West Berlin. Both Nazi grand admirals Raeder and Donitz were incarcerated in Spandau. The other Nazi prisoners in Spandau called them the admiralty. Raeder, in failing health and seemingly close to death, was released in 1955. He died in 1960. They had both been key targets for Room 39.

Harold "Kim" Philby

 Harold "Kim" Philby, Ian Fleming's point of contact in MI6 and SOE, was one of the Cambridge Five spy ring, with Guy Burgess, Anthony Blunt, Donald MacLean, and John Cairncross. Educated at Westminster School and Trinity College, Cambridge, he was recruited by the Soviet KGB in 1934 and joined MI6 in 1940. By 1949, he was a first secretary in the British embassy in Washington, liaising with US intelligence. He tipped off Burgess and MacLean that they were under suspicion, and they fled to Moscow in May 1951. Philby was suspected, and he resigned from MI6 in July 1951, and after an inquiry, he was exonerated of wrongdoing in 1955. However, the evidence mounted, and before he could be arrested, he fled to Moscow in January 1963, and he was then exposed as a Soviet spy. He died in Moscow on May 11, 1988, aged seventy-six.

Book Review: 'Room 39 and the Lisbon Connection'

ANITA L. SHERMAN

It's June 1940. The Battle of Dunkirk is over with a massive military evacuation from Britain's beachhead. Germany has occupied France. What of Britain's longtime ally Portugal and its key port in Lisbon? Prime Minister Winston Churchill along with British intelligence sees the security of Portugal as key in his continuing efforts to unseat Hitler and his instruments of Nazi control.

Many of Churchill's behind-closed-doors strategic planning sessions take place in Room 39 located in the British Admiralty near Whitehall. While "Room 39 and the Lisbon Connection" is a fictional account; here readers will meet key historical figures such as Britain's Vice Adm. Sir Norman "Ned" Denning, Sir John Cecil Masterman, and Vice Adm. John Henry Godfrey along with the author's main hero, Lt. Cmdr. Ian Fleming of the Royal Naval Volunteer Reserve.

Author Anthony Wells is uniquely positioned to tell the story of Fleming's role in British intelligence. Wells is the only living person to have worked for British intelligence as a British citizen and U.S. intelligence as a U.S. citizen. He also served in uniform at sea and ashore with both the Royal Navy and the U.S. Navy. Wells is a 55-year veteran of the Five Eyes intelligence community. The Five Eyes (FVEY) is an intelligence alliance comprising Australia, Canada, New Zealand, the United Kingdom, and the United States.

In addition to his extensive publications of reports and articles, Wells's most no-

table works of nonfiction include "A Tale of Two Navies: Geopolitics, Technology, and Strategy in the United States and the Royal Navy, 1960–2015" (2017) and "Between Five Eyes" (2020).

Sir Harry Hinsley, a mentor to author Anthony Wells, was a key member of the cryptanalyst team at Bletchley Park during World War II, noted for his code-breaking expertise, and in the late '60s introduced Wells to the Enigma data. The German Enigma machine enabled secret Nazi communications. Efforts to break that encoding system ultimately helped make D-Day possible. The Allies could learn of the location of U-boats and either sink them or reroute around them.

Wells's work of fiction takes the readers inside Room 39 and beyond as Churchill and his key strategists engage in conversations, revealing their characters as well as their intent to undermine the Nazi regime.

Who can be trusted? Traitors and treachery abound as the plot unfolds, taking our hero Fleming to Lisbon at that time, a place filled with British and German spies, many frequenting the best hotels and casinos.

Fleming touched many lives both directly and indirectly. His stellar naval career would serve to create one of our leading spy heroes—James Bond. Bond's boss, M, is based on the life of Vice Adm. John Godfrey, who served as director of British Naval Intelligence from 1939 to 1942.

Fleming hails from a wealthy family. He's educated at Eton and attends the

'Room 39 and the Lisbon Connection'

Author
Anthony Wells

Publisher
Xlibris, 2021

Pages
246

Author Anthony Wells is the only living person to have worked for British intelligence as a British citizen and U.S. intelligence as a U.S. citizen.

...or cohorts in Lisbon to counter a Nazi invasion.

Fleming was a spy. He seemed to have discovered his niche working for British intelligence. He was good at what he did.

So much so that Fleming visits Washington, D.C., during World War II to help with the framework of the budding U.S. intelligence agency, the Office of Strategic Services (precursor to the Central Intelligence Agency). There he meets with the head of the OSS, William "Wild Bill" Donovan, who got along very well with Churchill.

..., "Casino Royale," in 1953. It would be followed by 11 more novels plus two collections of short stories.

Fleming's home, which he had built in Jamaica, was simple, with plenty of open windows to let the breezes blow through. Overlooking a private beach on Oracabessa Bay, he named it after his covert operation in Lisbon, Goldeneye.

While not talked about in the book, a fun fact about Fleming and his alter-ego James Bond is the producer's choice of actor Sean Connery to play the part of Bond in the first film produced on the Bond series, "Dr. No." Set in Jamaica, this film launched the James Bond saga with Agent 007 becoming a legend.

Fleming wasn't keen on this little-known Scottish actor, who he felt was too much of a "tradesman." His visualization of James Bond was a more refined persona like actor David Niven.

A heavy drinker and smoker, Fleming died of a heart attack at age 56 in 1964, only a year after the release of "Dr. No" in 1963. Sadly, he wouldn't see the meteoric success of the films to follow and the literary of Bond portrayals over the decades.

Perhaps for most readers, Fleming is primarily known as the creator of James Bond, the fictionalized British Secret Service spy who has dazzling adventures, seemingly endless wealth, scores of beautiful women, amazing gadgets, and a talent for getting the bad guy.

Wells's novel lets us know that Bond is not so unlike his creator.

A cloak-and-dagger man who relishes adventure and has a way with the women, Fleming is very much an idea man and a fixer. While debonair and astute, Fleming is also very resourceful and definitely a value-added component of British intelligence during World War II.

"Room 39 and the Lisbon Connection" isn't just about Fleming, though it certainly gives readers a unique glimpse into the man that would set the spy standard for decades with his creation of James Bond, and Fleming's part in the novel is pivotal. His exploits are set against the broader background of World War II and the espionage scene in Lisbon.

Years after the war, Fleming would find

Anita L. Sherman is an award-winning journalist who has more than 20 years of experience as a writer and editor for local papers and regional publications in Virginia. She now works as a freelance writer and is working on her first novel. She is the mother of three grown children and grandmother to four, and she resides in Warrenton, Va. Anita can be reached at anitajusturite@gmail.com

Alan Turing

By contrast, Alan Turing, OBE, FRS, at Bletchley Park, was the great unsung hero and loyal patriot of World War II. After designing the Turing Machine, he was recognized after the war as the father of computer science. His work at Bletchley Park is estimated as having significantly shortened the war and saved millions of lives. He was accused of homosexual practices and was prosecuted in 1952. He died from the effects of cyanide poisoning on June 7, 1954, and to this day, the true reason for his death is unknown, as he had been subjected to brutal so-called therapy treatment. In 2013, Queen Elizabeth granted Turing a posthumous pardon, and in July 2019, the Bank of England announced that Turing would be depicted on the fifty-pound bank note. He is honored throughout the academic and scientific world in a wide variety of memorials, facilities, and awards. He is a legend and will be forever regarded as the mastermind behind Enigma.

Gordon Welchman

Gordon Welchman is probably the unsung hero of Bletchley Park, as the creator and master of the science and art of traffic analysis, a hugely innovative mathematical tool that permitted the British to figure out German intentions and operations before the full exploitation of Enigma, and therefore before the content of intercepted German messages could be decrypted.Welchman was born in June 1906 in Bristol, England, and after World War II, he went to the United States to design military communications systems. He died in Newburyport, Massachusetts, in October 1985, aged seventy-nine. Welchman studied mathematics at Trinity College, Cambridge, 1925–1928, and later became a fellow and dean at Sidney Sussex College, Cambridge. Together with Alan Turing, Hugh Alexander, and Stuart Milner-Barry at Bletchley Park, they became known as the Wicked Uncles. Welchman helped significantly in breaking the German Enigma code and was head of Hut 6 responsible for breaking German Army and Air Force Enigma ciphers. He left Hut 6 in 1943 and became assistant director for mechanization. He worked closely in cryptographic liaison with the United States. He helped in the development of machines for breaking into the later more advanced German ciphers such as the Geheimschreiber. In 1944, Welchman was awarded the Order of the British Empire in the King's Birthday Honors List, stating that it was for service in a Department of the Foreign Office. In 1982 his book *The Hut Six Story* was published in the US and Britain. The US National Security Agency disapproved, and his clearances were removed, a very sad ending to an extraordinary valuable career. On September 26, 2016, the director of GCHQ, Robert Hannigan, speaking at the unveiling of a plaque in his honor in Fishponds, Bristol, acknowledged the harsh treatment of Welchman by the US government and paid tribute to his immense contribution as a giant of his era.

Sir Harry Hinsley

Sir Harry (F. H.) Hinsley was a key member of the Hut 4 cryptanalyst team at Bletchley Park. Born in November 1918, he died in Cambridge, England, in February 1998, aged seventy-nine. In 1937, he won a scholarship to St. John's College, Cambridge, from Queen Mary's Grammar School in Walsall. He had a distinguished undergraduate academic career, and in October 1939, Commander Alastair Denniston, Royal Navy, the director of the Government Code and Cipher School, recruited him to join Hut 4, the naval section, at Bletchley Park. He made an outstanding contribution to highly sensitive intelligence operations, particularly against the Kriegsmarine and Donitz's U-boat force. In late 1943, he visited the Office of Naval Intelligence in Washington that led to an important exchange agreement in January 1944, a precursor to the growth of the Five Eyes intelligence community. In April 1946, he married Hilary Brett-Smith, who was a graduate of Somerville College, Oxford, and had worked in Hut 8 at Bletchley during the war. After the war, Harry Hinsley was elected a fellow of St. John's College, Cambridge, subsequently becoming professor of the history of international relations in 1969; master of St. John's College, 1979–1989; and vice chancellor of Cambridge University, 1981–1983. His major historical work is regarded as *Power and the Pursuit of Peace*, published in 1962. The British government invited him to lead the team that published the official history of British intelligence in World War II. Hinsley stated that Enigma speeded the Allied victory, and therefore shorted the war. The volumes were published as follows: Volume 1 (1979); Volume 2 (1981); Volume 3, Part 1 (1984); Volume 3, Part 2 (1988); and Volume 4 (1990). An abridged version, or composite volume, was published by both Her Majesty's printing office and Cambridge University Press in 1993. These volumes constitute to this day the most thorough record of intelligence in World War II. An annual Hinsley Memorial Lecture at St. John's College, Cambridge, on international relations related subjects is given in his honor. He was knighted for his outstanding services. Harry Hinsley was the author's mentor and, in the late 1960s, introduced him to the Enigma data, several years before Hinsley's first volume was published in 1979, changing completely interpretations of the conduct and outcome of World War II. Hinsley refers to the author's work in volume 1 of British intelligence in the Second World War.

Sir John Masterman

Sir John Cecil Masterman (January 12, 1891–June 6, 1977) joined the Royal Navy at Osborne Naval College and moved on its opening to Britannia Royal Naval College, Dartmouth. He later graduated from Worcester College, Oxford, with a degree in modern history. He lectured at the University of Freiburg im Breisgau just before World War I broke out and was interned in Ruhleben Internment Camp for the duration of World War I. He had a distinguished tennis career at Wimbledon in the 1920s. He became a tutor in modern history at Christ Church, Oxford, after World War I. After World War II, Masterman returned to academic life at Oxford, becoming provost of Worcester College 1946–1961 and the vice chancellor of Oxford University 1957–1958. He was knighted for his services to education. During World War II, he was chairman of the Twenty Committee that ran the Double Cross System, controlling German double agents from Britain and contributing significantly to deceiving the Nazis.

Vice Admiral Sir Norman "Ned" Denning

Vice Admiral Sir Norman "Ned" Denning (November 19, 1904–December 27, 1979), KBE, CB, served in the Royal Navy 1921–1967. He was in Room 39 in World War II and is regarded as a pioneering figure in British Naval Intelligence. He worked closely with the DNI throughout World War II and specifically with Ian Fleming. After the war, he became director of naval planning; director at the Royal

Naval College, Greenwich, 1956–1958; and was the last director of Naval Intelligence from 1960–1964. From 1964 to 1965, he was the first deputy chief of the Defense Staff in the newly constituted Ministry of Defense and Central Defense Staff. When he retired from the Royal Navy, he became head of the Defense and Security Media Advisory Committee, or D Notices Committee. Your author met Admiral Denning in the late 1960s, and he was a mentor for several years until his sad passing in 1979 after being bitten by a dog on the hand and dying subsequently from a heart attack after receiving a tetanus injection. One of his four brothers was Lord Justice Alfred Thompson "Tom" Denning (January 23, 1899–March 5, 1999, aged 100), the famous Master of the Rolls, 1962–1982.

Gold Received by Salazar's government from the Nazis

At the end of World War II, British intelligence calculated how much gold Salazar's regime had received from the Nazis. This was based on intelligence from both Switzerland and Portugal. They estimated that 123.8 tons of gold were received by Portugal for wolfram and other commodities during World War II. The issue of residual gold deposits became a postwar problem for Salazar. However, the Allies treated Portugal generously, and on June 24, 1953, after much negotiation, Portugal was allowed to return only four tons of gold as a result of an agreement negotiated by the US State Department on behalf of the Allied Powers in Europe. Portugal had indeed made a massive profit.

Antonio de Oliveira Salazar

Antonio Salazar (April 28, 1889–July 27, 1970, died aged 81) was prime minister of Portugal from 1932 to 1968. He was the founder of the Estado Novo (New State), the corporatist authoritarian government that ruled Portugal until 1974. He was succeeded by Marcelo Caetano. Salazar was a trained economist. He studied law at the University of Coimbra, graduating in 1914 with distinction and specializing in finance and economic policy. Salazar had a distinguished academic career in his early years, receiving a doctorate. He became an assistant professor of economic policy in the Coimbra Law School, becoming in 1917 the regent of economic policy and finance. He became well-known because of his clear intellectual ability. He was conservative and nationalist in his politics and was a dedicated opponent of democracy, communism, socialism, and any form of anarchic or liberal regimes. Salazar distanced himself from both fascism and Nazism. He supported Catholicism on the grounds that it performed valuable social responsibilities but should not be politically active. He used censorship and a secret police force to quell opposition, especially communist influence. He supported Franco during the Spanish Civil War and kept Portugal neutral during World War II, providing both sides with war materials. Salazar took Portugal, as one of the twelve founding nations, into the North Atlantic Treaty Organization (NATO) in 1949, joined the European Payments Union in 1950, and was a founding member of the European Free Trade Association (EFTA) in 1960. In 1961, he helped found the Organization for Economic Cooperation and Development. In 1962, he took Portugal into the General Agreement on Tariffs and Trade. He led several colonial wars. In 1974, the Estado Novo collapsed with the Carnation Revolution in Portugal. His dictatorship lasted forty-eight years.

During the 1974 political coup that ended the legacy left by Salazar, the Carnation Revolution released political prisoners, legalized a free press, abolished the Secret Police, and legalized the Socialist and Communist parties. The Azores became strategically significant during the Cold War, mirroring World War II, providing naval facilities and air bases for NATO maritime forces. The various islands, 400 miles apart at their widest, provided a critical location from which to mount operations against the Soviet and Warsaw Pact navies. The largest island, Sao Miguel, and capital, Ponta Delgada, play today a continuing key role in NATO naval operations.

The author J. K. Rowling spent time in Portugal, living in Oporto, and became immersed in Portuguese life and history. Her character Salazar Slytherin, in the Harry Potter series, is derived from the Salazar past. In her books, Slytherin builds the Chamber of Secrets.

Paul Fidrmuc

Paul Fidrmuc was born in Krnov in Czechia on June 28, 1898. He died from cancer in Barcelona, Spain, on October 20, 1958. He lived a double life, feeding the Abwehr totally made-up so-called intelligence in return for large sums of Reichmarks. He lived an extraordinarily good life in Lisbon during World War II, spending his ill-gotten gains from the Nazis on an extravagant lifestyle watched over by a British SIS agent, who was his seductress and mistress. He fed total fiction to Berlin, except that he did inform the Abwehr of one genuinely critical piece of intelligence, which in fact they ignored because of the effectiveness of Allied deception operations. He alerted Berlin to Operation Overlord, the D-Day Allied invasion of the Normandy beaches. Little, if anything, is known about how he knew this, unless it was an educated guess, which it most likely was, since the Allies themselves struggled hard to ensure that the Germans believed that the Pas de Calais area was the invasion area, not Normandy. The British novelist Graham Greene modeled his lead character, James Wormold, a vacuum cleaner retailer in Havana, Cuba, on Fidrmuc in his October 1958 novel *Our Man in*

Havana (published by Heinemann, London), in which his character, an SIS/MI6 agent in Cuba, feeds London with total fiction in return for payment. The novel was made into the 1959 film of the same name, staring Alec Guinness and Burl Ives, and produced by Carol Reed.

After World War II, Fidrmuc worked for Der Spiegel and other newspapers. Greene had worked for SOE during World War II and knew about Fidrmuc and his life of ill repute feeding off Nazi Reichsmarks in return for false intelligence.

William Joseph "Wild Bill" Donovan

William Donovan was the head of the United States' Office of Strategic Services (OSS) during World War II. OSS was the precursor to the Central Intelligence Agency (CIA). He is regarded as the founding father of the CIA. A statue of him stands in the lobby of the CIA headquarters building in Langley, Virginia. Donovan (January 1, 1883–February 8, 1959, died aged 76) was a soldier, lawyer, and diplomat in addition to his best known role as head of OSS from June 13, 1942, to October 1, 1945. Earlier he was President Franklin Roosevelt's coordinator of information from July 11, 1941, to June 13, 1942. Prior to President Roosevelt selecting him for these special assignments, Donovan had a distinguished career as a lawyer and soldier, reaching the rank of major general. He was a highly decorated war hero in World War I and is the only person to receive all four of the United States' highest awards: The Congressional Medal of Honor, the Distinguished Service Cross, the Distinguished Service Medal, and the National Security Medal. He also received the Silver Star and Purple Heart. Donovan got along famously with Winston Churchill. Churchill gave Donovan access to British intelligence classified information. On D-Day, Donovan was on one of the ships that took part in the Normandy landing. He and his commander of covert operations in Europe, Colonel David Bruce, had a very narrow escape from being captured or killed. On the war's conclusion, Donovan was a prime player in the instigation and conduct of the Nuremberg War Crimes trials. Despite many efforts by Donovan's supporters, President Harry Truman signed an executive order on September 20, 1945, abolishing the OSS. However, Donovan was successful in influencing what became the National Security Act of 1947. In the newly created CIA, several of Donavan's OSS protégés became leading lights at the new CIA, including Allen Dulles, William Casey, William Colby, and James Jesus Angleton. In August 1953, Donovan became the US ambassador to Thailand, resigning from that position on August 21, 1954. The remainder of his career was spent in law practice. He died from the complications of vascular dementia at Walter Reed Army Medical Center in Washington, DC, and is buried in Arlington National Cemetery.

Sir William Samuel Stephenson, Knight Bachelor, CC, MC, DFC

William Stephenson (January 23, 1897–January 31, 1989), whose World War II codename was Intrepid, was a Canadian soldier, airman, businessman, inventor, and spymaster. He was Prime Minister Winston Churchill's handpicked security coordinator for the entire western hemisphere during World War II. He was born in Winnipeg, Manitoba, and died aged ninety-two on the Goldeneye Estate in Tucker's Town, Bermuda. He was Churchill's key person for delivering scientific and intelligence secrets directly from the prime minister to President Franklin Roosevelt. He helped Roosevelt and his closest advisors in changing American public opinion from an isolationist position to a more aggressive stance regarding the Nazi threat. Stephenson was adopted, and his name was changed from Stanger (his original parents were a mother from Iceland and a father from the Orkney Islands, who could not care for him) to his foster parents' name, Stephenson. He had a most distinguished World War I military career, winning the Military Cross and the Distinguished Flying Cross. After World War I Stephenson had an outstanding business career and married, in 1924, the American tobacco heiress Mary French Simmons. He built a large array of international contacts such that by as early as April 1936, he was voluntarily providing Winston Churchill with confidential information on Hitler and the Third Reich and the latter's military buildup. Churchill used Stephenson's information to warn the British people of the dangers of appeasement. Against the objections of SIS (MI6) head Stewart Menzies, Churchill sent Stephenson to the United States on June 21, 1940, to secretly and covertly run British Security Coordination (BSC) based in New York City, over a year before the United States' entry into the war after the attack on Pearl Harbor, December 7, 1941. Stephenson and BSC operated from Room 3603, Rockefeller Center, officially known as the British Passport Control Office, and was registered with the US Department of State. Stephenson's operation handled highly sensitive information between British SOE and SIS and the Americans. He was also cleared by Churchill to pass selective Bletchley Park Ultra data to President Roosevelt. It was Stephenson who advised Roosevelt to appoint William Donovan as head of the US Office of Strategic Services (OSS). Stephenson worked without salary and paid from his own resources much of the large administrative and personnel costs of BSC. When he was made a Knight Bachelor in 1945, Winston Churchill wrote, "This one is dear to my heart." In November 1946, he was awarded the Medal of Merit by President Harry S. Truman, at that time the highest civilian award in the United States. General Wild Bill Donovan most appropriately presented the medal to Stephenson.

The quiet Canadian was made a companion of the Order of Canada on December 17, 1979, and invested on February 5, 1980. His book *A Man Called Intrepid* was first published in 1976.

Ian Fleming

Our hero, Ian Fleming, left the NID and Room 39 at the conclusion of World War II. Born May 28, 1908, in Green Street, London, he died August 12, 1964, in Canterbury, United Kingdom. Fleming came from a wealthy family, connected to the merchant bank Robert Fleming & Company. His father was the Member of Parliament for Henley from 1910 until his death on the Western Front in 1917. He was educated at Eton, the Royal Military Academy Sandhurst (the equivalent of the United States Military Academy at West Point), and the universities of Munich and Geneva. He wrote his first Bond novel, appropriately titled *Casino Royale*, started in January 1952 and completed on March 18, 1952, all sixty-two thousand words. It was an instant success. Fleming wrote eleven Bond novels and two collections of short stories between 1953 and 1964. He was a heavy smoker and drinker and succumbed to heart disease at the age of fifty-six. Two of his James Bond novels were published posthumously. In 1946, Fleming bought fifteen acres adjacent to the Golden Clouds estate in Jamaica. He built his house on the edge of a cliff overlooking a private beach on Oracabessa Bay. He named his home Golden Eye.

ABOUT THE AUTHOR

A NTHONY WELLS IS unique insofar as he is the only living person to have worked for British intelligence as a British citizen and US intelligence as a US citizen, and to have also served in uniform at sea and ashore with both the Royal Navy and the US Navy. He is a fifty-year veteran of the Five Eyes intelligence community. In 2017, he was the keynote speaker on board HMS *Victory* in Portsmouth, England, to commemorate the one hundredth anniversary of the famous Zimmermann Telegram intelligence coup by Blinker Hall and his Room 40 team in British Naval Intelligence. The guest of honor was Her Royal Highness Princess Anne, with the Five Eyes community, past and present, represented from the United States, the United Kingdom, Canada, Australia, and New Zealand. Dr. Wells, or Commander Wells as he is also, was trained and mentored in the late 1960s by the very best of the World War II intelligence community, including Sir Harry Hinsley, the famous Bletchley Park code breaker, official historian of British intelligence in the Second World War, Master of St. John's College, Cambridge, and Vice Chancellor of Cambridge University. Sir Harry Hinsley introduced Dr. Wells to the Enigma data before it became public knowledge. Dr. Wells received his PhD in war studies from King's College, University of London, in 1972. He is married to Professor Carol Evans, a former member of the CIA

STAP and current director of the Strategic Studies Institute (SSI) at the US Army War College. Anthony Wells has four children and eight grandchildren and lives on the family farm in rural Virginia. He is a retired veteran of the US National Ski patrol and is the president of The Plains, Virginia Volunteer Fire & Rescue Company. He writes a monthly "Letter from the Plains" for the *Middleburg Eccentric* newspaper. He is a certified FAA flight instructor, and he plays the saxophone and loves to play tennis now that his skiing days are over. His *Studies in British Naval Intelligence, 1880–1945* is still regarded, almost fifty years after publication, as the most well-researched and authoritative source. He has published extensively.

Dr. Anthony Wells
Unclassified Publications Since 1968

Literary Awards: In 2013 and 2017, the United States Submarine League presented Dr. Anthony R. Wells with literary awards for articles in the *Submarine Review.*

Books

German Public Opinion and Hitler's Policies, 1933–39. 1968. Electronic version available at Durham University Library, UK—access www to Durham University Library and enter data base with title and/or author name. Electronic and hard copy versions available.

Studies in British Naval Intelligence, 1880–1945. 1972. Electronic version available via the www British Library (ETHOS), and also King's College, London—www and then enter the data base with title and/or author name. Electronic and hard copy versions available. Also simply enter title and by Anthony Roland Wells, and a www edition is available on line.

Training and the Achievement of Management Objectives, the Solution of Management Problems, and as an Instrument of Organizational Change. 1974. The London School of Economics and Political Science.

Technical Change and British Naval Policy. Edited by Bryan Ranft, Hodder and Stoughton, London, 1977, and Holmes and Meier, New York, NY.

War and Society. Edited by Brian Bond and Ian Roy, Croom Helm, London, 1977, and Holmes and Meier, New York, NY.

Soviet Naval Diplomacy. Edited by B. Dismukes and J. McConnell, Pergamon Press, 1979.

The Soviet and Other Communist Navies. Edited by James George, Naval Institute Press, 1986.

Black Gold Finale. A novel. Dorrance Publishing Company, 2009.

The Golden Few. A novel. Dorrance Publishing Company, 2012.

A Tale of Two Navies: Geopolitics, Technology, and Strategy in the United States and the Royal Navy, 1960–2015. US Naval Institute Press, Annapolis, Maryland, January 2017.

Between Five Eyes. Casemate Publishers, Oxford, UK, and Havertown Pennsylvania, September 2020.

Room 39 & the Lisbon Connection. A novel. Xlibris, Bloomington, Indiana. To be published in 2021.

Articles

"Admirals Hall and Godfrey—Doyens of Naval Intelligence" (two parts). *The Naval Review*, 1973.

"Staff Training and the Royal Navy" (two parts). *The Naval Review* 1975, 1976.

"The 1967 June War: Soviet Naval Diplomacy and the Sixth Fleet—A Reappraisal." Center for Naval Analyses, Arlington, Virginia. Professional Paper 204, October 1977.

"The Center for Naval Analyses." Professional Paper Number 197, December 1977. Department of the Navy, Washington, DC, Center for Naval Analyses.

"The Soviet Navy in the Arctic and North Atlantic." *National Defense*, February 1986.

"Soviet Submarine Prospects 1985–2000." *The Submarine Review*, January 1986.

"A New Defense Strategy for Britain." Proceedings of the United States Naval Institute, March 1987.

"Presence and Military Strategies of the USSR in the Arctic." Quebec Center for International Relations, Laval University, 1986.

"Real Time Targeting: Myth or Reality." Proceedings of the United States Naval Institute, August 2001.

"Missing Magics Machine Material. New Insights on December 7, 1941, and Relevance for Today's Navy." *The Submarine Review*, April 2003.

"US Naval Power and the Pursuit of Peace in an Era of International Terrorism and Weapons of Mass Destruction." *The Submarine Review*, October 2002.

"Transformation—Some Insights and Observations for the Royal Navy from Across the Atlantic." *The Naval Review*, August 2003.

"They Did Not Die In Vain. USS Liberty Incident—Some Additional Perspectives." Proceedings of the United States Naval Institute, March 2005.

"Royal Navy at the Crossroads: Turn the Strategic Tide. A Way to Implement a Lasting Vision." *The Naval Review*, November 2010.

"The Royal Navy Is Key to Britain's Security Strategy." Proceedings of the United States Naval Institute, December 2010.

"The Survivability of the Royal Navy and a New Enlightened British Defense Strategy." *The Submarine Review*, January 2011

"A Strategy in East Asia that Can Endure." Proceedings of the United States Naval Institute, May 2011.

"A Strategy in East Asia that Can Endure." The Naval Review, August 2011. Reprinted by kind permission of the United States Naval Institute.

"The United States Navy, Jordan, and a Long Term Israeli-Palestinian Security Agreement." The *Submarine Review*, Spring 2012.

"Admiral Sir Herbert Richmond: What would he think, write and action today?" The *Naval Review*, February 2013—lead article in the Centenary Edition of *The Naval Review*.

"Postscript to Missing Magics Machine Material—Tribute to a Great Submariner: Captain Edward Beach, US Navy." *The Submarine Review*, 2013.

"Jordan, Israel, and US Need to Cooperate for Missile Defense." USNI News, March 26, 2103.

"A Tribute to Admiral Sir John "Sandy" Woodward." USNI News, August 8, 2013.

"USS LIBERTY Document Center." Edited by Anthony Wells and Thomas Schaaf. A website produced by SiteWhirks Inc., Warrenton, Virginia. September 2013. In April 2017, this website was transferred to the Library of Congress for permanent safekeeping for the use of future scholars and researchers.

"The Future of ISIS: A Joint US-Russian Assessment" with Dr. Andrey Chuprygin. *The Naval Review*, May 2015.

"The Zimmermann Telegram: 100ᵗʰ Anniversary." The Naval Review, February 2017 and *The Submarine Review*, 2017.

"Put the Guns in a Box" with Captain J W Phillips, US Navy retired. Proceedings of the US Naval Institute, June 2018.

"Quo Vadis China? A View from Across the Atlantic Part 1." *The Naval Review*. November 2019.

"Quo Vadis China?" *The Submarine Review*. December 2019.

"USS Amberjack and the Attack on USS Liberty," with Mr. Larry Taylor, ST1, USS Amberjack. US Naval Institute Naval History Blog, January 7, 2020.

"USS Amberjack & the Attack on USS Liberty," with Mr. Larry Taylor. *The Submarine Review*. March 2020.

"The UK's Strategic Defense & Security Review, a US Perspective." *The Submarine Review*. June 2020.

"The United Kingdom Needs a Maritime Strategy." *The Naval Review*, August 2020.

"Submarines and the Ring of Fire in the Indo Pacific Theater: A Strategic Analysis." *The Submarine Review*, December 2020.

"UK's Defense & Security Review—Some Final Observations." *The Naval Review*. Autumn 2020.

"A Brave New World of Next Generation Technologies: Warship World," Volume 17, Number 2, January/February 2021.

Reports

NATO and US Carrier Deployment Policies. Center for Naval Analyses, Arlington, Virginia, February 1977.

NATO and US Carrier Deployment Policies, Formation of a New Standing Naval Strike Force in NATO. Center for Naval Analyses, Arlington, Virginia, April 1977.

Sea War '85 Scenario, with Captain John L. Underwood, USN. Center for Naval Analyses, Arlington, Virginia, June 1977.

Submarine Construction Program for the State of Sabah, Malaysia. RDA Contract TR-188600-OOl, December 1984. Chief Minister of Sabah, Malaysia, and Government of Malaysia.

The Application of Drag Reduction and Boundary Layer Control Technologies in an Experimental Program. January 1985. For the Chief Naval Architect, Vickers Shipbuilding and Engineering Ltd, Barrow-in-Furness, UK.

The Strategic Importance and Advantages of Labuan, Federal Malaysian Territory, as a Naval Base with Special Reference to its Capabilities as the Royal Malaysian Navy Submarine Base, March 1985. Chief Minister of Sabah, Malaysia and Government of Malaysia.

Preliminary Overview of Soviet Merchant Ships in Anti-SSBN Operations and Soviet Merchant Ships and Submarine Masking. (Department of the Navy Contract N00016-85-C-0204).

SSBN Port Egress and the Non-Commercial Activities of the Soviet Merchant Fleet: Concepts of Operation and War Orders for Current and Future Anti-SSBN Operations. (Department of the Navy Contract 136400).

Overview Study of the Maritime Aspects of the Nuclear Balance in the European Theater (Department of Energy Study for the European Conflict Analysis Project). October 1986.

Soviet Submarine Warfare Strategy Assessment and Future US Submarine and Anti-Submarine Warfare Technologies (Defense Advanced Research Projects Agency, March 1988, RDA Contract 146601).

Limited Objective Experiment ZERO, July 2000. The Naval Air Systems Command, US Navy, Department of Defense. 2002.

Operational factors Associated with the Software Nuclear Safety Analysis for the UGM-109A Tomahawk Submarine-Launched Land Attack Cruise Missile Combat Control System Mark I. United States Navy and Logicon Inc., 1989.

Operation Bahrain, March 2003. The Assistant Director of Central Intelligence, the Central Intelligence Agency.

Distributed Data Analysis with Bayesian Networks: A Preliminary Study for Non-Proliferation of Radioactive Devices, December 2003 (with F. Dowla and G. Larson). The Lawrence Livermore National Laboratory, Livermore, California, December 2003.

Fiber Reinforced Pumice Protective barriers—To Mitigate the Effects of Suicide and Truck Bombs. Final Report and Recommendations. United States Navy, Washington, DC. With Professor Vistasp Kharbari, Professor of Structural Engineering, University of California, San Diego. August 2006.

Weapon Target Centric Model: Preliminary Modules and Applications, in two volumes. United States Navy, Principal Executive Officer Submarines, Washington, DC, August 2007.

Tactical Decision Aid (TDA): Multi intelligence capability for National, Theater, and Tactical intelligence in real time across geographic space and time. The National Intelligence Community, Washington, DC, May 2012.

Submarine Industrial Base Model: Key industrial base model for the US Virginia Class nuclear powered attack submarine, Principal Executive Officer Submarines, Washington Navy Yard, Washington, DC, October 2012.

Manuals

Astro-Navigation: A Programmed Course in 6 Volumes for Training UK and Commonwealth Naval Officers in the Use of Astronomical Navigation at Sea. Royal Navy, Ministry of Defence, UK, 1969.

The Battle of Trafalgar: A Programmed Course in One Volume in Naval Strategy and Tactics. Royal Navy, Ministry of Defence, 1969.

The Double Cross System: A Programmed Course In One Volume for British, Foreign and Commonwealth Naval Officers Attending the Royal Naval Staff College, Greenwich, UK. Royal Navy, Ministry of Defence, 1973.

Unclassified Titles for Technology and Operational Areas—Covering Classified Programs—and Publications (Generic Areas)

Airborne Mine Clearance
Streak Tube Imaging LIDAR
Magic Lantern Program
Tritium Micro sphere Technology
Classified Applications of the Naval Simulation System
Naval Surface Fire Support and the Extended Range Guided Munition (ERGM)
Non Acoustic Antisubmarine Warfare
Battlefield Awareness and Data Dissemination (BADD Program)
Joint Stars Program Special Applications
Naval Fires Network
Littoral Surveillance System
Fleet Battle Experiment Operations (Technical Director FBE Alpha and FBE Bravo) Third Fleet, US Pacific Fleet
Ocean Surveillance (radar and optics)
Multi Spectral Applications
Space Based Sensors and Surveillance
Microwave Radiometry Applications
Detection, Locating and Tracking
Clandestine Operations and Intelligence Collection Operations
Support to Special Forces
Special Submarine Operations
Tagging Tracking and Surveillance
Battlespace Shaping and Real Time Targeting
Covert and Clandestine Operations against Weapons of Mass Destruction and
Other major threats to US Security
Special Sensor Technology
Covert & Overt Operations Planning and Execution

Reports and MOUs for Commander-in-Chief and Secretary level actions

Airborne Infrared Measurement System

Stealth and Counter Stealth

Counter Intelligence Operations

Tactical Exploitation System and Joint Fires Network

Asymmetric Warfare Initiative—2003

Hairy Buffalo Program

Tracking of the al Qai'da Terrorist Network and Operations

Tactical Decision Aid (TDA) for Submarine ISR operations

Advanced Cyber Attack and Defense Technologies and Operations

Shrouded Lightning Special Program

Non Linear Junction Radar and Adaptive Regenerative Controller Special Program

Special Program in Jordan

Special Program in Malaysia

Special Program in Bahrain

Special Program in Abu Dhabi

Special Program in Saudi Arabia

Special Program with Commander United States Pacific Fleet

Special Tests at the US Naval Air Station Patuxent River, Maryland, September 2012

LISAC Special Program

Applications of the Robust Laser Interferometry (RLI) system and technology

Special Support to a combined Cheltenham UK and Maryland US Group

Special Support for Indo-Pacific Operations

Classified Titles and Publications

1968–2018, Dr. Wells has been the author, lead author, or a key author of multiple highly classified code word documents at the Top Secret SCI level in both the United Kingdom and the United States.